MW01531748

To M,

Welcome & Bon Appetit!!

Chef Joe

Mississippi Gulfcoast Casino & Local Restaurants

Post Hurricane Katrina

LEE & LINDA ESCHLER

Copyright © 2010 Linda Eschler
All rights reserved.

ISBN: 1439267375
ISBN-13: 9781439267370

DEDICATION

"There is a light in the world; a healing spirit more powerful than any darkness we may encounter. We sometimes lose sight of this force when there is suffering and too much pain, and then suddenly, the spirit will emerge among the lives of ordinary people who hear the call and answer in extraordinary ways."
~ *Richard Attenborough*

Hurricane Katrina brought a darkness upon our Mississippi Coast and many never believed they would recover from this darkness; yet, the spirit emerged among the lives of these ordinary people we call our fellow Mississippians; they heard the call, and they answered in extraordinary ways. They used their pain and suffering as a healing force to bring light back to our beautiful Mississippi Gulf Coast. Volunteers throughout the United States heard the call as well and they answered with the words, *what can we do to help?*

This book is dedicated to everyone that was affected by Hurricane Katrina and to those that extended a helping hand.

ACKNOWLEDGEMENTS

We would like to thank the restaurants on the Mississippi Gulf Coast for making this book possible.

To all of you who provided a feature story, we thank you as well.

A special thank you goes out to Ken Combs II for sharing his personal Hurricane Katrina story.

To our friends and neighbors that shared their special recipes, thank you one and all.

As always, we thank Andrea Yeager, Community Relations Manager for *Barnes and Noble*, Gulfport, Mississippi. Her continued support of local authors is greatly appreciated and to our editor and daughter, Kim Stewart, who takes a special interest in all of our projects, *thank you* and *we love you*.

FOREWORD

August Twenty Ninth, 2005 is a day that will never be forgotten by the residents of the Mississippi Gulf Coast for this was a day that drastically changed our lives.

Hurricane Katrina was one of the deadliest hurricanes in the history of the United States, killing over 1,800 people.

Katrina was the largest hurricane of its strength to approach the United States in recorded history; its sheer size caused devastation over 100 miles from the storm's center and over ninety thousand square miles were affected by Katrina. The storm surge caused major or catastrophic damage along the coastlines of Louisiana, Mississippi and Alabama.

Katrina was the eleventh named storm, fifth hurricane, third major hurricane and second category five hurricane of the 2005 Atlantic hurricane season. It was also the sixth strongest hurricane ever recorded, and the third strongest hurricane to make landfall in the U.S. ever recorded.

Hurricane Katrina was the costliest hurricane in U.S. history, with $75 billion in estimated damages.

Hundreds of thousands of local residents were left unemployed and more than one million Gulf Coast residents were displaced.

Many of our restaurants owners along the coast; not only lost their homes, but their livelihood as well. Some rebuilt, while others relocated and within a few years, many new restaurants came to be. This book is about the resilience of these restaurateurs and their determination to rebuild the Mississippi Gulf Coast in the face of such adversity.

Once you dine in the wonderful restaurants inside this book, you will understand why the Mississippi Gulf Coast restaurants are second to none in the world.

LOCAL ATTRACTIONS

Beauvoir, Jefferson Davis Home & Presidential Library

2244 Beach Blvd

Biloxi, MS 39531

Phone: 228 388-4400

Fax: 228 388-7800

Website: http://www.beauvoir.org/

Biloxi Shrimping Trip

P.O. Box 1315 / Slip 104

Biloxi, MS 39531

Phone: 228-385-1182

Fax: 228-388-6693

Website: www.biloxishrimpingtrip.com

Gulf Islands WaterPark

13100 16th St

Gulfport, MS 39503

Phone: 866-485-3386

Website: www.gulfislandswaterpark.com

Gulfport Dragway

17085 Race Track Road

Gulfport, MS 39503

Phone: 228-863-4408

Website: http://www.gulfportdragway.com/

Gulf Islands WaterPark
Maritime & Seafood Industry Museum

P O Box 1907

Biloxi, MS 39533

Phone: 228-435-6320

Fax: 228-435-6309

Website: http://www.maritimemuseum.org/

Lighthouse Tours & Receptive Services

PO Box 454

Biloxi, MS 39533

Phone: 228-872-5611

Fax: 228-872-0611

Call toll free: 888-219-7211.

Lynn Meadows Discovery Center

246 Dolan Ave

Gulfport, MS 39507

Phone: 228-897-6039

Fax: 228-248-0071

Website: http://www.lmdc.org/

Ohr-O`Keefe Museum of Art

1596 Glenn Swetman Dr

Biloxi, MS 39530

Phone: 228-374-5547

Fax: 228-436-3641

Website: http://www.georgeohr.org/

Ship Island Excursions/Pan Isles Inc.

P.O. Box 1467

Gulfport, MS 39502-1467

Phone: 866-466-7386

Fax: 228-864-3797

Website: http://www.msshipisland.com/

Walter Anderson Museum of Art

510 Washington Ave

Ocean Springs, MS 39564

Phone: 228-872-3164

Website: www.walterandersonmuseum.org

RESTAURANT & CASINO
CONTRIBUTORS

Beau Rivage

875 Beach Boulevard Biloxi, Ms. 39530

Phone: 228. 386.7111

guestservices@beaurivage.com

www.beaurivage.com

Restaurants at Beau Rivage:
B R Prime – Steakhouse
The Buffet
Coast
Fallen Oak
Jia – Pan – Asian cuisine
Memphis Q
Terrace Cafe

anjac's Barbeque & Burger Company

34A 29th Street

Gulfport, MS 39507

Phone: 228.868.6560 | Fax: 228.868.6514

www.anjacsbbq.com

anjac's # 2

1621 Pass Road

Biloxi, Ms. 39531

Phone: 228.267-3525

www.anjacsbbq.com

anjac's # 3

12407 Highway 49 North Suite 5

Gulfport, Ms. 39503

Phone: not yet available

www.anjacsbbq.com

Back Bay Seafood Restaurant

1458 Magnolia Street

Gulfport, MS 39503

Phone: 228.248.0505

www.backbayseafoodrestaurant.com

Capone's

2113 Government Street

Ocean Springs, MS

Phone: 228.818.8941

www.caponesoceansprings.com

Chili Willie's Pizzeria

Norwood Village shopping center

12100 Hwy 49 Suite 612 Gulfport, ms. 39503

Phone: 228. 831.9117

www.chiliwilliespizzeria.com

Chili Willie's Pizzeria

124 Davis Avenue Pass Christian, Ms. 39571

Phone: 228. 452.7757

www.chiliwilliespizzeria.com

Clay Oven

2101 14th Street Gulfport, Ms. 3950

Phone: 228. 214.5111

www.clayovenms.com & www.indiafood4u

Cuz's Fresh Seafood & Poboys,

10408 Hwy 603

Bay Saint Louis, MS 39520

Phone: 228. 4673707

Half Shell Oyster House

2500 13th Street

Gulfport, MS 39501

Phone: 228.867.7001

www.halfshelloysterhouse.com

Lil Ray's PoBoys & Seafood

500 A Courthouse Road

Gulfport, Ms. 39507

Phone: 228.896-9601

www.lilraysrestaurant.com

Mediterraneo

1314 Government Street

Ocean Springs, MS 39564

Phone: 228.872.3311

www.oceanspringsrestaurant.com

Mugshots Grill & Bar

2650 Beach Blvd, Suite 20

Biloxi, MS 39531

Phone: 228.385.4626

www.mugshotsgrillandbar.com

Nezaty's Café

360 Courthouse Road

Gulfport, Ms. 39507

Phone: 228. 8971139

www.nezatys.com

Port City Café

2418 14th Street

Gulfport, MS 39501

Phone: 228.868.0037

The Quarter

2504 13th street

Gulfport, Ms. 39501

Phone: 228. 863-2650

Taranto's Crawfish, PoBoys & Seafood

12404 John Lee Road

Biloxi, MS 39532

Phone: 228.392.0990

Vintage Station

302 Courthouse Road Suite D

Gulfport, Ms. 39507

Phone: 228. 8944420

www.vintahestation.com

FEATURE STORIES ~

Food Quotes ~Trivia ~ Famous Mississippians

- ◆ Beauvoir
- ◆ Blessing of the Fleet
- ◆ Broadcast Media Personalities from Mississippi
- ◆ Championship Golf on the Mississippi Gulf Coast
- ◆ Coast History
- ◆ Famous Mississippians
- ◆ Famous Food Quotes
- ◆ Food Trivia
- ◆ Gulf Coast Writer's Association
- ◆ Gulfport – Biloxi International Airport
- ◆ The History of Gambling
- ◆ The Katrina Dolphins
- ◆ Lake Vista
- ◆ Linda's Stories and Family Recipes
- ◆ Local Attractions
- ◆ Learn and Laugh -At The Lynn Meadows Discovery Center
- ◆ Mardi Gras Trivia
- ◆ Maritime & Seafood Industry Museum
- ◆ Marlin Miller - Wood Sculptor
- ◆ Mississippi Gulf Coast Local Recipes
- ◆ Mississippi Trivia
- ◆ MO-JOE foundation
- ◆ Ohr-O`Keefe Museum
- ◆ Rob Stinson
- ◆ Robin Roberts & GMA
- ◆ Southern Food
- ◆ WLOX – Television

WELCOME BACK

In our first book, we took you inside many of our local restaurants along the Mississippi Gulf Coast.

You read the history of these restaurants and you took the journey with each and every one of them as they described what it was like to go through the most devastating natural disaster to ever hit the United States.

The resilience of these restaurants will be remembered for many years, as will the wonderful recipes they provided.

In this second installment of *Mississippi Gulf Coast Restaurants* we have not only added many more restaurants along the Mississippi Gulf Coast; not included in the first book, we have also added our casino restaurants that were devastated or destroyed by Katrina, so please step inside and allow these restaurants to take you on another journey as they tell their stories and share with us their happy endings as well as many more delectable recipes from each and every one of them.

As an added feature, we included more recipes and stories from our local residents, more local history, feature stories and information on fun things to do on the Mississippi Gulf Coast.

He may live without books
- what is knowledge but grieving?
He may live without hope
- what is hope but deceiving?
He may live without love
- what is passion but pining?
But where is the man that can live without dining?

Edward R. Bulwer-Lytton "Lucille"

Enjoy!

MISSISSIPPI

Gulf Coast

Gulfport/Biloxi
www.gulfcoast.org

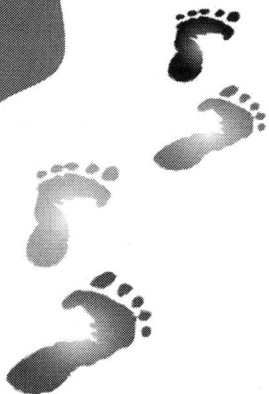

RELAX, IT'S
THE MISSISSIPPI
GULF COAST.

Gulfport/Biloxi
www.gulfcoast.org

MISSISSIPPI GULF COAST CONVENTION & VISITORS BUREAU

Welcome to the Mississippi Gulf Coast, the exciting "Playground of the South," where your perfect vacation awaits.

No matter what your idea of a heavenly getaway is, you're sure to find it on the Mississippi Gulf Coast. From 26 miles of sugar-white beaches to non-stop casino action, sophisticated shopping, culture, history, arts, delectable cuisine and championship golf courses, the Playground of the South has it all and everything in between.

Whether you're vacationing solo, as a couple or a family, you'll find plenty to entertain every member of your group.

Among the Coast's exciting entertainment mix is the high-spirited fun of casino gaming. Thirteen casinos have brought the excitement of Las Vegas to the beach, with table games and slot machines galore. All casinos are open 24 hours a day, seven days a week. Some of the casinos offer supervised activities for children; some are complete resort complexes with golf courses and hotels as part of their package, and more casino developments are on the way.

If outdoor fun is high on your list, you need look no further than the beach for adventure. Get a bird's-eye view of the entire shoreline with a parasail ride or an aerial tour over the Gulf. Or, you can hop on a jet ski; try your hand at windsurfing, sailing, skiing or motor boating. Water parks with everything from a wave pool, slides, and amusements such as miniature golf, rides and arcades are also among the outdoor set's list of favorite places on the Coast. The ultimate beach experience - spending a day on a barrier island - is only a ferry ride away.

For lovers of sports, there's no better place to be than the "Playground of the South." A temperate climate and generally pleasant weather mean year-round fun.

Sports fishermen can plan a day-long or overnight trip into Gulf waters where some of the best deep-sea fishing in the world can be found, or they can fish the area's many lakes and rivers.

For those who believe a great day is a day on the links, over 24 golf courses offer challenges for every skill level, and the greens fees are surprisingly lower than those of comparable golf resort areas. With several courses recently refurbished and new courses either under construction or in the planning stages, the Gulf Coast is a choice destination for golf lovers near and far.

For a little peace and quiet, a simple drive along the beach will treat visitors to the unparalleled beauty of graceful live oaks, unique landmarks and antebellum homes. Historic neighborhoods provide a lesson in the notable architecture of the past and annual pilgrimages offer an inside glimpse of the area's gracious homes, some of which have stood for more than a century.

Art and history play an important role in the character of the Gulf Coast. Two museums are dedicated to the works of two of the area's most famous artists, potter George E. Ohr and painter/sculptor Walter Inglis Anderson. A seafood industry museum commemorates the significant role that the seafood industry has played in shaping the region, and a marine education center teaches visitors about the Coast's environment and displays aquatic life native to the Gulf of Mexico in a 42,000-gallon aquarium. At another marine attraction, Marine Life, visitors can see daily shows of trained dolphins and can view other types of marine life.

If a shopping expedition is what it takes to put a smile on your face, you'll have plenty to rave about along the coast. Edgewater Mall and Edgewater Village in Biloxi offer a mix of department stores and specialty boutiques. There is also the fabulous Crossroads Center and the factory outlet mall, Gulfport Factory Stores just off I-10, brings shoppers bargains in name-brand clothing, home accessories, jewelry, books, music and more. For those in search of unique finds, visit the quaint shops in historic downtown Ocean Springs or Bay St. Louis.

For party people, rest assured there's a celebration somewhere along the Coast you can enjoy. Locals sometimes say that the Gulf Coast has a celebration for every crustacean, and that's not far from the truth. The abundance of fresh seafood - crabs, shrimp, oysters, fish, crawfish - is reason enough to have a party. Add the area's diverse cultural mix, season it with music, heritage and an overall spirit of fun, and you've got enough festivals to fill practically every weekend of the year.

Among the highlights each fall is the "Cruisin' the Coast" event where thousands of custom cars, hotrods and custom performance car enthusiasts from around the country meet in a week-long Coast-wide party.

Combine all there is to see and do with the hospitality here on the Gulf Coast, and you'll know in an instant that you've brought your vacation fantasy to the right place: The Playground of the South.

For more information contact:
Mississippi Gulf Coast Convention & Visitors Bureau
P.O. Box 6128
Gulfport, MS 39506
PH: 228-896-6699
800-237-9493 U.S./Canada
E-mail tourism@gulfcoast.org

COAST HISTORY

PASCAGOULA MISSISSIPPI

The name Pascagoula, which means "bread eaters," is taken from a group of Native Americans found in villages along the Pascagoula River some distance above its mouth. Hernando De Soto seems to have made first contact with them in the 1540s, though little is known of that encounter. Pierre Le Moyne d'Iberville, founder of the colony of Louisiana, left a more detailed account from an expedition of this region in 1700. The first detailed account comes from Jean-Baptiste Le Moyne de Bienville, younger brother of Iberville, whom the Pascagoula visited, at Fort Maurepas, in present-day Ocean Springs, shortly after it was settled and while the older brother was away in France.

The first settlers of Pascagoula were Jean Baptiste Baudreau Dit Graveline, Joseph Simon De La Pointe and his aunt, the Madame Chaumont

Pascagoula has three historic districts and more than 30 individual structures listed in the National Register of Historic Places.

GAUTIER MISSISSIPPI

The City of Gautier was incorporated in 1986 and is currently one of the 50 largest cities in the State of Mississippi. The City of Gautier is very proud of its history and has been able to preserve a prehistoric Indian burial mound at the end of Graveline Road. This is an accomplishment in itself as there are very few of these preserved East of the Mississippi River.

GRAVELINE BAYOU INDIAN MOUND

Prehistoric Native Americans once lived in Gautier as evidenced by garbage dumps of broken pottery, bones and oyster shells, particularly along the beach.

The earliest identifiable group, the Woodlands Indians, who are believed to have migrated originally from Asia into Alaska as early as 30,000 years ago and then across the whole of the Americas, also left evidence of their occupation by building mounds for ceremonial and burial purposes.

Most of these mounds have been destroyed by urban development, but one may be seen on Barracuda Drive. It is thought by archaeologists to have been built circa 400 to 600 A.D. The Mississippi historic marker erected at the site reads:

"Graveline Bayou Indian Mound -- The nearby eastern mound was built by prehistoric Indians during the Late Woodland Period between 400 and 700, A.D. The mound's flat summit was used for ceremonial purposes. Listed in the National Register of Historic Places, it is one of the few remaining Native American mounds on the Mississippi Gulf Coast."

A 2000 archaeological report by John H. Blitz and C. Baxter Mann for the Mississippi Department of Archives and History gives more details on the small, ramped, platform mound located on an undeveloped lot.

The original mound contours have been modified by erosion, but it is clear that the mound was constructed in a rectangular shape.

Six other mounds were found near the mouth of the Graveline Bayou in earlier investigations, suggesting that the Graveline Mound is the largest of what may be a multiple-mound center. If true, Graveline would be the only known coastal multiple-mound center between the northwest Florida coast and Louisiana.

Early excavations yielded highly decorated ceramics and, in some cases, evidence of communal feasting. The mound was added to the National Register of Historic Places as the "Graveline Mound site" in 1987.

OCEAN SPRINGS MISSISSIPPI

Ocean Springs, Mississippi, lies at the heart of the beautiful Mississippi Gulf Coast on the eastern shore of Biloxi Bay. It's known as the City of Discovery in recognition of the French establishment of a settlement here in 1699. Long before the French arrived, however, the area was appreciated for its beauty and natural resources by Native Americans. The attributes that brought these early residents have attracted a diverse stream of people during the past 300 years.

BILOXI MISSISSIPPI

Biloxi is an Indian word that means "First People." The French established the first European settlement in the lower Mississippi Valley in 1699 across the bay at Old Biloxi. Old Biloxi is now known as Ocean Springs, Mississippi. New Biloxi was founded in 1719. New Biloxi was the capital of French Louisiana until 1722, when New Orleans replaced it.

Biloxi, Mississippi was incorporated as a town in 1838 and as a city in 1896. . Biloxi is located on a peninsula between the Biloxi Bay and the Mississippi Sound on the beautiful Gulf of Mexico. Industries in Biloxi include fishing and boat building, the packing and shipping of shrimp and oysters and several small manufactures. Casinos have made Biloxi the center of a booming gambling district with thousands of new hotel rooms. Biloxi is the third largest gaming site in the United States.

The western islands of the Gulf Islands National Seashore, which include Ship Island, a Union fort during the Civil War are located off the coast of Biloxi.

The Biloxi Lighthouse built in 1848 is the only lighthouse in the United States to stand in the middle of a four-lane highway. The lighthouse survived Hurricane Katrina and is reported to be the most photographed landmark on the Mississippi Gulf Coast. This historic landmark and others can still be seen aboard Biloxi's oldest and best historic tour, *The Biloxi Tour Train*.

THE BILOXI TOUR TRAIN

Established in 1962 the *TourTrain* has treated thousands of visitors to a historical journey through one the oldest towns in America, Biloxi, Mississippi. The Tour Train will entertain you with a 90 minute narrated tour through Biloxi's Historical District, beginning at the Biloxi Lighthouse and traveling the neighborhood streets lined with 18th and 19th century architecture.

GULFPORT MISSISSIPPI

Gulfport was incorporated in 1898. In 1902, the harbor was completed, and the Port of Gulfport became a working seaport.

The Port of Gulfport has flourished over the years and today accounts for millions of dollars in annual sales and tax revenue for the state of Mississippi.

Gulfport has evolved into a diversified community with about 6.7 miles of man-made white sandy beaches along the Gulf of Mexico and is one of the fastest growing areas in the state, due in part to recent gaming activities. Home of the annual "Worlds Largest Fishing Rodeo," Gulfport is a residential community that is blessed with a strong business center.

Gulfport, Mississippi is a picturesque beachfront city on the Gulf of Mexico with a diverse culture and safe family oriented neighborhoods supported by a progressive economy where everyone feels welcome and at home!

LONG BEACH

History:

Long Beach began as an agricultural town, based much around its radish industry. But on August 10, 1905, Long Beach incorporated and became another city on the Mississippi Gulf Coast. As the years went on, the city moved from its agricultural heritage and moved toward tourism with the beach and high-rise condominiums becoming increasingly popular.

"The Radish Capital of the World"

Long Beach's early economy was largely agriculture-based. Logging initially drove the local economy, but when the area's virgin yellow pine forests became depleted, row crops were planted on the newly cleared land.

A productive truck farming town in the early 20th century, citizens of Long Beach proclaimed the city to be the "Radish Capital of the World." The city was especially known for its cultivation of the Long Red radish variety, a favorite beer hall staple in the northern US at the time. In 1921, a bumper crop resulted in the shipment of over 300 train loads of Long Beach's Long Red radishes to northern states.

Eventually, the Long Red radishes for which Long Beach was known fell into disfavor, and the rise of the common button radish caused a dramatic decline in the cultivation of this crop in the area.

PASS CHRISTIAN

Pass Christian was named for a nearby deepwater pass, which in turn was named for Nicholas Christian L'Adnier who lived on nearby Cat Island beginning in 1746. (Another nearby pass, Pass Marianne, was named for L'Adnier's wife Marianne Paquet.)

The town was a famous resort prior to the American Civil War and the site where the first yacht club of the South (and second in the US) was established in 1849. The town was a favorite location for the beach and summer homes of the wealthy of New Orleans. The row of historic mansions along the town's shoreline, especially Scenic Drive, was one of the country's notable historic districts. Tarpon Hole, offshore of Pass Christian in the Mississippi Sound, was the location where a world record Black Sea Bass was caught by Captain John T. McDonald. Captain McDonald operated The Schooner "Queen of the Fleet"

The fishing vessel was noted for its nearly spotless racing record throughout the 1890s and early 1900s until being replaced by larger, faster schooners built for the Biloxi fisheries during World War I. The two-masted 42-foot (13 m) vessel was purchased in 1895 by Mrs. Bidwell, later given to John McDonald, and years later, was lost at sea on October 16, 1923 during a storm. John T. McDonald had been a city alderman in 1888, and served as mayor for three 2-year terms from 1890 to 1895, and served another term in 1903.

Pass Christian was in the path of two of the most intense hurricanes ever to hit the United States--Hurricane Camille in 1969 and Hurricane Katrina on August 29, 2005. Both hurricanes caused the near total destruction of the city.

BAY ST. LOUIS

Bay St. Louis lies along the Mississippi Sound (an embayment of the Gulf of Mexico) at the entrance to St. Louis Bay, 58 miles northeast of New Orleans, Louisiana.

The site was part of a 1789 Spanish land grant to Thomas Shields. The village soon became a resort for wealthy planters and, later, for tourists who arrived after the New Orleans, Mobile and Chattanooga Railroad was completed in 1869. The town was incorporated as Shieldsborough in 1818 and as the city of Bay Saint Louis in 1882. During the War of 1812, the bay (named in 1699 for Louis IX of France) was the scene (1814) of the naval engagement against the British known as the Battle of Pass Christian. In the late 20th century, casino gambling fueled the growth of the city, significantly increasing tourism's importance to the local economy.

The John C. Stennis Space Center of the National Aeronautics and Space Administration (NASA) is about 15 miles west.

CHAMPIONSHIP GOLF ON THE MISSISSIPPI GULF COAST

With over 20 golf courses, the Mississippi Gulf Coast has been welcoming golfers for over 100 years and is home to the first golf course in Mississippi in 1908. With golf courses by Nicklaus, Palmer, Love, Pate and many more - there is a golf course for every skill level or budget. All the best golf course architects in the world built their best here and you can play golf here year-round

Pascagoula:

Pascagoula Country Club
150 Country Club Drive – Pascagoula, Ms. 39567
(228) 762-1466

Gautier

Mississippi National Golf Club
900 Hickory Hill Drive, Gautier, MS 39553
(228) 497-2372

Shell Landing Golf Club
3499 Shell Landing Blvd., Gautier, MS 39553
(228) 497-LOVE | 866-851-0541

Vancleave:

The Preserve Golf Club
8901 Hwy 57 Vancleave, MS 39565
(228) 386-2500 | 877-MSGOLF 9

Ocean Springs:

Gulf Hills Golf Club
13700 Paso Road Ocean Springs, MS 39564
(228) 872.9663 | Fax: 228.872.6447

St. Andrews Golf Course

#2 Golfing Green Drive, Ocean Springs, MS 39564

(228) 875-7730 | 888-875-7730

Biloxi:

Dogwood Hills GC

17476 Dogwood Hills Drive, Biloxi, MS 39532

(228) 392-9805

Fallen Oak – Beau Rivage Casino

24400 Hwy 15, Biloxi, Ms. 39532

(228) 386-7111 Toll free (877) 805-4657

KAFB – Bay Bridge Golf Course

Keesler Air Force Base – Biloxi (Civilian Play with proper identification)

(228) – 377-3832

Sunkist Country Club

2381 Sunkist Country Club Road, Biloxi, MS 39532

(228) 388-3961

Gulfport:

Bayou Vista Golf Course

13756 Washington Avenue
Gulfport, Ms. 39503
(228) 868-9953

Mississippi's Oldest Golf Course - Historic Great Southern Golf Club

Great Southern Golf Club

2000 Beach Drive, Gulfport, MS 39507

(228) 896-3536

NCBC Pine Bayou Golf Course-Naval Construction Battalion Center

1706 Bainbridge Avenue-Bldg 418 Gulfport, MS 39501 Phone: 228.871.2494 | Fax: (228)871.2539

Windance Country Club

19385 Champions Cir, Gulfport, MS 39503

(228) 832-4871

Saucier:

Grand Bear Golf Club

12040 Grand Way Blvd.,Saucier, MS 39574

(228) 539-7806 | 888-946-1946

Diamondhead:

Diamondhead C.C. - Pine

7600 Golf Club Drive, Diamondhead, MS 39525

(228) 255-3910 | 800-346-8741

Diamondhead - Cardinal

7600 Country Club Circle, Diamondhead, MS 39525

(228) 255-3910 | 800-346-8741

Pass Christian:

The Oaks Golf Club

24384 Clubhouse Drive, Pass Christian, MS 39571

(228) 452-0909

Pass Christian Isles Golf Club

150 Country Club Drive, Pass Christian, MS 39571

(228) 452-4851

Bay St. Louis:

The Bridges Golf Club at Hollywood Casino

711 Hollywood Boulevard, Bay Saint Louis, MS 39520

(228) 463-4047 | 1-866-7-LUCKY-1

Hurley:

Whispering Pines Golf Course

18412 Hwy 613 — Hurley, Ms. 39555

(228) 588- 6111

RESTAURANT CONTRIBUTORS

anjac's Barbeque & Burger Company

34A 29th Street
Gulfport, MS 39507
Phone: 228.868.6560 | Fax: 228.868.6514
www.anjacsbbq.com

anjac's # 2

1621 Pass Road
Biloxi, Ms. 39531
Phone: 228.267-3525
www.anjacsbbq.com

anjac's # 3

12407 Highway 49 North Suite 5
Gulfport, Ms. 39503
Phone: not yet available
www.anjacsbbq.com

Back Bay Seafood Restaurant

1458 Magnolia Street
Gulfport, MS 39503
Phone: 228.248.0505
www.backbayseafoodrestaurant.com

Beau Rivage

875 Beach Boulevard Biloxi, Ms. 39530
Phone: 228. 386.7111
guestservices@beaurivage.com
www.beaurivage.com

Restaurants at Beau Rivage:

B R Prime – Steakhouse

The Buffet

Coast

Fallen Oak

Memphis Q

Jia – Pan – Asian cuisine

Terrace Cafe

Capone's

2113 Government Street

Ocean Springs, MS

Phone: 228.818.8941

www.caponesoceansprings.com

Chili Willie's Pizzeria

Norwood Village shopping center

12100 Hwy 49 Suite 612 Gulfport, ms. 39503

Phone: 228. 831.9117

www.chiliwilliespizzeria.com

Chili Willie's Pizzeria

124 Davis Avenue Pass Christian, Ms. 39571

Phone: 228. 452.7757

www.chiliwilliespizzeria.com

Clay Oven

2101 14th Street Gulfport, Ms. 3950

Phone: 228. 214.5111

www.clayovenms.com & www.indiafood4u

Cuz's Fresh Seafood & Poboys,

10408 Hwy 603
Bay Saint Louis, MS 39520
Phone: 228. 4673707

Half Shell Oyster House

2500 13th Street
Gulfport, MS 39501
Phone: 228.867.7001
www.halfshelloysterhouse.com

Lil Ray's PoBoys & Seafood

500 A Courthouse Road
Gulfport, Ms. 39507
Phone: 228.896-9601
www.lilraysrestaurant.com

Mediterraneo

1314 Government Street
Ocean Springs, MS 39564
Phone: 228.872.3311
www.oceanspringsrestaurant.com

Mugshots Grill & Bar

2650 Beach Blvd, Suite 20
Biloxi, MS 39531
Phone: 228.385.4626
www.mugshotsgrillandbar.com

Nezaty's Café

360 Courthouse Road

Gulfport, Ms. 39507

Phone: 228. 8971139

www.nezatys.com

Port City Café

2418 14th Street

Gulfport, MS 39501

Phone: 228.868.0037

The Quarter

2504 13th street

Gulfport, Ms. 39501

Phone: 228. 863-2650

Taranto's Crawfish, PoBoys & Seafood

12404 John Lee Road

Biloxi, MS 39532

Phone: 228.392.0990

Vintage Station

302 Courthouse Road Suite D

Gulfport, Ms. 39507

Phone: 228. 8944420

www.vintahestation.com

FEATURE STORIES

- ◆ **BEAUVOIR**
- ◆ **Blessing of the Fleet**
- ◆ **Broadcast Media Personalities from Mississippi**
- ◆ **Famous Food Quotes**
- ◆ **Food Trivia**
- ◆ **The History of Gambling**
- ◆ **Learn and Laugh -At The Lynn Meadows Discovery Center**
- ◆ **Mardi Gras Trivia**
- ◆ **Marlin Miller - Wood Sculptor**
- ◆ **Maritime & Seafood Industry Museum**
- ◆ **Mississippi Trivia**
- ◆ **MO-JOE foundation**
- ◆ **The Katrina Dolphins**
- ◆ **Ohr-O`Keefe Museum**
- ◆ **Rob Stinson**
- ◆ **Robin Roberts & GMA**
- ◆ **WLOX – Television**
- ◆ **Southern Food**
- ◆ **Championship Golf on the Mississippi Gulf Coast**
- ◆ **Local Attractions**
- ◆ **Gulfport – Biloxi International Airport**
- ◆ **Coast History**
- ◆ **Gulf Coast Writer's Association**
- ◆ **Lake Vista**
- ◆ **Mississippi Gulf Coast Local Recipes**
- ◆ **Linda's Stories and Family Recipes**

Beau Rivage Resort & Casino – Biloxi Mississippi

BEAU RIVAGE RESORT & CASINO

BEAU RIVAGE HISTORY/BACKGROUND

Casual elegance is redefined at Beau Rivage, MGM Resorts International's destination resort on the Mississippi Gulf Coast. Named one of the top hotels in the United States by both *Conde Nast Traveler* and *Travel + Leisure,* Beau Rivage blends world-class amenities with world-famous Southern hospitality.

French for "beautiful shore," Beau Rivage opened in March of 1999 and was destined to forever change the face of tourism on the Mississippi Gulf Coast. At the time, the 32-story, 1,740-room luxury resort was the largest hotel casino in the United States outside of Nevada and its $750million+ investment made it the largest one time single investment in Mississippi's history. But it wasn't the cost or size alone that made Beau Rivage's contribution to its home state so significant. Upon opening, the Beau employed more than 4,000 people, making it one of the largest employers in the state.

Hurricane Katrina, the worst natural disaster in United States history, closed the property on August 29, 2005. Committed in its efforts to rebuild and renew the Gulf Coast, MGM Resorts International set an ambitious goal— to reopen the resort just one year after Katrina made landfall. With the support of the Gulf Coast community and to the astonishment of many, Beau Rivage Resort & Casino reopened for business on the one-year anniversary of the storm, following a dramatic $550-million renovation. New amenities and experiences have been added but the Beau's legendary Southern charm is still ever-present and welcoming. Today, beauty and elegance truly transcend every space just as they have since Beau Rivage originally opened in 1999.

Executive Chef Joseph Friel

CHEF JOSEPH FRIEL, EXECUTIVE CHEF, BEAU RIVAGE

Joseph Friel, Executive Chef at the Beau Rivage Resort & Casino, may be new to the Mississippi Coast region but is no stranger to the fine dining industry. With over 20 years of Executive Chef experience in some of New York's most prestigious restaurants and hotels, Joe brings to the Beau his expertise on classical fine dining as well as a fresh new perspective on trend setting menus. His culinary highlights include being honored as one of the Great Chefs of New York and being invited to cook at the renowned James Beard House. Most recently, Joe was lured away from the highly acclaimed "3 Star" New York restaurant, Town, where he worked alongside Chef/owner Geoffrey Zakarian.

Originally hired as Assistant Executive Chef, nine months later Joe was appointed as Executive Chef when his boss left to take another position out of state. Not many people could have made the transition so smoothly nor assumed the additional responsibilities with such ease. For Joe, after the initial surprise, the role was just a natural progression of his upbringing.

Born in the small Gaelic speaking area of Donegal in northwest Ireland, Joe got his first exposure to the hotel/restaurant business working for his parents who owned a hotel. With both parents busy operating the hotel, the young Friel, the eldest of five children, had no choice but to help out, mainly in the kitchen. Working alongside professional chefs, he learned the basics of sauces and kitchen management. He remarks, "Our family had a very strong work ethic. I grew up in a big family. You either worked or didn't eat. My dad always made sure there was plenty of work for us to do whether at home or at the hotel. Also, while in Ireland, I grew up attending boarding schools. It's not as though you can just go to the fridge whenever you want. The boarding school would feed us three times a day, but it was more the case, you get what you get. I was always hungry."

It was this strong work ethic that helped him to persevere when he first arrived on the shores of San Francisco in 1974. With no work visa permit, Joe took jobs bartending or working in construction to get by. Eventually, he landed a cooking job at a local restaurant/bar where he slept upstairs in exchange for receiving the morning's bread delivery. There, he made friends with a wine sales agent who educated him in fine wines. He later moved to New York, where he met his former wife, only to have to return to Ireland. A year later, in 1977, he returned to the United States, this time legally, working at the renowned Pierre Hotel. He worked in the storeroom until a kitchen position became available. In 1979 his only son Evan was born. By 1986, he worked his way up through the kitchen organization from Breakfast Cook to Chef Entremetier and Chef Saucier. The laid back, amiable cook from Ireland had established himself as one of the Great Chefs of New York.

His professional career underway, Joe moved on to New York's famous "21" Club as Executive Sous Chef. There he oversaw all operations of the restaurant, working alongside notable chefs Chef Sailhac and Chef Rosensweig. Two years later, he left the Club to open the intimate and exclusive northern Italian restaurant, San Domenico, to which the New York Times awarded the coveted "3 Star" recognition. There he honed his culinary and management skills, training under the direction of Chef Valentino, a "2 Star" Michelin Chef.

In 1988, he became The Plaza Hotel's Executive Banquet Chef. His leadership role expanded to include 50 chefs under his direction. Here he utilized his artistic and administrative skills designing and overseeing all The Plaza's high-profile fund-raising functions, extravagant weddings and social events for celebrities, such as Donald and Ivana Trump, Eddie Murphy and Joan Rivers. Joe also planned and coordinated gala events for big name corporations such as Time Magazine's 75th Anniversary celebration and Tiffany's Feather Ball.

After twelve years, and with the start of a new millennia, Joe felt the need for fresh challenges. He assumed his new leadership role as Executive Chef at the Old Westbury Golf & Country Club for a year before becoming Executive Sous Chef at the New York restaurant Town.

Whether in New York or the Coast, Joe is very much in his element, a natural leader. With his calm, patient demeanor, quick wit and Irish charm, Joe brings to the Beau Rivage a solid culinary reputation and strong interpersonal skills. He possesses a rare ability to build a sense of team and confidence with his staff, as well as the ability to establish an easy rapport with hotel clients. His easy-going character belies a highly organized, efficient culinary master with a very hands-on management style. When asked about his management philosophy, Joe laughs, remarking, "Firm but fair. I grew up working for my father, for God's sake. There was no philosophy. You just worked. I've certainly mellowed over the years. I'm now more interested in creating a nurturing environment. It is very fulfilling for me when I find someone even halfway interested in learning."

When he is not working at the Beau, Joe can be found gardening and fixing up his house in Biloxi or just relaxing. His hobbies include collecting and reading an eclectic mix of cookbooks, mysteries and Irish history books, as well as travel, cooking and listening to a broad range of music from classical to jazz.

B R Prime

DINING AT BEAU RIVAGE

The culinary standard at Beau Rivage is on par with the world's finest resorts. From traditional cooking to exotic international cuisine, Beau Rivage's 10 distinctive restaurants and cafes offer a multitude of dining experiences and the resort's award-winning gourmet restaurants set a culinary standard that pleases even the most sophisticated palates.

Savor the chic ambiance where classic meets contemporary at **BR Prime**, Beau Rivage's signature steak and seafood restaurant. Only two percent of all beef produced in the U.S. is certified prime grade by the USDA and BR Prime serves nothing but this premium grade. The menu features classic American steakhouse fare including both wet-aged and dry-aged prime beef, Gulf shrimp, succulent lobster tail and stone crab, all prepared with expertise and regional flair. This synergy of substance and style is as apparent in the restaurant's design as it is in the outstanding dishes coming from its open kitchen. A *Wine Spectator* magazine Best of Award of Excellence winner, BR Prime complements its delectable cuisine with an extensive wine selection in its 3,500-bottle wine floor-to-ceiling towers.

BR Prime New Orleans Barbeque Shrimp

3 Jumbo Shrimp (U10).

1 tablespoon blackening spice.

½ tablespoon diced fresh rosemary.

½ tablespoon diced fresh thyme.

6 oz. light beer.

1 tablespoon Worcestershire sauce

1 tablespoon hot sauce.

1 clove garlic (thin slice).

2 tablespoons whole butter.

Garlic toast.

Season shrimp with blackening spice. Sear on one side in a hot pan with a small amount of butter or oil. Flip shrimp and add beer, rosemary, thyme, and garlic. Reduce to a syrup consistency, swirl in butter. Arrange shrimp on the toast, serve with sauce.

The Beau Rivage Buffet

THE BEAU RIVAGE BUFFET

The Buffet at Beau Rivage offers an enticing collection of specialty foods and southern favorites. This extraordinary dining atmosphere takes buffet dining to a new level with live-action stations, the freshest ingredients and meals custom prepared to meet every guest craving.

Seafood Gumbo

Makes 1 gallon

1 ½ cups diced Onion

1 ½ cups diced bell pepper

1 ½ cups diced celery

1 ½ cups chopped celery

1/3 cup shrimp base

¼ cup crab base

1 ½ cups andouille sausage

1 ½ cusps alligator sausage

dark roux (1 cup of oil to 1 cup of flour)

¼ cup tobacco sauce

1 ½ cups cut okra

¼ cup ounces kitchen bouquet

1 teaspoon coarse pepper

¼ teaspoon cayenne pepper

1 teaspoon gumbo filet

½ teaspoon old bay

0.18 ounces blackening sea

1/4 teaspoon dried thyme

blonde roux (including in dark roux)

4 cups gallons water

½ pound each shrimp & crawfish

Gather all of the ingredients. Heat the pot to 180°F. Add one tablespoon of cottonseed oil to the pot, add onions, celery, and bell pepper and fresh garlic. Add flour roux and all seasonings, add chicken bouquet, add tobacco, mix well add water. Add sausage and all bases to the water and let cook for one hour. Add okra and cook for 30 minutes. Pump in 1.5-gallon increments.

COAST
NIGHTCLUB & RESTAURANT

COAST
NIGHTCLUB & RESTAURANT

Coast

COAST

Beau Rivage's Coast fuels the appetite and the soul with hearty appetizers, plump and juicy hamburgers, brick-oven pizzas and savory entrees. When the sun goes down, Coast lights up as the hottest nightclub on the Gulf Coast with an energetic mix of people and the best live entertainment in town.

Queso Fundito with Pico Degallo

1block Pepper jack cheese　　　　　　*4 quarts heavy whipping cream*

In medium pot add cream and bring to a boil. Meanwhile, grate block of pepper jack cheese for easy melting. After you add the cheese, turn fire down on low to prevent scorching. When the cheese is completely melted it's ready.

Pico De Gallo

2 whole tomatoes
½ red onion
½ cup green onion
2 ounces cilantro
1 ounce olive oil
Pinch of salt
Pinch of pepper

Dice tomato, red onion and green onion and add to bowl. Rough chop cilantro and add. Drizzle olive oil and mix in salt and pepper. You can add more salt and pepper depending on your taste.

Fallen oak

FALLEN OAK

Fallen Oak continues to draw praise from golfers of all abilities and experiences for its inherent beauty and playability. The Beau Rivage-owned Tom Fazio-designed golf course was recognized by *Golf Digest* as having one of the "50 Best 19th Holes" in golf. Fallen Oak's 12,000-square foot Southern mansion clubhouse features a 19th hole that provides patrons panoramic views of the signature 18th hole and the course's namesake fallen oak and signature infused Bloody Mary's and Kobe Beef Sliders. Once golfers finish tackling the rugged par-4 18th and drive through the oak canopy to the clubhouse, they can repose to a 70-seat lounge that offers a world of cocktail and culinary comforts.

Golf Digest selected the best 19th holes based on places "golfers often would rather spend time there than in their own home." The magazine selected Fallen Oak based on a clubhouse mansion that "has an Old South feel" with service that "is Southern hospitality at its best."

Fallen Oak's Infused Bloody Mary Recipe

FALLEN OAK'S AWARD WINNING BLOODY MARY

Vodka slowly infused for six days with fresh oregano basil thyme garlic peppers onions and tomatoes. The infusion will use one liter of premium vodka in a gallon infusion jar/chamber and yield about 20oz. The herbs and vegetables will be added to taste and preference.

Kobe Beef Sliders

8 oz. ground Kobe beef

3 mini Brioche burger buns

3 Roma tomato slices

1 piece red leaf lettuce, cut into three pieces

1 oz. julienned red onion

1 sliced, aged, cheddar cheese

Salt & pepper

Take Kobe and dived it up into three even portions. Set to the side. Heat up a skillet, and then season the Kobe with salt and pepper. Place the Kobe into the heated skillet. Brown the meat until the whole patty is brown. Cook to preferred temperature of medium rare. Take the three brioche buns and brush with butter and flattop the buns until brown. Then pull off the flattop and place on the plate. On the plate, place the buns on the bun bottom place the lettuce and the tomato slice. After the Kobe has been cooked top with cheese and melt. Place burger on top of lettuce and tomato add the julienned onion top and serve with French fries.

Julienned Red Onions

1 red onion

8oz sugar

8oz white vinegar

Cut the red onion in half and turn on its side. Then slice thinly and set to the side. In a heated saucepan add the white vinegar and then the sugar. Blend in the sugar until the vinegar absorbs it. Add the red onion until they become translucent or bright purple in color. Pull from the burner drain and cool them down. After the onions are cool place into a container until served.

Waffle Fries

1 medium –sized Yukon Gold Potato (one serving)

Trim one side of the potato off with a chef's knife. With a mandolin using the crinkle side, run the potato over it. Turn the potato 180* and then down the mandolin to achieve the waffle cut. Then place into a container of water. Drain the water and rinse the potato off. Fry potato in the fryer at 350° until golden brown season and serve.

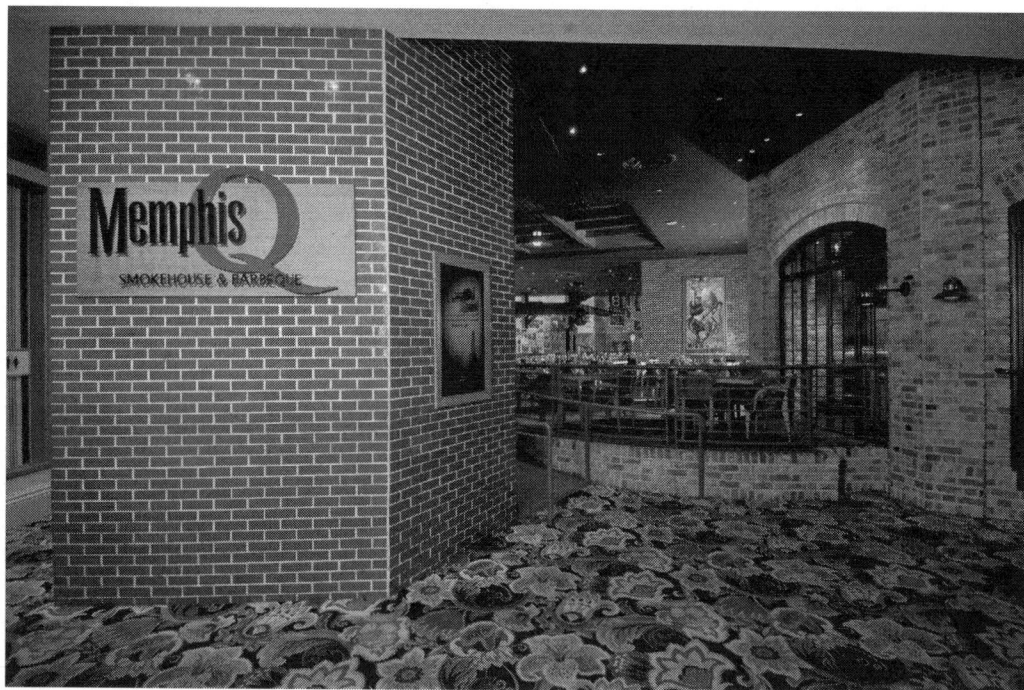

Memphis Q Smokehouse & Barbecue

MEMPHIS Q SMOKEHOUSE & BARBECUE

Cool Blues and hot barbecue are synonymous with Beau Rivage's Memphis Q. Guests enjoy thick, juicy steaks and Memphis traditions such as house-smoked chicken, fried delta catfish and deliciously tempting southern desserts.

Brisket Stuffed Mushrooms

10 large button mushrooms

1 teaspoon chopped garlic

2 tablespoons butter

2 cups smoked beef brisket meat

2 tablespoons shredded Mont. Jack Cheese

½ a diced onion

1 pinch of chopped fresh thyme

2 oz Sour cream

1 teaspoon of salt

1 teaspoon of pepper

3 teaspoons of BBQ spice

Pull stems from mushrooms and set aside. Melt butter in a medium fry pan. Cook half of the chopped garlic in the butter until browned. Add the mushroom caps to the fry pan and cook until done but not falling apart. Make stuffing in a food processor. Mix beef brisket, the rest of the garlic, the stems from the mushrooms, Mont. Jack cheese, diced onion, fresh thyme, sour cream, salt, pepper, and BBQ spice. Stuff mushrooms with stuffing and cook in the oven at 375° for about ten minutes. Serve with BBQ sauce.

Jia

JIA

Jia – Japanese for "beautiful" - dishes out authentic sushi, teppanyaki and pan-Asian cuisine created from simple, quality ingredients. Enveloped in Asian-Zen modern décor, *Jia* offers three distinct dining experiences – sushi bar, teppanyaki-style or a la carte dining. Artfully combining the best culinary traditions of Japan, China, Thailand, Vietnam and Hong Kong in one modern, sophisticated space, Jia's architecture blends traditionally celebrated elements of nature with modern materials. At the sushi bar, Jia serves only the highest quality sushi. For teppanyaki, Jia honors Japanese tradition with a separate traditional Ryokan structure teppanyaki room.

Peking Style Duck Breast Appetizer

4 oz duck breast	.5 oz Chinese mustard
1 oz soy sauce	1 pinch of b & w sesame seeds
1 oz sugar	1 whole sweet potato (peeled & diced)
1 teaspoon garlic	1/8 cup of butter
1 teaspoon fresh ginger	1 teaspoon brown sugar
1 teaspoon Hoisin sauce	1 Braised Baby Bok Choy
1 oz Mey Ploy sweet chili sauce	Salt & pepper to taste

Trim fat off the duck breast and remove any silver skin. Score the skin on X to make the skin cook faster. Mix soy sauce, garlic, ginger & hoisin sauce in a bowl, add the duck breast into the bowl and let marinate at least 15 to 20 minutes. In a sauté pan at medium heat place the duck breast skin side down until receiving a nice dark char and most of the fat has been rendered. In a saucepan cook your sweet potato until it is fork tender, add to a mixing bowl with the butter and brown sugar and smash until well incorporated. Let the duck breast rest for a few minutes so all the fat will run out then slice in small pieces and cook until medium rare - medium in an oven at 400° for 2 minutes more or less. Braised Bock Choy and sweet potato in the middle of the plate with the sliced duck on top, add Mey Ploy Chili Sauce on the side with the Chinese hot mustard and sesame seeds. Garnish with seasonal micro greens and fruit chutney.

Terrace Café

Terrace Cafe

TERRACE CAFÉ

Nestled in the lobby's atrium among dazzling garden displays, the Terrace Café provides the ideal locale for guests to relax in a casual setting as they enjoy an array of contemporary and classic American cuisine. This 24-hour café delivers a tempting selection of appetizers, entrees, sandwiches, salads and mouth-watering desserts.

Deviled Crab Louis

8 servings

> 2 heads of Romaine lettuce, one shredded.
>
> 1 head of iceberg lettuce, shredded.
>
> ½ bunch parsley, chopped.
>
> 4 red endives, separated into leaves
>
> 2 pounds jumbo lump crab.
>
> 8 hard boiled eggs, cut into quarters
>
> 1bunch chives, chopped

Shred one head of Romaine and iceberg lettuce. Line each salad with Romaine leaves and five red endives leaves. Mix shredded Romaine, iceberg and chopped parsley with enough Louis Dressing (below) to bind. Place shredded lettuce mixture in center of endive star. Place 4 oz. of picked jumbo lump crab on lettuce. Alternate hard-boiled eggs and tomatoes around endives star. Coat crabmeat with one tablespoon of Louis Dressing and sprinkle with chopped chives. Garnish with lemon wedges.

Deviled Louis Dressing

> 3½ cups
>
> 1 cup of your favorite salsa
>
> 1 tablespoon chipotle pepper
>
> 2 cups mayonnaise
>
> 2 tablespoons fresh lemon juice
>
> 1 teaspoon sugar
>
> ¼ cup water or milk

Mix everything, but the mayonnaise, in a blender until smooth. Pour into a bowl and stir in mayonnaise.

anjac's Barbecue

ANJAC'S BARBEQUE

The History of anjacs

If you're wondering how *anjac's BBQ* acquired its name, well the story goes something like this:

Over sixty years ago, in the country of Germany, Mr. Jack Meaks met Ann, his soon to be wife.

After Jack and Ann married, they moved to Gulfport Mississippi and opened a convenience store and named it *anjac's,* of course.

The store was doing well so Jack and Ann decided to create their own barbecue sauce and to start serving barbecue sandwiches, using their homemade barbecue sauce. The sandwiches were selling so well that the Meaks decided to add pork to their menu. Ribs came next and the menu continued to grow.

Years later, Jack and Ann passed away, leaving *anjac's* to their son, Michael, who continue to run the restaurant until 1988 when it burned to the ground.

After a year and a half, *anjac's* relocated to 29th street in Gulfport, right off Courthouse Road, but the restaurant soon suffered financial problems and was lost to the owner's of the building.

For the next seven months, due to name rights, *anjac's BBQ* operated under the name of Jac's BBQ. But when David and Lacy Vickers decided to purchase the restaurant, the name was immediately changed back to *anjac's BBQ and Burger Company*.

Since David and Lacy took over *anjac's*, the recipes have all been up-dated, and improved, all but the barbecue sauce, that is. *anjac's* still serves the original barbecue sauce created by Jack and Ann Meaks, the founder's of *anjac's*.

Thirteen days after hurricane Katrina hit the Mississippi Gulf Coast, *anjac's* was back in business and it has been an incredible journey ever since.

Besides their incredible barbecue, *anjac's* serves Po-Boys, shrimp, catfish, gumbo, potato salad, baked beans, cole slaw, potato cut fries and red beans and rice. For dessert, *anjac's* serves cobbler, bread pudding, cheesecake and more. They also offer full service catering and since *anjac's* BBQ sauce has become so popular, David and Lacy are offering it on their website, www. anjacsbbq.com.

Twice Baked Potatoes

(adjust recipe according to number of potatoes you need)

> *10 potatoes*
>
> *2 1/2 pounds sour cream*
>
> *1 pound butter*
>
> *2 ounces granulated garlic*
>
> *1/2 ounce white pepper*
>
> *4 ounces bacon bits*
>
> *1/4 quart half and half*
>
> *1 ounce dried parsley flakes*
>
> *8 ounces cheddar cheese*

Wrap potatoes in foil and bake until tender. Approximately an hour and a half at 350° Remove foil, cut potatoes in half. Scoop the potato meat out into a bowl, mash. Add all other ingredients and incorporate. Using a spatula, place in potato shells, cover, refrigerate. Place cheddar cheese on top of potato and microwave for one minute.

Pulled Pork

> *1 each pork butt,*
>
> *Approximately 6-7lbs.*
>
> *BBQ rub*

Rub pork butt all over, covering well. Place in smoker for about 8-10 hours. Remove and place on pan, remove excess fat. Sprinkle pork with a little more rub and pull pork apart. It is best to pull the pork while it is hot!

anjac's chicken and sausage gumbo

1 cup oil

1 cup flour

2/3 cups chopped bell peppers

2 cups chopped onions

1/2 cup parsley

1 chicken

2 pounds sausage

2 bay leaves

2 ounces granulated garlic

8 ounces chicken base

2 to 3 small cans diced tomatoes

Browning sauce

Black pepper

Heat oil in steamer; add flour to make roux, stirring constantly until smooth. Cook chicken for 1 hour on high heat, drain and pick off chicken, no bones!! Add 2 gallons of hot water, stir well. Cook for two hours, stirring often.

anjac's # 2

ANJAC'S BARBECUE #2

This new location of anjac's is immediately outside Keesler Air Force base's gate seven at the east end of Pass road in Biloxi, Mississippi. "The biggest comment I am getting" said owner, David Vickers is, *Thank God I won't have to drive all the way to Gulfport, ya'll are finally here.*" The menu is basically the same as anjac's number one; however they do have a larger dining area.

anjac's red beans

5 pounds red kidney beans

3 chopped bell peppers

2 chopped yellow onions

1 ounce parsley-dry

2 ounces granulated garlic

1 1/2 ounce black pepper

8 ounces chicken base

3 ounces oil

2 pounds sausage

2 gallons water

2 bay leaves

Place bell peppers, onions and oil in steam kettle, sauté until tender. Add all seasonings, mix well with a long handle spoon, cook for 5 minutes. Add red beans. Add 2 gallons water, stir. Cook until beans are very tender, approximately 2-2 1/2 hours, stirring every 15 minutes.

Bread Pudding

15 cups bread, torn in pieces

9 eggs

2 1/2 cups sugar

1 quart heavy cream

3 tablespoons vanilla

1 tablespoon nutmeg

1 tablespoon cinnamon

Mix all ingredients and pour into greased pan. Bake at 400° for 35 minutes

Anjac's # 3

ANJAC'S #3

Home of the biggest burger on the Mississippi Gulf Coast. Located 12407 Highway 49 North, Orange Grove, Mississippi

Back Bay Seafood Restaurant

BACK BAY SEAFOOD

Rob Stinson, Executive Chef and Owner of Gulfport's Back Bay Seafood, Lookout 49, Salute Italian Restaurant and formerly Long Beach Lookout and has made a huge impact on the Mississippi Gulf Coast in the past seven years. Lookout 49 was voted "Best Seafood Restaurant on the Gulf Coast 2006." Rob trained under Cordon Bleu Chef Gerald Thabuis, former Chef for President of France, Charles DeGaulle, Master Italian Chef Ciro Cuomo, and Creole Chef extraordinaire Nathaniel Burton. He has three TV cooking segments weekly, "Lunch at the Lookout," and "Salute!" on WLOX-ABC TV and "That's What I Like About The South," on FOX TV WXXV. His spectrum of work has spanned from 5-star dining at Windsor Court Hotel Grill Room, to managing the highest volume restaurant in the world, Orlando Planet Hollywood. Rob's community involvement has separated him from other businesses on the Gulf Coast as he serves as president of the Long Beach Rotary and former president of the Long Beach Chamber of Commerce, and sits on the board of many other committees. Rob was chosen by Governor Barbour to represent the State of Mississippi as their official Chef in the Great American Seafood Cook-off in New Orleans in 2007 and 2009. Rob was born in Mount Vernon, New York, grew up in Shaker Heights, Ohio and attended Miami University in Oxford Ohio. Rob, his wife Paige, children Samuel and Abigail live in Long Beach Mississippi.

LONG BEACH LOOKOUT, LOOKOUT 49 & SALUTE ITALIAN RESTAURANTS

A team history...

Long Beach Lookout began as a dream of Rob Stinson, Joe Jefferson and Steve Huber. In April of 2002 this trio acquired the location that was formerly known as "Fish & Bones," on beautiful Long Beach Harbor by the boat launch. It was a beautiful building with one of the best panoramic views of the Gulf. The Lookout, its familiar name to locals, struggled at the outset because of the prior restaurant's reputation. Rob utilized the variety of cuisines he had learned in New Orleans, working under great chefs like: Gerald Thabuis, Cordon Bleu Chef of France, Ciro Cuomo, Master Chef of Italy and Nataniel Burton, Creole Chef extraordinaire, to create a menu that separated the Lookout from other Coast restaurants. The menu evolved by listening to the customers and refining the changes to accommodate their tastes.

The Team:

While the Lookout's menu was building so was the staff. Denis Trochesset was a waiter when Rob opened the Lookout. Denis separated himself from other employees by arriving at 8am and reading novels in his car. Awesome on the floor, willing to accept change and adapt, and leading others, Denis quickly became an indispensable asset to the company. Denis was promoted through the ranks from waiter, to manager, to general manager, and finally offered the opportunity to buy in as a working partner of the restaurant by Rob, Joe and Steve. He has continued to be Rob's right hand in business and a great friend.

In July of 2004, Rob searched New Orleans for an old restaurant friend and great chef, Cory Fazzio. By the luck of fate, Cory was unhappy in his current job (his last paycheck had bounced-ugh!) and willing to relocate to the Gulf Coast. Cory walked into Lookout on the busy July 4th weekend and when the current chef quit, he quickly assumed the helm and has never looked back. Helping to open Lookout 49 and Salute, Cory has established himself as an equity partner in Salute.

Rachel Edwards. Who can say enough about Rachel! Smiling face, Southern drawl, great bartender, and everyone's personal psychologist who sits at her bar, she has a long history at

Lookout as well. Working as a server at Fish & Bones briefly, while she bartended at Outback (9 years) Rob met her and was dismayed when she quit after he bought the restaurant. Determined to get her back, after the Lookout gathered steam and was getting busy before Katrina, Rob got his wish. Offering her the bar managing position she came on board with Lookout and built a great bar clientele on the beach. Friday night at the bar with Rachel became a way of life for many Long Beach residents. Moving on and helping rebuild the bar at Lookout 49, and now an equity partner in Salute, Rachel is a key player on the team.

Long Beach Lookout was in the third year of operation in August of 2005, and sales were great.

Sales were increasing every month compared to the previous year and the partners and team were excited. Rob had planned a massive advertising campaign in August to overcome the dreaded month of September- the slowest month of the year. "Meat- The Menu," was the promotion and new dishes like lamb, veal and pork chops were the ammunition. TV, radio and newspaper ads were all in place for the Lookout. Orders were in, menus designed and new preparations for the staff were all ready for the promotion. The kitchen had just been redesigned to accommodate the additional business and then came the warning...

Samuel Stinson, Rob's 10 year old son, woke Rob up at 5am Sunday morning, August 28th. "Dad it's a category 5 hurricane and it is coming right for us!!!" Lookout had planned to open for business Sunday because so many times hurricanes had been false alarms. People were living the proverbial "boy who cried wolf," when it came to evacuating for hurricanes. This time is was different. Rob called the forces and started removing all computers, catering equipment and liquor from the restaurant. Rob knew three things: the restaurant would be gone and he needed records for insurance and sales, they would be serving relief workers with the catering equipment and that his staff and friends would want the liquor to keep their sanity!

As we all know now, Katrina smashed the Gulf Coast and life changed forever. Lookout was gone, and so was just about everything else from the railroad tracks south. Devastating, horrible, catastrophic are just a few of the words used to describe the aftermath of Katrina. Pork chops, lamb and veal were scattered in the remains of Dad's Super Pawn in Long Beach. Marketing promotions became a thought of the past. After replacing the roof at his house, Rob packed his family and was off to Ohio to stay with his mother in Chagrin Falls. Hoping to begin a new life, Rob and family cuddled and regrouped in the sanctity of a different area where hurricanes are not a factor. All that changed after Rob called the insurance company for the restaurant. The 150k loss of income policy that would pay the bills while deciding what to do was not going to pay. Insurance companies became a hated word after Katrina. Wind not flood, flood not wind, whatever the way out was, it seemed that insurance companies would use it so as not to pay the policies. Rob panicked. What are we going to do? Rob, Joe, Steve and Denis (now a partner) had just purchased the lease and rights of Long Beach Lookout. They had not even paid one note. How would they pay the $7500/month note? Rob realized that they would have to find another location immediately and get back in business. Where? How?

The Lookout 49...

Denis stayed on the Coast after the hurricane. Denis's priorities were helping friends and family while attempting to gain some sense of normalcy. Rob had received notice from his Sysco rep that there was a possible location in Orange Grove to utilize for the Lookout. Rob called Denis to explain that there was no insurance coming to cover their down time, and that they needed to get back in the game. Time was of the essence because so many restaurants were destroyed and there were other restaurateurs looking for a location. Rob asked Denis to go give a check to secure the location the next day. 21 days later the Lookout 49 was born.

The team is the reason for the quick opening. Denis, Rachel, Cory and team worked day and night to renovate the location while Rob handled getting the myriad of permits necessary for a restaurant. The State of Mississippi was unbelievably helpful to local businesses trying to reopen. Rob traveled to Jackson, Hattiesburg, while Denis bought equipment out of state. The team decided that the Lookout was going to be a full menu restaurant (many operations after Katrina served only 4 or 5 items at exorbitant prices) serving reasonably priced food, with cable TV, taking credit cards and offering a complete bar. The first restaurant to relocate and reopen, Lookout 49 was incredibly busy. Feeding relief workers, church volunteers and homeless families, Lookout saw many tears of happiness in the first days.

The Team Grows...

Debra Williams, a former employee of Chimney's Restaurant, asserted herself from day one at Lookout 49. Helping rebuild the bar, clean the restaurant and hire and train the staff, Debra was the obvious choice to manage the Lookout. Debra and team allowed the busy restaurant to do the impossible- Keep a staff when everyone on the Gulf Coast was looking for help. People didn't want to work after Katrina. Sitting on money given by FEMA, many workers simply didn't decide to get back into the routine of daily work. Lookout 49, through great leadership and teamwork was able to keep a staff and maintain the highest level of service possible in extremely difficult times. The success of Lookout 49 is due to the incredible teamwork of the staff.

Catering Emerges and the Team Grows...

Ron Craven walked into Lookout 49 two weeks after the storm looking for work as a waiter. Rob spotted him and immediately screamed "you're hired!" Ron had waited on Rob at Chimney's restaurant before the storm and was the best waiter he had seen in Mississippi. Calm, well organized and personable, Ron Craven emerged as the Lookout 49's catering director. Large relief groups became a daily event at Lookout. There were very few restaurants that could handle weddings, business groups and government agencies that wanted catered parties. Ron became the go to person for parties and has grown into an incredible asset for the Lookout 49 and Salute Italian restaurants. Training Juanita Shaw as his assistant, they became the team called upon to satisfy large groups both on premise and off.

Lookout 49 became an oasis in the desert of the Gulf Coast.

Salute!!!

Fema, Mema, grants, permits, contractors and insurance companies all seemed to move at a snail's pace when rebuilding the Gulf Coast was concerned. The lease of Lookout 49 was in question so another location was a must. Rob had been in touch with the city of Long Beach, and unfortunately all of the above agencies kept the harbor off limits until all utilities could be completely rebuilt. Over a year after Katrina, Long Beach Lookout couldn't be constructed, so Rob and Denis decided to look elsewhere. Denis had been in communication with Jeanie from Blue Cross of Mississippi, and she mentioned a location on the beach in Gulfport. Rob started the lease negotiations for a magnificent location in the fabulous 15th Place building of Mark Davis and Ron Feder. 15th Place had been the home of "The Irish Coast Pub," and "Java Jean's Coffee Shop" before the storm. The rest of the building houses three law firms, and was finished about two years before the hurricane. The building resembles a "Mediterranean, Italian structure" and may just be the finest architectural specimen on the Gulf Coast. Perfect for the Italian restaurant that Mark and Ron wanted, Rob and crew started the design for a great Italian fare restaurant. Salute was the perfect chance to design the perfect restaurant. Rob sat down on a Friday night at six o'clock, and at midnight had the plans laid out for the restaurant. A long bar overlooking the Gulf was the starting point. Next was the open air kitchen perfected by Cory and Rob. Booths and tables fell into place and in June of 2007 "Salute Italian Restaurant" opened. Unable to maintain a full staff because of the lack of a work force on the Gulf Coast, Salute started with dinner only. It was extremely busy. Well received, Salute began to gain popularity. Rachel's bar now became one of the hot spots on the Coast. With a magnificent view of the water, Salute's martini bar quickly became a favorite of the Gulfport elite. Judges, attorneys, business owners and the like frequented the bar. Giving their input, with Rachel and team listening, the bar has prospered. Cory and team perfected the food. Cooking out of an exhibition kitchen, the food evolved and became a mixed menu of Italian and local fare

The Team Grows...

James Crumbley is the current chef at Lookout 49. Terry Ftizpatrick has been the rock of Gibralter in the prep kitchen. Chad Henson, a bartender and server from Lookout, became the manager at Salute while the front of the house team grew. Juanita Shaw is now the Catering Director of Lookout 49. Too many more to list in this book, it needs to be said- the success of Lookout and Salute has been because of the great team.

The Future...

Focused on getting back to Long Beach harbor, Rob, Denis, Steve and Joe will be designing a new building for Long Beach Lookout. Having obtained an additional term to their lease (52 years total) the team will be planning their return to the original location sometime in 2009. Great young talent like Michael Sigafoose and others will help shape the daily operation of this new restaurant, menu and staff. This long awaited return to the location where the team began will be the next chapter in this story. Stay tuned for the details....

The Hidden Team...

It needs to be said that in the midst of all this turmoil, there have been unsung heroes in the shadows of our team. The wives and girlfriend of the owners need their own praise. Paige Stinson, Andrea Trochesset, Katie Jefferson and Darcy Lequerre have been the ones to console, counsel and often participate in the daily operation of the restaurants. It is only through their happiness, that the team has been allowed to prosper.

Back Bay Begins...

Opportunity lurks in the strangest of places... Rob Stinson watched a beautiful restaurant being built on the site of the old Kremer Marine in Gulfport. Hurricane Katrina had destroyed so many restaurants on the Gulf Coast, so when a new one was built it gained a lot of attention. The intersection of Cowan and Magnolia road appeared to be the perfect location for a new restaurant called Tugs Wharf. The restaurant was designed to have a great view of the water where Bayou Bernard flows from Back Bay (Big Lake) to the Three Rivers area. Surrounded by some of the finest houses on the entire Coast, Tug's Wharf appeared to have a great location. Unfortunately this magnificent building did not fare well for the owner Joe Tuggle, and Rob began the discussion of taking this location and creating a new restaurant. It seems that the team of Rob Stinson, Denis Trochesset and Cory Fazzio, have a habit of taking locations that haven't fared well and turning them around into successful operating restaurants. The "team concept" is the secret behind the success that has helped transform these locations into profitable operations. There are many team players who help with the huge job of creating and opening a new restaurant.

The Name

Back Bay has traditionally been associated to the Biloxi Big Lake, but Rob thought the alliteration of Back Bay would be remembered better than Bayou Bernard. The fact that the bayou meanders into Back Bay was enough to capitalize on, and the name was born. Back Bay in large red neon would be the essence of the new sign on top of the restaurant so it would be easily seen from the bridge on Cowan road.

The Theme

Back Bay, being located on the water, would have to feature local seafood and to give some "pizzazz" Boston lobster was added. A unique logo with red claws of shellfish was created by the graphic genius of Dave Johnson in New Orleans. Dave is the artist that creates the annual Mardi Gras Poster for Arthur Hardy's Mardi Gras Guide book. Dave has a unique talent of combining brilliant colors and appropriate themes through graphic art.

Casual dining with great food at affordable prices has been the recipe for success with all the restaurants the team has opened on the Coast. Long Beach Lookout, Lookout 49 and Salute Italian restaurants have all featured these characteristics. Back Bay would obviously do the same. A comfortable environment was also important. A vibrant mustard yellow, rich cream, complemented by natural woodwork would be reminiscent of the original restaurant: Long Beach Lookout. Lookout was also located on the water and Rob and Denis felt that choosing the same colors might make some of the customers feel at home. Menu development came next and this is Cory's strong point.

The Menu

Where Lookout was known for its Creole seafood menu, and Salute its Italian fare, Back Bay wasn't constrained by any preconceived notion of menu. Back Bay would have some Creole, Seafood, Burgers, Asian, wraps & po-boys. Affordable prices, coupled with great portions is a great way to build customer loyalty. Featuring many dishes that regular customers know from the other restaurants, would give the clientele the feeling that they had come home.

The Opening

In June of 2009, Back Bay Seafood Restaurant was officially born. Cory and Denis were ready with a great menu, the décor and sign were in place and the staff came from Lookout, Salute and elsewhere. It was an immediate hit! People were excited that a new operation was started and they came to check out the menu. Dining on the deck, sitting inside and viewing the sunsets from the bar all fell into place. In the first few months open, the menu was perfected to accommodate the desires of the customers. It has become a "neighborhood restaurant" and the local clientele has taken ownership of the concept. Perhaps the best burger on the Coast has evolved. Who would have thought that a seafood restaurant would become known for the best hand-formed fresh burger, char-grilled to order!

Long Beach Shrimp & Grits

1 small box grits　　　　　　　　　　　　　　*¼ cup butter*

2 cups water

Make grit recipe according to box. Pour hot grits into a greased cake pan 9 X 12. Let cool in fridge till firm and easy to cut. These cakes can be colored with puree spinach and red bell peppers to make them holiday colored if you like. Place grit cakes (cold) on heated skillet and brown in butter on both sides till warm inside

2 tablespoons oil

4 ounces garlic

8 ounces WASI Shrimp

4 ounces portabella mushrooms

4 ounces bacon

1 teaspoon Italian seasoning

2 ounces wine

8 ounces cream

2 ounces parmesan cheese

2 ounces tomato, chopped

1 ounce green onion, chopped

Heat oil in sauté' pan. Add garlic and lightly brown. Add shrimp, mushrooms and bacon. Deglaze with wine and add Italian seasoning and cream. Let reduce and add parmesan. Ladle over grit cake in a bowl. Garnish with fresh chopped tomato and green onion.

Back Bay Shrimp Mediterranean

3 ounces extra virgin olive oil

8 ounces shrimp

4 ounces artichoke hearts

4 ounces portabella mushrooms

2 ounces kalamata olives

2 ounces capers

4 ounces sun-dried tomatoes

2-4 ounces garlic

2 ounces white wine

4 ounces feta cheese

1 bag mescaline mix (mixed greens)

2 pieces kale

2 each lemon wheel

In Italy this dish is cooked sway sway: fast fast. It is flavorful and fun to cook and great for summer dinner or lunch parties where you don't want to waste time or heat-UGH! In skillet place oil and garlic. Lightly brown garlic and add shrimp, artichoke, portabella, olives, capers and sun-dried tomatoes. Deglaze with wine and place on top of mixed greens. Top with feta cheese for a treat. Garnish with kale and lemon and perhaps a slice of grilled bread.

Capone's Italian Ristorante

CAPONE'S

Italian Ristorante

Chef Danie opened Capone's Italian Ristorante in Ocean Springs, Mississippi on April 26, 2009. Capone's was built as a replica of Del Castle; a house that Al Capone was said to have stayed in. "We kind of make a joke out of it" say Chef Danie, "we say it's like one of Capone's hideouts. It kind of becomes part of the whole mystique"

Capone's restaurant was the second for Chef Danie and was opened to be closer to a customer base that had been driving to Pappa Roni's Italian Foods in Vancleave for 14 years.

"We thought it would be nicer to be close to our guests that have supported us for so long" said Chef Danie

Chef Danie has always enjoyed working with young people who have an interest in the culinary field and has raised her family in the business. Her son, Ferrill, works as her sous chef, her daughter, Jillian, works as a hostess and her husband, Chuck, moonlights as a bartender at night, after his day job as a barber at *Hair Razors;* one of their other businesses.

"My father's family is Italian" says Chef Danie, "which is where most of my inspiration comes from. We just play around, basically, with creating and developing recipes, always; that's the fun part, that's the creative part, when we actually get to do that

"We have been totally self employed for 20 years and owned a total of four businesses at one time.

Capone's and Pappa Roni's are very dear to our hearts and we strive to put out the best Italian Foods possible. We use local ingredients and cook by the seasons. Our menu changes every 6 months."

Chef Danie teaches pasta classes on Monday nights at the restaurant and shares with everyone how they make their own fresh pasta; she has her own cooking show called *Capone's Kitchen,* in conjunction with REI Productions, which airs twice a week where she shares all of the recipes from the restaurant and family, and she works with young people and the teachers at Ocean Springs Culinary dept to encourage their culinary career.

Chef Danie sets up every Saturday at the Fresh Market in Ocean Springs and sells all of the fresh products from Capone's as well as sharing recipes and ideas for meals that guests at the market can make at home using the products they purchase at the market; she is very passionate about bringing the freshest food possible to her guests at Capone's and all of the products made in house are sold and shipped all over the country and can be ordered on their website; **Capone-soceansprings.com.**

Appetizers at Capone's include Foccacia Dip, which is an in house specialty, Clams in garlic sauce and baked onion topped with garlic and Gorgonzola. The salads are served in a fresh bread bowl with in house dressing. The entrees include Veal Parmesan and Chicken or veal Marsala, Shrimp Pomodoro, Manicotti, Mediterranean Pesce and so much more.

Capone's also serves pizza with many toppings to choose from as well as Gourmet pizzas such as Margherita pizza, Pesto Pizza and make your own pizza. Capone's full menu can be viewed on their website.

Look for us on facebook at Chef Danie

Chef Danie's Bolognese Lasagna

1 lb. ground veal	*1 teaspoon ground oregano (can substitute*
2 lb. ground chuck	*Italian Seasoning)*
½ yellow onion chopped	*Salt & pepper to taste*
3 cloves garlic chopped	*2 tablespoons extra virgin olive oil*
3 cups tomato sauce	*1 container ricotta cheese*
1 tablespoon granulated garlic	*3 cups mozzarella cheese*
1 tablespoon onion powder	*Sheets of fresh pasta or store bought lasagna*

In a cast iron pot (preferable) add extra virgin oil and garlic and onions. Cook until slightly translucent then add veal and ground chuck, salt, pepper and other seasonings. Cook until all meat is browned, add tomato sauce and season again. Let cook about 30 minutes. In a lasagna pan that is buttered, start your first layer with Bolognese sauce (thin layer). Top with pasta sheets and more Bolognese and ¼ mozzarella. Next layer of pasta and container of ricotta cheese and ¼ of the mozzarella. Then another layer of pasta and Bolognese and ¼ of the mozzarella. Last layer is pasta and Bolognese and mozzarella. Bake 375° for 35 minutes for fresh pasta and 45 minutes for store bought pasta. Let the lasagna set before cutting. About 20 minutes. Serves 6-8

Chef Danie's Pesto Chicken Lasagna

1 jar rotisserie chicken, picked from the bone

1 jar roasted red bell peppers

1 jar Chef Danie's Four Cheese Sauce or store bought Alfredo

sauce

1 jar Chef Danie's Basil Pesto or store bought pesto

3 cups mozzarella cheese

Fresh sheets of pasta or store bought lasagna

In a lasagna pan that has been buttered, start by putting a thin layer of cheese sauce on the bottom, followed by a layer of fresh pasta. Top the fresh pasta with 1/3 of the cheese sauce, ½ of the chicken, ½ of the bell peppers and ½ of the pesto and ¼ of the mozzarella. The next layer is fresh pasta, ricotta cheese and ¼ of the mozzarella topped with another layer of fresh pasta. On top of this, add 1/3 of the cheese sauce, the rest of the chicken, bell peppers and pesto and ¼ of the mozzarella. Top this with fresh pasta and cheese sauce and the last of the mozzarella. Bake 375° for 20-30 minutes. Let the lasagna rest before serving.

Pappardelle Pasta

3 cups flour
5-6 eggs
¼ cup extra virgin olive oil
Thyme leaves

Blend all ingredients together in food processor until it forms a ball. Remove from processor and allow to rest 5 minutes. Roll dough out in small sections. Roll to about 1/8 inch then cut into strips about 1 ½ in-2 in wide. Lay on a pan to hold until water comes to a rolling boil. Cook pasta for about 8 minutes. Serve topped with rabbit spezzatini.

Rabbit Spezzatini with Thyme Pappardelle Pasta

1 whole rabbit cut up
Mushrooms
1 onion
6 cloves garlic
Granulated garlic
granulated onion
Spinach
1 green bell pepper (sliced)
1 cup flour
Salt & pepper
4 cups tomato sauce

Put flour in a bowl and season with salt & pepper. Add about ½ cup olive oil to a pan and turn on heat. When pan is warm put floured pieces of rabbit into the pan and fry until slightly browned on both sides. Remove from the pan and set aside. In a dutch oven add olive oil and the rest of the garlic cloves coarsely chopped. Add rabbit to the pan and all the veggies. Add tomato sauce to cover everything. You may need a little bit of water also. Season sauce with 2 tablespoons garlic and 2 tablespoon onion and salt & pepper to taste. Let cook covered for about 1 hour.

Chili Willie's Pizzeria ~

CHILI WILLIE'S PIZZERIA ~

Chili Willie's Pizzeria

Orange Grove location

Willie Orr grew up in Riverhead, New York (long Island) and has been a resident of the Mississippi Gulf Coast since 1979; the last four years in Pass Christian.

Willie wanted to bring the flavor of the pizzas he grew up with in New York to the coast and to offer a full service restaurant feel so he opened *Chili Willie's Pizzeria* in Norwood shopping center in Orange Grove, November of 2007.

Besides pizza, *Chili Willie's Pizzeria* has many sandwiches and pastas on the menu as well as half pound burgers, hot wings, salads, subs, hero's garlic knots, and they make their own dough and marinara fresh daily. They also blend two types of mozzarella cheese to get that *just right flavor*. *Chili Willie's Pizzeria* offers a **VIP club email program** that gives coupons to their regular guests who sign up on their website.

www.chiliwilliespizzeria.com

Baked Ziti

2 tablespoon olive oil

1.2 cup onion, coarsely chopped

2 teaspoons dried oregano

2 teaspoons dried basil, crumbled

8 ounces ricotta

1 teaspoon salt

2 tablespoons dried parsley

1 pound Italian sausage, casing removed

3 ½ cup tomato sauce

½ cup grated Parmesan

1 pound ziti or penne pasta

½ pound mozzarella, shredded

(about 2 cups)

In a large sauté pan, warm olive oil over medium-high heat for 1 minute. Add onion and sauté, stirring, 2 minutes. Add Italian sausage and cook and stir, crumbling sausage, 5-6 minutes, or until sausage is cooked through. Remove from heat and drain odd excess grease. Add tomato sauce, oregano, and basil. Cook sauce at a steady simmer while preparing the rest of the dish. In a large bowl, combine ricotta, salt, parsley and parmesan. Set aside (refrigerate if any unused for longer than 30 minutes. Cook pasta in plenty of boiling salted water until about half cooked. Drain pasta, shock, then set aside to dry further if you have time. Add pasta to ricotta cheese mixture and stir well to combine. Preheat oven to 400°. Remove sauce from heat and allow to cool, about 5 minutes. Add sauce to the pasta and ricotta mixture and combine well. Pour pasta sauce mixture into a full size pan. Level top with the back of a spatula or spoon. Spread mozzarella evenly over pasta. Tent some foil over the dish and bake about 15 minutes or until sauce starts to bubble. Remove foil and bake an additional 5 minutes, or until cheese starts to brown. Cool and prepare like Lasagna.

Zucchini Lasagna

3 zucchini

½ container of ricotta cheese

1 lb. of shredded mozzarella

Four cheese blend (equal parts of Parmesan, Assiago, Provolone, and whole milk Mozzarella)

1box pre-cooked lasagna noodles

Marinara

(yields 1 tray of lasagna)

Using a green handled ladle, scoop two ladles of marinara onto bottom of pan spreading evenly. Place two pre-cooked lasagna noodles side by side in pan. Add two scoops of marinara and spread evenly on noodles. Add zucchini by spreading out evenly. Cover with mozzarella. Repeat. Two noodles, add marinara, spread ricotta cheese (about a centimeter in thickness). Two noodles, add marinara. Add zucchini by spreading out evenly. Cover with four cheese blend. Sprinkle with pizza dust. Put in oven at 375°. Watch until top is a light golden brown.

Pass Christian location

Chili Willie's Pizzeria in Pass Christian opened the latter part of February, 2009, following a yearlong desire to open in that area. The holdup was finding an affordable location; however, they were fortunate enough to get the former Lizzy's Cafe' location on Davis Avenue.

Willie Orr lives in the Pass and felt the one thing missing in Pass Christian was pizza. He felt it was the place to grow and has not been disappointed. The reception from the citizens of Pass Christian has been overwhelming. *"They are such nice people and though we had to downsize our menu a bit due to the small kitchen, we still have a good diverse menu."*

Caprese Salad

Thick slices of fresh mozzarella
Thick slices of fresh Roma tomato (long way)
Fresh basil

Coarsely ground pepper
Olive oil
Balsamic Vinegar

Place slices of tomato on dish topped with a whole leave of basil then place mozzarella slice on top. Drizzle with olive oil and Balsamic vinegar, top off with ground black pepper.

Zeppole

Take your favorite pizza dough and roll out. Cut triangles and deep fry in 350° oil until floating and lightly browned. Be sure to turn over for even cooking. Remove and drain and lightly sprinkle powdered sugar on top, eat while warm…Very Good!

Willie Orr
President
Chili Willie's Pizzeria
12100 Hwy 49, Suite 612
Gulfport, MS. 39503
228-831-9117
228-547-4005 Cell
www.chiliwilliespizzeria.com

Clay Oven Indian and Mexican Restaurant

CLAY OVEN
INDIAN AND MEXICAN
RESTAURANT

Akarsh Kolaprath started his journey as a pastry chef at Leela's hotel in Bombay, India. He was amongst five graduates from a batch of one hundred seventy five that was selected to work for a five star rated hotel. Akarsh worked at Leela's for eight months before he was selected to work for Carnival cruise lines. He was one of the youngest chefs at Leela's to be chosen by Carnival cruises. During his career with Carnival, Akarsh worked as a pastry chef, a bar manager and finally an assistant food and beverage manager. His hard work and dedication shined through the years and he finally decided to move on and open his own restaurant, a dream that every chef has. He opened an Indian restaurant in Mandeville, Louisiana called *India 4 U*. His talent and the food was well recognized by everyone. In a short time, his dream was a success.

Akarsh was determined to open another restaurant. He always loved the Gulf Coast and knew that he would want to settle by the beach someday so for about six months, he searched for the right location and finally found what he was looking for. When he first saw the location, there was nothing left but four walls because everything else was destroyed by Hurricane Katrina; however, Akarsh had faith in the city and wanted to be a part of the post development of Gulfport. Akarsh had a vision of remodeling the building and opening an Indian and Mexican restaurant with an Equinox lounge and bar upstairs. On October Twenty Fourth, 2009, his vision became a reality and *Clay Oven* opened its doors to the public. People were instantly fascinated by the restaurant and its beautiful décor and couldn't wait to try Indian food.

Clay Oven serves authentic Indian and Mexican food. Indian cuisine is very time consuming and requires years of experience to perfect. Akarsh has that experience after many years of preparing Indian food and his dishes are truly perfection.

Indian cuisine has various spices and many ingredients so the flavors are bold and fragrant. Spices and aromatics are the very heart if Indian cooking.

Since there are a large variety of Indian food choices on the menu, everyone can find something they would like to try.

Flowers, leaves, roots, bark, seeds and bulbs; the simplest of natural ingredients, are used in endless combinations to produce an infinite variety of flavors; sweet, sharp, hot, spicy, aromatic, tart, mild, fragrant or pungent. Their tastes and aromas combine to create a kaleidoscope of exotic flavors to delight the palate. Indian spices also offer significant health benefits. They also add flavor and nutrients to dishes, without adding fat or calories. Another unique thing about Indian cooking is the traditional clay oven, which is only found in restaurants. All the breads and some of the meats and shrimp dishes are prepared in the clay oven. The taste and texture of the food achieved with a traditional clay oven cannot be compared to any microwave or regular oven cooking. *Clay Oven's* famous *Garlic naan* is to die for.

Here are some of our customer's favorite dishes:

Malai Kofta – Potato and vegetable croquets cooked in a creamy herb sauce

Palak Paneer – Creamy spinach with Indian spice and cubes of Indian cheese

Chicken Tikka Masala – Clay oven cooked, white meat chicken, cooked in a creamy tomato and onion based sauce

Indian Style Talapia – Pan seared with Indian herbs and spices; a very healthy choice

Seared Tuna Steak – Garlic marinated yellow fin tuna, drizzled with spicy Indian cheese sauce

Catfish Vindaloo – Crispy fried catfish, served with a fiery red tangy tomato based sauce with potatoes (very spicy)

Shrimp Malabar – Fresh Gulf coast shrimp, grilled to perfection and cooked with a special coconut flavored sauce

Lamb Korma – Diced lamb cooked in a creamy, mildly spiced, Indian curry sauce with ground nuts and raisins

Goat Curry – Tender pieces of goat, cooked in a mild and flavorful curry sauce

Tandoori Chicken – Half chicken breast and leg marinated overnight in yogurt and cooked with Tandoori spices in a traditional clay oven.

These are just some of the dishes amongst a variety of others to choose from. Indian appetizers are also very popular and unique. Vegetable Samosa and Chili are a couple of the favorites of the customers. Oh !! Don't forget the desserts. Kulfi and Mango ice cream is a definite must to try.

The Mexican food at the *Clay Oven* is excellent. Some of the favorites are; Fajitas, Fried Ice – cream and caramel flan.

EQUINOX LOUNGE AND BAR

Located upstairs from the restaurant, the *Equinox Lounge and Bar* is a perfect spot for a dinner and dancing. You can have a scrumptious meal and burn it all off on the dance floor.

Equinox is the new happening club in downtown Gulfport. It is equipped with two pool tables, a fuse ball table, darts, juke box, punch master, DJ station and a private lounge area. *Equinox* is a perfect place for you and your friends to chill, relax and have some fun.

Our next location will be in Orlando Florida.

Tandoori Chicken

1 (800 gms) of chicken

1 teaspoon of Kashmiri red chili powder

1 tablespoon of lemon juice

Salt to taste

For Marination

200 gms of yogurt

1 teaspoon of Kashmiri red chili powder

Salt to taste

2 tablespoons of ginger paste

2 tablespoons of garlic paste

2 tablespoons of lemon juice

1 teaspoon of garam masala powder

2 tablespoons of mustard oil

For basting of butter

2 teaspoons of chaat masala

For garnishing

Onion rings and lemon wedges

Skin, wash and clean the chicken. Make incisions with a sharp knife on beast and leg pieces. Apply a mixture of Kashmiri red chili powder, lemon juice and salt to the chicken and keep it aside for half an hour. Remove whey of yogurt by hanging it in a muslin cloth for fifteen to twenty minutes. Mix Kashmiri red chili powder, salt, ginger-garlic paste, lemon juice, garam masala powder and mustard oil to the yogurt. Apply this marinade onto the chicken pieces and refrigerate for three to four hours. Put the chicken onto the skewers and cook in a moderately hot tandoor or a pre-heated oven (200° Celsius) for ten to twelve minutes or until almost done. Baste it with butter and cook for another four minutes. Sprinkle chaat masala powder and serve with four onion rings and lemon wedges.

Chicken Tikka Masala

4 free-range skinless chicken
breasts cut into ½" 1 cm cubes
1 fresh ginger, peeled and grated
1 garlic clove, finely diced
Salt and pepper

½ cup, small handful fresh
coriander, finely chopped, plus
extra for garnish
Juice and zest of 1 lime
3 tablespoons vegetable oil

1 teaspoon chili powder
1 red onion, roughly chopped
2 teaspoons ground turmeric
1 teaspoon ground cumin
10 fl. Oz. /250ml light/single
cream or plain yogurt
1 dessertspoon tomato puree
Juice of ½ lemon

In a large stainless steel or glass bowl, place the chicken with the ginger, garlic, salt, pepper, chopped coriander, lime juice and zest with 1 tablespoon of the oil. Stir, then cover with a clean cloth, leave to one side for 30 minutes. After 30 minutes, heat one tablespoon of oil in a large frying pan or wok, add the chicken and cook for 8-10 minutes until browned all over. Remove the chicken from the pan and put to one side. In the same pan, heat the remaining oil and gently cook the onion and chili powder for 5 minutes. Add the turmeric and ground cumin, stir and cook for another minute. Stir in the cream and gently simmer for 5 minutes. Add the chicken and simmer for another 5 minutes. Add the tomato puree, stir, and then add the lemon juice. Cook for one minute more, then serve, garnished with fresh coriander. Boiled rice, warm naan bread or chapattis are delicious served alongside.

Saag Paneer

1 large onion
6 cloves garlic
1 oz. fresh ginger
1 pound frozen spinach, thawed
1 cup plain yogurt
4 oz. buttermilk

2 teaspoon red chili powder
2 teaspoon garam masala
1 cup half and half
6 oz. paneer, a homemade cheese
Salt to taste

Grind the onion, garlic and ginger into a fine paste. In a medium saucepan, combine the paste, spinach, yogurt, buttermilk, chili powder, and garam masala. Simmer at medium heat for 20-30 minutes. Mash the ingredients with a potato masher. Add half and half. Simmer until the mixture has a creamy consistency, 10-15 minutes. Add the cheese, simmer 5 minutes. Season with salt. Makes 4 to 6 servings.

Lamb Biryani

½ teaspoon saffron strands, pounded

25 ml boiling milk

75 gm ghee or unsalted butter

1 5cm cassia bark or cinnamon sticks

8 green cardamom pods. (split the top of

each pod to release flavor)

8 cloves

10 black peppercorns; up to 12

3 bay leaves

1 large onion, finely sliced

1 tablespoon garlic paste

1 tablespoon ginger paste

1 tablespoon ground cumin

1 tablespoon ground coriander

¼ teaspoon salt, or to taste

125 gm natural yogurt

1 kg boned leg of lamb; cut into 5cm 1 cubes

450 gm basmati rice; washed and drained

1 toasted flaked almonds

Soak the pounded saffron in the hot milk and set aside. In a heavy-based saucepan (large enough to hold the mean and rice together), melt the ghee or butter over a low heat and sizzle the cassia or cinnamon, cardamoms, cloves, peppercorns and bay leaves for 15-20 seconds. Add the onions and increase the heat to medium. Stir and fry the onions for 4-5 minutes. Add garlic and ginger, stir and cook for a further 2-3 minutes, then add the spices and chili. Stir and cook for 12 minutes. Add the salt, yogurt, meat and half the saffron milk. Stir to distribute well and switch off the stove. Put the rice in a pan with plenty of hot water and 2 teaspoons salt. Bring to the boil for 1 minute. Drain the rice and pile it on top of the meat. Drizzle the remaining saffron milk on the rice. Soak a large piece of grease-proof paper and squeeze out the water. Spread this on top of the rice. Now soak a clean tea towel, squeeze out the water and spread it on top of the grease-proof paper. Put the lid on the pan. Now seal the top of the saucepan with a large piece of kitchen foil so that no steam can escape. Place the pan over a very low heat and cook for 1 hour. Use a heat diffuser if necessary and do not peep during cooking! Remove the biryani from the heat and allow to stand for 15 minutes. Stir gently with a fork to mix the meat and the rice and serve immediately, garnish with the toasted flaked almonds.

Chimichanga

½ pound chopped bacon pieces &
grease cooked
1 pound premium ground or
shredded beef
½ onion, diced
2 tomatoes, chopped
1 can chopped green chilies
Sour cream
Salsa

1 teaspoon salt
1 ½ teaspoons oregano
1 to 2 teaspoon chili powder
2 tablespoons minced, fresh cilantro
12 large flour tortillas, warmed
Vegetable oil
Shredded cheese
Shredded lettuce
Sliced black olives

In skillet, cook bacon & grease, breaking into pieces as it cooks. As bacon nears completion, add onion and sauté. Lower heat & add chilies, salt, oregano, chili powder and cilantro; simmer 2 to 3 minutes. Add meat and tomatoes mix well, simmer 2 to 3 minutes. Place ½ cup meat filling on each tortilla. Fold envelope style (like a burrito). Fry, seam side down, in ½ inch of hot oil, until mildly crispy and tan. Turn over and brown other side. Drain briefly on paper towels. Place on plate and top with shredded cheese, sour cream and salsa. Place shredded lettuce around the chimichanga and top lettuce with chopped tomatoes and sliced black olives.

Cuz's Seafood

CUZ'S SEAFOOD

Where you can find the best boiled seafood in town! Our poboys are overstuffed and our plates runneth over! We slow cook prime roast for hours to slice up and serve to you with gravy on hot, toasted French bread or over French fried potatoes with lots of gravy and cheese - sloppy fries! Our unique boiled shrimp poboys with jumbo boiled shrimp are also a favorite among customers who prefer a lighter meal.

Cuz has made an art out of boiling seafood and it shows! We can't keep count of how many people have told us that our crawfish are the best they have ever had! We also boil shrimp and crabs and open oysters to serve on the half shell as you order them.

You can come in and sit at the bar to order a drink or enjoy our back deck overlooking the bayou! The atmosphere is casual and fun. As a family owned business, you'll probably be served by one of Cuz's daughters and you can find Cuz's raven haired wife, Christine, called Red by Cuz in the kitchen cookin' up something good!

With something good always playing on the radio, our good food, and fun, family hospitality, you won't be disappointed at Cuz's!

Cuz's Potato Salad with Boiled Shrimp or Crawfish

5 pounds of small red potatoes
6 eggs
1 cup of mayonnaise
½ cup of green onions chopped
1 ½ cups of chopped boiled shrimp
½ cup of celery, chopped
½ cup of onions, chopped
Old Bay® seasoning
salt and pepper
or crawfish

Boil potatoes, uncut, with eggs, for about 20 minutes. Put boiled potatoes and peeled boiled eggs in a mixing bowl along with celery, green onions, and mayonnaise. Mix well and add Old Bay® seasoning and salt and pepper to taste. Serve and enjoy.

Oysters Cuz-a-Fella

1 dozen raw oysters on the ½ shell
2 sticks Land O' Lakes® butter
(always, always, always use real
butter when you cook)
lemon juice
minced garlic
Italian bread crumbs
hot sauce
Parmesan cheese
Old Bay® seasoning

In a skillet melt butter and add minced garlic, hot sauce, and lemon juice. Place oysters, on the ½ shell, in a cooking tray lined with aluminum foil. Pour sauce over oysters, filling the shell. A small ladle works best for this. Place tray in an oven pre-heated to 350°. Cook until oysters begin to curl. Sprinkle bread crumbs then parmesan cheese and Old Bay® seasoning on top. Remove from oven and serve.

Cuz's Shrimp and Crab Stuffed Potatoes

6 to 12 large potatoes
2 cups shredded cheddar cheese
1 cup of sour cream
½ cup butter, softened
1 pound boiled shrimp, peeled and
deveined
1 pound of crabmeat
1 package of cream cheese

Preheat oven to 350°. Place potatoes on heavy baking sheet and bake for 1 hour. Cut off top of potatoes and scoop out the meat. Mix the potato meat with cheese, sour cream, and butter. Spoon the mixture back into potato shells. Bake for 30 minutes then add a layer of shrimp and crabmeat. Top with green onions and Old Bay® seasoning.

Our address is 10408 highway 603 in Bay Saint Louis.

Our website is cuzsseafood.com.

And we are on facebook @ cuz's seafood.

Half Shell Oyster House

HALF SHELL OYSTER HOUSE

In 1994, Bob Taylor moved to the Mississippi Gulf Coast and quickly made it his home.

"I fell in love with the coast when I moved here. The people are great," he said. We have developed good relations with the government, police and fire departments, legislators and vendors."

Bob moved here from Memphis to become managing partner for the Outback Steakhouse and now owns *High Cotton Grills* in Gulfport and D'Iberville, a catering business, *Half Shell Oyster House* and *The Quarter* in downtown Gulfport.

"I love seeing people who were my regulars from the Outback days," he says. "Working with schools and charities has been an uplifting experience and I love seeing those people come in too."

"I like meeting customers, building relations, helping out the community and mentoring people under me. Every day is different, not like an office job."

High Cotton Grill opened in Gulfport, shortly after Hurricane Katrina and next came *High Cotton Grill* in D'Iberville. The *Half Shell Oyster House* opened in 2009 in the historic Kremer building. The 110 year old building has original brick walls, exposed beams, 17- foot ceilings and large windows. "I see tremendous potential in the downtown area, especially with the façade program and streetscape project," Taylor said. "We're excited to be a part of the revitalization of downtown."

BBQ Shrimp

12 oz. liquid margarine

4 tablespoons olive oil

¼ cup Worcestershire sauce

2 tablespoons crystal hot sauce

1 teaspoon paprika

1 teaspoon salt

2 teaspoons black pepper

¼ cup chopped parsley

1 tablespoon Zatarain's

¼ cup minced garlic

3 pounds large shrimp, head on.

Combine all ingredients, margarine first, except for minced garlic, in mixing bowl. Whisk until blended well. Fold in garlic. Place butter mixture in stockpot and add shrimp. Cook on low heat for about 10 minutes or until shrimp is cooked thoroughly. Turn off heat and soak for 10 minutes before serving.

Grilled Asparagus with Gorgonzola Butter

Gorgonzola Butter

> 1 cup Gorgonzola cheese
> ¼ pound softened butter
> ½ tablespoon lemon juice
>
> ½ teaspoon salt
> ½ teaspoon black pepper

Combine all ingredients in mixing bowl and mix well with rubber spatula.

Asparagus

> 2 bunches of asparagus
> ¼ cup olive oil
> 2 tablespoons chopped fresh
> basil
> 1 tablespoon minced garlic

Snap ends off asparagus. Place asparagus in large pan and mix with olive oil, by hand, until evenly coated. Place asparagus on grill; cook only long enough to char each side. Transfer to casserole dish, top with gorgonzola butter and broil until butter melts.

Lil Ray's PoBoys and Seafood

LIL RAY'S
POBOYS AND SEAFOOD

Ray Kidd Sr; known to everyone as Daddy Ray, opened his first restaurant in Bay St. Louis, Mississippi; the restaurant was called Ray's and was truly a family business. Ray supported his family of nine with the help of his wife, Lorraine and their sons and daughters.

Lil Ray's, owned by Ray Jr., opened in Waveland, May of 1970 and soon after, the "Lil Ray's PoBoy" concept was born.

In 2005, Hurricane Katrina destroyed Lil Ray's in Waveland; however, the tradition is being carried on in the Long Beach location by Ray Jr.'s son, Trey and the Courthouse Road location is being run by David and his daughter, Jennifer.

Lil Rays has been a Coast tradition for serving quality grilled, fried, and boiled seafood for the last thirty plus years. As a self owned and managed restaurant we have strived to maintain the individuality that has attracted generations of locals to us. Our French bread is still delivered daily from New Orleans, as it has been since opening day over thirty years ago. Even Hurricane Katrina couldn't change that!

Along with our daily delivered bread, our seafood is as fresh as it gets...often times having spent the previous night in the nearby Gulf waters.

Our customers love coming to spend time with friends and family in our relaxed and casual atmosphere, where they can sit and order a cold pitcher of beer with their oysters on the half shell, boiled shrimp or crawfish!

Did you know?.....

The French bread for our PoBoys is delivered fresh daily from New Orleans to both location; Courthouse Road and Long Beach.

Lil Ray's on Courthouse road makes their tuna dip from scratch, along with their red beans, gumbo, tartar sauce, shrimp Creole, and jumbo lump crab cakes.

We are currently in our 35th year at the Courthouse Road location; So come see us doing what we do best...great seafood for the past thirty years and still a Gulf Coast tradition!

Louisiana Shrimp Creole

¼ pound butter

1 cup chopped onions

1 cup diced shallots

1 cup tomato puree or 2 tablespoon

tomato paste

1 oz. lemon juice

1 oz. cornstarch

1 cup chopped green peppers

1 cup diced celery

2 cups chopped canned tomatoes

2 bay leaves

3 pounds peeled and deveined

shrimp

Salt, pepper and cayenne

Melt butter, sauté pepper, onions, celery, and shallots for 5 minutes. Add canned tomatoes, tomato puree or paste, bay leaves, simmer for 15 minutes. Add shrimp and simmer for 15 minutes, dissolve cornstarch in one pint water, add and simmer for 5 minutes. Add lemon juice, salt and pepper to taste, add pinch of cayenne, simmer for 15 minutes. Serve over steamed rice.

Shrimp Remoulade Sauce

1 cup olive oil

1/3 cup vinegar

1 bunch green onion

2 cloves garlic

2 tablespoons paprika

5 tablespoons Creole mustard

1 stalk celery

1 sprig parsley

Salt and pepper

Ketchup to taste

Grind very fine, all the vegetables, then add mustard, paprika, salt and pepper. Mix all ingredients thoroughly with vinegar and then add the olive oil gradually. After the shrimp are boiled and peeled, let them soak in this sauce for a few minutes. Shrimp should be served on shredded lettuce and tomatoes as a garnish.

Shrimp Salad

5 pounds peeled shrimp
3 eggs
1 bunch green onions
3 stalks celery
½ cup dill relish
1 cup mayonnaise
½ cup Creole mustard
Tony Chachere's, salt, pepper

Boil shrimp and eggs, chop celery, green onions, and add dill relish, mayonnaise, Creole mustard. Season to taste.

Mediterraneo

MEDITERRANEO

The owners of *Mediterraneo;* Angelos Apeitos and Kal Zayed are both from Mediterranean families; one being from Cyprus, the other from Egypt. They both enjoyed their mother's cooking so opening a Mediterranean restaurant was a dream for both of them; however, making their dream come true, required traveling to several different countries in order to make the *Mediterraneo's* atmosphere authentic. The chandeliers in the dinning room as well as the Mother of pearl wooden check presenters were found in Cairo, Egypt, at the oldest market in the world. (Khalili market). The Fleur De Lis tiles that surround the chair rail in the dining room were found in the south of Spain, in Andalucia.

Many of the spices used at *Mediterraneo;* such as Saffron and sweet smoked paprika, are purchased in Spain and Egypt. The dried mint used for their Moroccan tea comes from Egypt as well.

Mediterraneo Staff:

Executive Chef, Kurt Anderson joined Angelos and Kal at the beginning of their journey, collaborating with them even before the restaurant was set up. Kurt Anderson is a talented young chef, hailing from Homer, Louisiana. He learned the Culinary Arts as Sous Chef under John at the Louisiana State University faculty club. Kurt originally specialized in Cajun and Creole cuisine, but has expanded his scope through training and study in order to specialize in the preparation of Mediterranean cuisine. Kurt is a very vocal chef and the front of the house crew knows to do exactly as he directs or they are certain to receive an *earful.*

Angelos and Kal say that whenever anyone asks them about Kurt, they tell them that he fed the tigers before he came to the *Mediterraneo* and though people look at them as if they have lost their minds, it's actually true. Kurt and Kal were responsible for catering to the World Champion LSU Tigers football team in 2007 and 2008. They provided good eats for the coaches, staff, players, and new recruits during special recruiting events and during the holidays as well; which could very well be the reason they won the National championship that year.

Mediterraneos's employees are what give the restaurant a family environment. So many of the staff has been with them from day one,

The kitchen is a combination of eclectic personalities, including Executive Chef; Kurt Anderson, Michael "Biggie" Lacoste, and Benjamin "Bennie" Caraballo. These three chefs have brought so much to the plates of *Mediterraneo's* customers. Each has a unique background in the culinary arts.

The Food:

The food at *Mediterraneo* includes a variety of Mediterranean dishes; as well as Spanish, Greek and Italian cuisine, all based on coastal Mediterranean seafood.

The appetizers include grape leaves, Pita bread, and hummus as well as smoked tuna dip and mixed olives with cheese.

There is an extensive wine selection available with more than fifty kinds of wines, some recognizable and others more exotic.

Main dishes at *Mediterraneo* include Souvlaki-grilled pork tenderloin with vegetables and poblano apricot chutney, Spanakopita – spinach and feta chesses stuffed in a filo dough pastry, lamb chops seasoned with Rosemary and Thyme and served with Tahini sauce, seared Tuna slices with artichoke and ginger soy sauce, and eggplant stuffed with ground beef and Béchamel sauce and topped with parmesan cheese.

Mediterraneo is one of Ocean Spring's finest dining experiences.

Mediterraneo Salad

Romaine lettuce
Half cucumber, small dice
2 medium tomatoes, chopped
1/4 cup chopped mint leaves
Half red onion, sliced

1 loaf large Pita bread from fryer
precut like hummus pieces.
2 teaspoons pomegranate
molasses
Grilled chicken

Dressing: pre make once a week

1/2 cup lemon juice
1 1/2 cups Olive oil
2 cloves garlic paste

1 teaspoon salt
Pinch pepper
3 teaspoons sumac

Mix all ingredients and serve over salad

House Salad Dressing

2 1/2 cups Olive oil blend
1 teaspoon fresh Thyme
20 Mint leaves
1 1/2 teaspoons Kosher salt

1 cup orange juice
1 cup lemon juice
1 teaspoon orange zest
4 tablespoons brown sugar

Combine all ingredients except oil. Slowly add oil until combined

LINDA ESCHLER

Chocolate Molten

20 ounces chocolate chips

16 ounces melted butter

12 egg yolks

1 cup sugar

12 eggs

12 tablespoons flour

Melt chocolate and butter in a double boiler. Beat eggs, yolks, and sugar until pale yellow. Add egg mixture to chocolate 1/3 at a time until combined. Add flour to mixture, 3 tablespoons at a time until combines. Pour into buttered and floured cups, pushing 5 or 6 chocolate chips into the center. Bake at 350 (low fan) for 12 – 13 minutes

Mugshots Grill & Bar

MUGSHOTS GRILL & BAR

Ron Savell and Chris McDonald opened the first MugShots in Hattiesburg, near the University of Southern Mississippi; they had little money to start the restaurant so friends and family chipped in labor to help make their dream a reality. Ron and Chris rewarded everyone that helped out; buy taking their photograph or Mugshot and displaying them on the wall in the restaurant. Customers are also encouraged to send in their MugShots from places they visit, with the MugShots logo in hand. The first one was so successful they decided to open one in Starkville, near Mississippi State University, followed by one in Flowood, near Jackson and yet another one in Tuscaloosa, Alabama.

The newest MugShots opened in Edgewater Village in Biloxi, Mississippi and is being run by Ron; he tells this very funny story of how he and MugShots ended up in Biloxi.

Ron and his bride; Caitlin were honeymooning in the Bahamas when they met three Biloxians sitting around the pool. When they learned that Ron was from Mississippi, they advised him to try a restaurant near Mississippi State University called MugShots. They said this place had "the best hamburgers in Mississippi."

Ron headed to his hotel room and returned with three drink huggies with the MugShots logo. Of course everyone had a good laugh and when Ron returned home, he knew it was time to open their next restaurant, in Biloxi, Mississippi.

The Savells decided on Edgewater Village as the location for MugShots because the strip mall flooded in 2005 during Hurricane Katrina and they felt they could be a part of the recovery process.

The front room of the restaurant is very family oriented, complete with high chairs for the little ones. The back room is a sports bar with 33 beers on tap, pool tables and lots of television sets. On weekends, an acoustic guitar plays.

Hamburgers are the main attraction at MugShots Grill and Bar; half pound of fresh seasoned beef served on a signature sourdough bun, accompanied by crispy beer battered fries. The burgers come any way you can imagine; bacon, red onions, sautéed mushrooms, chili, blue cheese, sour cream, jalapenos Thousand Island and even peanut butter.

Chuck Savell; Ron's father, says, "Above all else, we try and have fun with our menu so our customers can have fun as well. We're into fun, fresh affordable food with great service; and we do make everything fresh; even the fries and onion rings are battered when you order them"

MugShots also offers a Portobello burger, a turkey patty, a Mahi fish, and more than a dozen other sandwiches; their signature salads and pastas are available along with appetizers of fried cheese wedges, nachos, wings, and fried dill pickles.

Bring your mug to Mugshots

Savell Gourmet Burger

1 toasted sourdough bun
1 half pound choice ground round burger
patty, seasoned and grilled to perfection
1 Slice Cheddar Cheese
2 Slices of cooked hickory smoked bacon
Mayo, Diced red onions, lettuce,
sliced tomato

Apply mayo generously to the bottom half of your sourdough bun, apply red onion, lettuce and tomato to your liking. Approximately 2 minutes before removing your burger from the grill place bacon and cheese on top so it can melt. Remove the burger from the grill, place on the dressed bottom bun, place toasted top bun on and enjoy.

McDonald Gourmet Burger

1 toasted sourdough bun
1 half pound choice ground round burger
patty, seasoned and grilled to perfection
1 Slice Cheddar Cheese
2 Slices of cooked hickory smoked bacon
Smokey BBQ Sauce
Ranch dressing, Diced red onions, lettuce,
sliced tomato

Apply ranch generously to the bottom half of your sourdough bun, apply red onion, lettuce and tomato to your liking. After flipping your burger on the grill, apply bbq sauce to the top of the patty. Two minutes before removing your burger from the grill place bacon and cheese on top so it can melt. Remove the burger from the grill, place on the dressed bottom bun, top with the toasted top bun, grab a napkin and dig in.

Picou Gourmet Sandwich

1 toasted sourdough bun
1 6 ounce marinated, seasoned and
grilled to perfection
1 Slice Swiss Cheese
2 Slices of cooked hickory smoked
bacon
Honey Mustard Dressing, lettuce,
sliced tomato

Apply Honey Mustard generously to the top and bottom of your sourdough bun, apply lettuce and tomato to your liking. Approximately 2 minutes before removing your chicken breast from the grill place bacon and cheese on top so it can melt. Remove the chicken from the grill, place on the dressed bottom bun, place toasted top bun on and devour.

Nezaty's Cafè

NEZATY'S CAFÉ

Nezaty's Café is a local favorite coffee and sandwich shop located just off the beach on Courthouse Road*in Gulfport. The menu includes specialty coffee drinks, all natural smoothies, Paninis, sandwiches on artisan breads, soups, fresh salads, and gourmet desserts.

HISTORY OF CAFE

The current owner, Joanne Bullard O'Keefe, purchased the café the summer of 2005 a month before Hurricane Katrina. Joanne, a Gulfport native, had lived in Atlanta for 15 years with a career in environmental and waste management before moving back to the coast in 2003. While working on her real estate license, the opportunity to buy Nezaty's and start a second career in her hometown became available. The location was great with unique menu items; so, Joanne's second career started, as a café owner. With paperwork done, management in place, she started to learn the business. Then Katrina hit.

The Cafe sustained heavy wind and rain damage. After many long hard hours, Nezaty's reopened at the end of December with a handful of employees and friends and an old fashioned cash register. The café opened with a very limited menu and limited hours with cash only. The lines were out the door daily and the staff worked hard. Good friends also stepped in to help and serve food, bus tables, and clean. In addition to staff and friends, other restaurant owners shared their experience and contacts with Joanne, who was still a "freshman" in a new industry. Everyone's help and expertise was invaluable in getting the café up and running.

THE CAFE TODAY

Joanne is still learning the business and relies on her great staff who all takes pride and ownership in their work. The Café today has a friendly warm atmosphere filled with local art purchased after Katrina. Nezaty's is a "hidden charm" in terms of ambience, convenient location, and consistently great food.

The café is a favorite among locals for the first coffee of the day. The door opens to the wonderful smell of croissants, breads, and cookies baking while mingling with the aroma of fresh coffee. Customers pour their coffee at the coffee bar or have the barrista make their drinks. Coffees and all natural smoothies are available throughout the day.

Stuffed breakfast croissant (great for overnight fishing trips-prepared and packed), scones, muffins, meat frittatas and spinach frittatas are served Monday through Friday from 7am until they run out!

For lunch or an early dinner the Panini grillers and sandwiches are made to order on Artisan breads. From classic French dips to the Mushrooms Gone Wild, Nezaty's Café can cover anyone's craving. The salads are fresh with generous portions. The signature black bean soup is made daily. The best muffalatta this side of New Orleans can be found here; along with a huge Reuben on generous slices of fresh baked rye bread. *See their website for full menu.*

The coffee is brewed all day long. A large inventory of some of the finest coffees from around the world and flavor infused coffees are sold by the pound. Many of the coffees are locally roasted in New Orleans. The staff is happy to assist in customers in selecting just the right coffee or blend for their palate.

Nezaty's is located in Gulfport on Courthouse Road across from the Post Office — less then ½ mile north, off Hwy 90. Open Monday through Friday 7 to 5; Saturday 10 to 3. www.nezatys.com

*HISTORY OF COURTHOUSE ROAD

Courthouse Road was home to the original Harrison County Courthouse in Mississippi City, the first coast town to receive a charter and the county seat for 62 years, from 1849 until 1903.

In 1888, Jefferson Davis, the ex president of the Confederate States, made his famous post civil war speech on the property of the old courthouse.

In 1903 Gulfport annexed Mississippi City and the courthouse building was abandoned as the county seat. The courthouse (built 1856) was demolished in 1916. The remaining structure, the clerks' office and grand jury room built in 1893, was intended for demolition in the mid 1980's. In 1986, the building was saved and became home to the Tourism Commission.

Katrina severely damaged the building, which has since been rebuilt and is located just north of the Ken Combs Pier on Courthouse Road off of Hwy 90.

Today Courthouse Road is a main thoroughfare home to some of the most unique shops on the Coast. A variety of clothing shops offering fishing attire to formal elegance. Local artists are featured in galleries and gift shops. Spa services can also be found along with a Wine bar.

Nezaty's Black Bean Soup

Black beans (6lb 15oz can)

Rotel tomatoes (28oz can)

1 ½ tablespoons cumin

2 tablespoons Tones Cajun

Seasoning

Drain half of the liquid from the black beans. Pour can of Rotel Tomatoes into blender (with liquid). Add ½ can of black beans to Rotel tomatoes in the blender (other ½ goes into soup pot). Blend Rotel tomatoes and black beans in blender for approximately 45 seconds. Add puree to soup pot with the ½ can of whole black beans. Season with cumin and Tones Cajun Seasoning adjusting to taste. Simmer for about 15 to 30 minutes. Stir every few minutes. Serve with shredded sharp cheddar cheese and sour cream. Other toppings may be added including chopped green onions, cilantro, or jalapeno peppers.

Nezaty's Signature Chicken Salad

3 to 3 ½ lbs chicken breast meat

(either 3lb 2oz can or equal amount

of cooked cubed chicken breast)

1 cup mandarin orange sections

1 cup pineapple tidbits

¾ to 1 cup Blue Plate Mayonnaise

1 tablespoon cinnamon

Drain water from chicken — add shredded canned chicken and/or cubed cooked chicken breast into mixing bowl. Add Pineapple tidbits (after draining liquid). Add ¾ to 1 cup Blue Plate Mayonnaise adjusting to taste. Add cinnamon. Mix. After mixture is mixed and correct consistency GENTLY FOLD in mandarin orange slices. Serve on fresh baked sandwich croissants.

Nezaty's Rotini Pasta Salad

1 lb uncooked rotini pasta

3 to 4 roma tomatoes

1 cucumber seeded

½ cup feta cheese crumbles

½ cup ripe, sliced black olives

Approximately ½ cup creamy Italian

or similar dressing

Cook rotini pasta according to directions on package. Add rinsed, cooled pasta to large mixing bowl. Add Italian dressing to cooled pasta and mix well. Remove seeds from tomatoes, dice tomato flesh, and add to pasta. Peel half of skin off of cucumbers in strips, remove seeds, then cut into small cubes and add to pasta. Mix well being careful not to break up pasta (remember pasta needs to be COOL). Add black olives and feta cheese. Mix cheese. Serve chilled. If pasta seems to "dry out" after refrigerated add a little more Italian dressing to taste.

Port City Cafe

PORT CITY CAFÉ

Port City Café opened in downtown Gulfport, June 1st, 2000. What began as a small downtown business; seating forty people, eventually grew into a well known local restaurant seating 120.

Although *Port City Cafe* did receive some damage from Hurricane Katrina, they were one of the luckiest businesses south of the railroad tracks. The restaurant had two broken windows and only six inches of water. The owner, Ernest Ulrich and his son Anthony began working on clean-up the next morning and they worked from Sun-up till sun-down with no power whatsoever.

On the third day of clean-up, a man walked into the café and introduced himself as *Harry Smith* with *CBS Early News*. He expressed his amazement at how we were able to perform such major clean-up in such a short period of time and he couldn't believe that we were planning on re-opening in a week.

Port City Café was the first restaurant to re-open in downtown Gulfport and they immediately began serving six hundred lunches and six hundred dinners daily to the power company.

When Ernest told his employees that their break was over, they were ready and happy to be returning to work. Ernest said there were some long, hot days for everyone; however, everyone worked together and they managed to pull it off. He said he could not have done it without the help of all of his dedicated employees and family working together for one common cause; feeding all the men and women working to clean up the devastation that Hurricane Katrina left behind.

Port City Café has continued to prosper for almost ten years and Ernest Ulrich, his family and friends look forward to many more years watching downtown Gulfport grow.

Port City Mashed Potatoes

1 1/2 bags red potatoes
1 1/4 quarts heavy cream
1 teaspoon salt

1/2 teaspoon black pepper
1/ lb butter

Bring potatoes to boil in large pot. Boil for 45 minutes. Drain water, add rest of ingredients. Mash thoroughly, place on steam table or put in storage container to cool.

Port City Green Beans

1 1/2 bags frozen green beans

2 packages of Lipton onion soup mix

1 teaspoon Tony Chachere's

Cover green beans in pot with water. Add other ingredients and bring to a boil. Place on steam table or put into a container to cool

Port City Lima Bean

1 bag frozen Lima beans

2 packages Lipton onion soup mix

1 teaspoon Tony Chachere's

Cover beans in pot with water. Add other ingredients. Add bacon from breakfast bacon as it comes out of the oven. Bring to boil and stir occasionally for 20 minutes. Place on steam table or put in storage container to cool.

Port City Baby Back Ribs

3 slabs pork baby back ribs

Tony Chachere's

Onion powder

Garlic powder

Black pepper

Brown Sugar

Barbecue sauce

Peel the silver skin off the back of the ribs. Coat generously with Tony Chachere's, onion powder, garlic powder, brown sugar and black pepper. Put ribs in baking pan and pour enough water to cover 1/3 of the pan. Cover with aluminum foil and bake at 300° for 3 hours. Take foil off and baste with barbecue sauce and return to oven for 20 minutes. Put on steam table or in storage container to cool.

Port City Meatloaf

10 pound hamburger roll

2 yellow onions (diced)

2 green peppers (diced)

1 cup heavy cream

2 large eggs

2 cups Italian bread crumbs

1 cup brown sugar

1 teaspoon Italian seasoning

1 teaspoon Tony Chachere's

1/2 teaspoon black pepper

In a large metal bowl, mix all ingredients together until smooth. Form two meatloaves to fit into a baking pan. Bake uncovered at 300° for two hours. Remove from oven and coat top with brown sugar and ketchup (wearing a rubber glove, rub the sugar and ketchup mixture onto the loaf to cover the entire surface area with a glaze) return to oven for 30 minutes. Cut the two loaves into 25 pieces (approximately 6 ounces per person) Put on steam table or in storage container to cool

Port City Corn

1/2 bag frozen corn

Pinch dried parsley

1/2 teaspoon Tony Chachere's

Cover corn in pot with water. Add Tony Chachere's and bring to a boil. Place on steam table or put in storage container to cool.

Port City Brown Gravy

1/2 pot water

4 packs Lipton Onion soup mix

1/2 teaspoon Tony Chachere's

Pinch black pepper

2 cups flour to thicken

Bring water and Lipton Onion soup mix to a boil and reduce heat to simmer. Add flour and whisk continually until flour is dissolved and gravy is desired thickness. Add Tony Chachere's and black pepper. You can use the pot roast jus to loosen and darken gravy if needed. Place in crock pot or put in storage container to cool.

Port City White (Sawmill) gravy

8 cups water

3 packs white gravy mix

Bring water to a boil and reduce to simmer. Add gravy mix and stir continually until gravy is smooth and desired thickness. Place in crock pot or in storage container to cool.

Port City Sauce Marinara

1 bottle Ragu tomato sauce

1 yellow onion (diced)

2 green bell peppers (diced)

1 teaspoon fresh granulated garlic

2 teaspoons Italian seasoning

1 teaspoonTony Chachere's

1/2 teaspoon black pepper

In pot sauté the garlic, onion and bell pepper until tender. Add tomato sauce, Italian seasoning, Tony Chachere's and black pepper. Bring to boil, stirring occasionally. Put in storage container to cool.

Port City Buffalo sauce

1/2 pound butter (melted)   *2 teaspoons Louisiana hot sauce*

Stir until mixed together well. Put in storage container to cool and heat in microwave when needed.

Port City Red Beans

1/4 pot red beans   *1 teaspoon Tony Chachere's*
10 cups water   *1 teaspoon black pepper*
2 packs Lipton Onion soup mix   *2 teaspoons Italian seasoning*
2 teaspoons fresh granulated garlic

Cover beans with water in pot. Water level should be six inches above the top of the beans. Add Lipton Onion soup mix, garlic, Tony C's and black pepper. Bring to a boil and stir occasionally for one hour. Reduce heat to simmer and add Italian seasoning. Continue to stir occasionally for 2 hours. Put in crock pot or storage container to cool.

Port City Chicken and Sausage Gumbo

3 cups vegetable oil   *1 teaspoon Tony Chachere's*
2 cups flour   *1 teaspoon fresh granulated garlic*
1 yellow onion   *2 teaspoons Italian seasoning*
2 green bell peppers (diced)   *1/2 teaspoon black pepper*
1/2 pack Andouille sausage (diced)   *10 cups chicken jus (broth)*
4 cups baked chicken

Make a dark chocolate colored roux in a cast iron pot. Sauté Andouille, onions and bell pepper in a separate pot. Once roux is dark enough, add sautéed from other pot. Add the chicken jus (or water if no jus is on hand), bring to a boil and then reduce to simmer, stirring every ten minutes. Add Tony Chachere's, garlic, Italian seasoning and black pepper and continue to stir while simmering for 45 minutes. Add water to loosen if needed. Put in crock pot or storage container to cool.

Port City Baked Chicken

2 packs of chicken breasts
1 teaspoon Tony Chachere's

2 cups water

Place chicken in baking pan and sprinkle Tony Chachere's over top. Add water to pan (half — way up pan). Cover with foil and bake at 300° for 2 1/2 hours. Put on steam table or in storage container to cool.

Port City Pot Roast

2 packs Angus beef tips
2 packs Lipton onion soup mix

2 teaspoons fresh granulated garlic
1 teaspoon Tony Chachere's

Put beef tips in cast iron pot and cover with water. Add the Lipton onion soup mix, garlic and Tony Chachere's, bring to a boil and stir occasionally for 45 minutes. Reduce heat to simmer and continue to stir occasionally for 2 hours. Put on steam table or in storage container to cool.

Port City Hamburgers/Hamburger Steak

10 lb hamburger roll
Tony Chachere's

Lipton onion soup mix

Roll the 10 pounds of beef into 25 hamburger patties (rounded edges and flat) — 1/2 inch thick and weighing approximately 6 ounces. Sprinkle hamburgers with Tony Chachere's. Sprinkle Hamburger Steaks with Lipton onion soup mix. Bake on sheet pan at 300° for 30 minutes. Put on steam table or in storage container to cool.

The Quarter

THE QUARTER

The *Quarter* opened just west of the *Half Shell* last December. The bar and music venue brings a little bit of New Orleans to the area. The *Quarter* has eclectic décor that includes exposed brick, salvaged doors and architectural remnants and folk art.

"There is a growing variety of new restaurants and bars in the area," Taylor said, "and we hope downtown Gulfport becomes a destination for good times like the *French Quarter.*"

Voodoo Rita

1 oz. Cuervo tequila

.5 oz. Blue Curacao

.5 oz. Chambord

1 splash lime juice

Sour mix

Cranberry juice

Salted rim and lime garnish

Marie Laveau's Love Potion

1 oz. Absolut

1 oz. Chambord

1/3 lemonade or sour mix

1/3 orange juice

1/3 cranberry juice

Garnish with 2 cherries

Barq's Bulldog

1/25 oz. Absolut

.75 oz. Kahlua

Ice milk

Barq's top

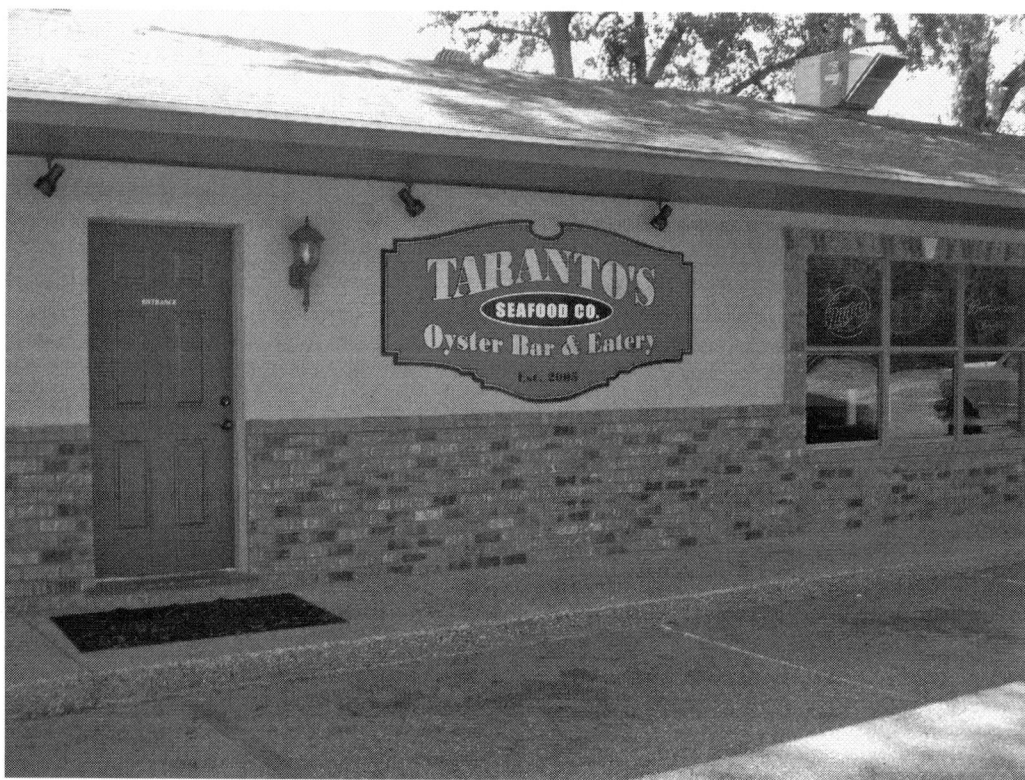

Taranto's Seafood Company

TARANTO'S SEAFOOD COMPANY
OYSTER BAR & EATERY

Pat Taranto grew up in D'Iberville, Mississippi and has been in the crawfish and Seafood business since the 1980's. His dream of owning his own seafood business came true when he opened *Taranto's Seafood Company* in 2005. *Taranto's* prepares dishes the old fashioned way, using some recipes that date back 100 years.

Everything is fresh, all the time because Pat buys his seafood from the local fishermen. He prides himself on the fact that the seafood he uses, *slept in the Gulf of Mexico the night before.*

Taranto's uses only Zatarains when they boil their crawfish, shrimp and crabs. The 8 inch Po-Boys are always made on Gambino's French bread from New Orleans. The Po-Boys are *dressed and pressed* with only the best ingredients and are among the finest on the Mississippi Gulf Coast.

The Oyster bar is now open and serves fresh oysters on the half shell, shucked right before your eyes. Grilled oysters are available as well.

Taranto's restaurant also offers soft shell crabs served year round and boiled King crabs as well.

Steaks or Surf and Turf combinations made with choice beef Rib-eye are also on the menu. All of their recipes are original and everyone is local.

Daily specials are offered and their drink prices are very reasonable.

Taranto's Seafood Company was voted BEST SEAFOOD ON THE COAST in 2007 AND 2009.

Shrimp Pasta Salad

1 pound Rotini pasta

1 ½ pound medium shrimp, peeled
and cooked

½ red onion, chopped fine

½ green bell pepper, chopped fine

1 tablespoon garlic powder

4 oz. Italian dressing

8 oz. mayonnaise

1 can Rotel tomatoes, drained

Boil pasta, rinse and set aside to cool. Mix all other ingredients together, toss with pasta and serve cold.

House Grilled Oysters

Fresh opened oysters on the half shell

Creole seasoning

Garlic powder

Butter

Parmesan cheese

Place oysters on the half shell on hot grill and cook until juices are bubbly. Do not overcook. Blend garlic powder and butter. Top oysters with garlic powder/butter blend and top with Parmesan cheese.

Pan Grilled Grouper

2 eight oz. grouper filets

Creole seasoning

Butter

Garlic

Sprinkle fillets with Creole seasonings. Place fillets in pan with butter and garlic sauce. Plan pan on grill and cook until firm. Do not overcook.

Vintage Station

VINTAGE STATION..
WHEN YOU WANT TO SEE..
OR BE SEEN!

A quiet and comfortable place to get away or discuss business.. you will find it here. Come in and enjoy the elegant and soothing atmosphere enhanced by a soft background of smooth jazz, blues, and light classical music.

Add to our spirits list an exquisite pairing menu, and you have a comfortable ambiance worthy of the most discriminating taste.

Impressive menu offerings.. think beef wellington, crab cakes, escargot, imported cheeses, and fresh fruits and breads

Vintage Station is the Mississippi Coast's premier wine bar. Wines from around the world are served by the glass, and bottle. Revered old world producers, rising stars, and exciting new world wineries are equally represented on our wine list.

You will also find a choice of fine liquors and beers, and a variety of appetizers and hors d'oeuvres to pair with your selection.

Enjoy the traditional Wine Bar or take a seat in a private nook and enjoy a quiet conversation.

Vintage Station provides a variety of cozy and communal seating options. Private niches, outside patio, or traditional wine bar, we are at your service.

Vintage Station is proud to offer a private event room, The West Wing for your private party or meeting. The room accommodates forty to sixty persons depending upon the venue.

The West Wing Vintage Station offers a private room for your party, meeting, or other event. The West Wing entrance is through two large sliding doors in the wine bar area. There is also a separate front entrance if needed for your event.

The room is fifty feet by twenty three feet, offering approximately twelve hundred square feet of space. We can arrange the West Wing to suit your needs.. We can provide tables and chairs for forty to fifty persons to accommodate dining, meetings, or parties.

We offer "turn key" events, providing everything that you may need including drinks, food, seating, decorations, and entertainment, or we will be glad to work with you in providing only the things that you need.

We can make the room available most any time of the day on a "per hour" or "per head" basis. The price and terms, obviously, depends on the time frame and the services that we provide.

Come by and check it out! We will be glad to show you around and discuss your needs.

Did you know?...

At Vintage Station your wine glass appears to be about half full when we pour it. There is a reason for this. Wine needs to combine with the air to fully develop in taste and smell. Swirling the wine in the glass allows the air and wine to mix. Also, the wine on the side of the glass helps in allowing the aroma to collect in the glass. Swirling would not be possible if the glass were poured to the top.

Also, we pour in large glasses. For example, our red wine glass is an eighteen and a quarter ounce glass. If we poured it full, it would hold three quarters of a bottle. That would, of course, raise the price of a glass considerably. We are very careful to pour five ounces in each glass and price our product according to the amount poured.

Just A Little More Trivia..

In the year 121 B.C. Italy had such a great vintage for wine it signaled the end to Greek dominance of the wine industry.

There is a 1600 year old bottle of wine on display in the Speyer Museum in Germany.

In the Middle Ages wine was used as currency.

The Egyptians attributed the gift of wine to their God, Osiris.

The first commercial U.S. winery, established in 1823, was located in Missouri.

Champagne is at its peak between four and ten years of age.

The Armenians claim Noah planted the first vineyards on earth in their country.

Grapes were first planted in California at Mission San Diego in 1769.

There were more than 700 wineries in California in 1920.

Louis Pasteur first determined the true nature of fermentation.

The term 'Blanc de Noir' refers to white wine made from red/black grapes.

When pouring wine, the glass should typically be no more than half full.

The descending tears of wine seen on the inside of a glass after it has been swirled are called legs.

Crab and Artichoke Melt

2 pounds artichoke hearts (whole or half)

1 pound jumbo lump crab meat

1 pound cream cheese

2 cups of a 5 cheese blend

1 cup of parmesan cheese

Salt and pepper to taste

Tony's seasoning to taste

Chop up artichokes and crab meat finely and place in saucepan. Heat all ingredients together until melted. Store in refrigerator. Can be served hot or cold.

Bananas Foster

In a small cooking pot, combine the following:

One and half tablespoons butter

2 oz rum

2 oz banana liquor

1 cup brown sugar

Sprinkle with cinnamon

Heat until butter is melted and sauce is warm. Add bananas and cook until bananas are tender. Place on top of ice cream and serve.

Smoked Oyster and Spinach Melt

2 lbs frozen spinach

3 jars of Reese's petite smoked oysters

1 lb cream cheese

2 cups of a 5 cheese blend

1 cup of parmesan cheese

Salt and pepper to taste

Cavenders seasoning to taste

Cook frozen spinach in cooking pot until not frozen and tender. Drain excess water from pot. Add smoked oysters and remaining ingredients and heat until melted. Store in refrigerator.

Smoked Salmon Mousse

1 Package Boursin Cheese

1/4 package cream cheese

1 tablespoon red onion

2 tablespoons capers

7 – 8 pieces Salmon

Mix all ingredients into a food processor until it has a mousse texture.

SEASONINGS – SPICES – HERBS

Basil – Sweet, spicy, slightly more minty than fresh basil. Use in salads, Mediterranean sauces, tomato sauces and casseroles.

Bay – Pungent; stronger if leaves are torn before use. Use in stocks, sauces, soups and stews.

Caraway Seeds – Pungent, bittersweet. Use in Austrian and German soups, stews, vegetable dishes and breads

Cardamom – Strong, with a lemonlike aftertaste. Use in Indian and Middle Eastern cooking, especially sweet dishes

Cayenne – Made from one of the hottest varieties of chilies. Use in Mexican and Cajun dishes.

Chili Powder – Blend of chilies, garlic, cumin and oregano. Use in Mexican, Indian and Southwestern dishes

Cinnamon – Subtle, spicy, sweet. Use in pies cakes and cookies

Cloves – Sweet, highly aromatic. Use in oranges and baked ham.

Coriander – Highly aromatic, with a mild hint of orange peel. Use in Indian dishes, poultry, meat and vegetables.

Cumin – Very distinctive flavor, slightly bitter, a little like caraway. Use in Mexican, African and Indian food, and with chicken and vegetables.

Curry Powder – Flavor varies from Indian through Chinese to Thai. Gives curries an authentic flavor, difficult to achieve by mixing spices together.

Dill – Subtle flavor, tones of aniseed. Less pungent than fresh dill. Use for marinades and dressings, especially in Northern and Eastern European cooking.

Ginger – Hot, pungent, warming. Use in desserts and baking, pickles and chutneys and in Indian and Chinese spice mixtures.

Nutmeg – Sweet, warm, quite powerful. Use in sweet dishes, savory sauces and with vegetables.

Oregano – Powerful, almost spicy. Use in Italian and Mediterranean dishes. Also frequently used in Mexican cooking.

Paprika – The mildest of the pepper family. Use in Hungarian and Spanish dishes and as a colorful garnish.

Rosemary – Pungent, spicy, yet refreshing. Use in casseroles, Italian dishes and marinades with lamb, pork, chicken and potatoes.

Saffron – Pungent, aromatic, faintly bitter. Use for coloring foods yellow, especially rice and fish dishes, sweet breads and cookies.

Sage — Slightly bitter. Good with pork, duck, sausage and veal. Also good in egg and cheese dishes.

Tumeric — Musky, peppery. Use to color foods yellow. Especially Indian curries and bean dishes.

OILS AND VINEGARS

Sunflower Oil — Very light and natural, virtually tasteless. Can be used for all cooking purposes. Mix half & half with Olive oil for extra flavor

Olive Oil — Mildly fruity. Virgin has low acidity level and is less refined. Use in Mediterranean dishes, marinades, barbecuing, broiling and sautéing.

Extra Virgin Olive Oil — Peppery, fruity. Use for dressing salads and cold dishes. Sprinkle over hot foods just before serving.

Wine Vinegar — Red and white are mildly fruity; sherry is nutty and brown. Balsamic is oak matured and musky. Use in dressing, sauces and marinades.

Cider Vinegar — Strong like acidic hard cider. Use with pork, liver, sausages and in pickles, chutneys and dressings.

COOKING TERMS

Al dente — An Italian expression applied in all western kitchens to pasta cooked just until enough resistance is left in it to be felt "by the tooth. The expression is also applied to vegetables that have been cooked crisp by steaming, boiling, or stir-frying.

Bain-marie — A bain-marie is a pan of water that is used to help mixtures such as custards bake evenly and to protect them from the direct heat of the oven or, in some cases, the stove.

Blanch — A method of cooking in which foods are plunged into boiling water for a few seconds, removed from the water and refreshed under cold water, which stops the cooking process. Used to heighten color and flavor, to firm flesh and to loosen skins.

Braise — To cook in a small amount of liquid (also called stewing or pot roasting). In contract to poaching, in which the food is completely submerged in simmering liquid, braised dishes use a relatively small amount of liquid. Usually, the purpose of braising is to concentrate the food's flavors in the surrounding liquid so that it can be made into a sauce, or allowed to reduce so that it coats or is reabsorbed by the foods being braised.

Butterfly — To cut and open out the edges of meat or seafood like a book or the wings of a butterfly.

Caramelize – The flavor of many foods, including vegetables, meats, and seafood, is often enhanced by a gentle browning that caramelizes natural sugars and other compounds and intensifies their flavor. Meats for stews, for example, are usually browned to caramelize juices that if not caramelized are much less flavorful. Chopped vegetables, especially aromatic ones such as carrots and onions, are often caramelized—sometimes with cubes of meat—in a small amount of fat before liquid is added to enhance the flavor of soups, stews, and sauces.

Deglaze – To add liquid to a pan in which foods have been sautéed or roasted in order to dissolve the caramelized juices stuck to the bottom of the pan. The purpose of deglazing is to make a quick sauce or gravy for a roast, steak, chop, or a piece of seafood fillet or steak. To make a pan-deglazed sauce, first pour out any fat left in the pan, and make sure that the juices clinging to the bottom of the pan haven't blackened and burned. Add a few tablespoons of flavorful liquid, such as wine, broth, or, in a pinch, water, to the pan. Gently scrape the bottom of the pan with a wooden spoon to loosen the caramelized juices. You can use such a sauce as is, or you can turn it into something richer and more elaborate by adding reduced broth, swirling in a few pieces of butter, adding a little heavy cream, or thickening it with a vegetable puree, such as garlic or tomato, and then reducing the sauce to the consistency like. You can add nuance and flavor to the sauce by adding chopped herbs or ingredients such as green peppercorns.

Flambé – To ignite a sauce or other liquid so that it flames. Most of the time flambéing has no real function other than to delight your guests. If you are going to flambé a dish keep in mind that it is impossible to flambé a cold dish by sprinkling it with spirits and trying to light it—the spirits only release their flammable fumes when hot. Do not pour flaming spirits.

Julienne – To cut into long thin matchstick size strips.

Panfry – Most cooks use the terms panfry and sauté interchangeably, but strictly speaking, there is a difference. Although both terms refer to cooking in a small amount of hot oil, butter, or other fat, sautéing means to toss foods over high heat, while pan-frying describes cooking pieces of meat, seafood, or large pieces of vegetables in a hot pan, turning with tongs, a spatula, or a fork only once or twice.

Reduce or Reduction – The technique of cooking liquids down so that some of the water they contain evaporates. Reduction is used to concentrate the flavor of a broth or sauce and, at times, to help thicken the sauce by concentrating ingredients such as natural gelatin.

Refresh – To rinse just-boiled vegetables under very cold water to stop their cooking.

Resting – Roasted meats should not be served straight out of the over, but should be allowed to rest in a warm place for 20 to 30 minutes, loosely covered with aluminum foil. (The foil keeps the meat warm; loose wrapping ensures that the outside of the meat doesn't steam and lose its crispness.) Resting allows the meat to relax so the juices become redistributed in the meat and aren't squeezed out onto the platter during carving.

Sauté – To cook over high heat in a small amount of fat in a sauté pan or skillet.

Scald – To heat milk just below the boiling point. Or, to immerse a vegetable or fruit in boiling water in order to remove its skin easily.

Restored House 2009

Beauvoir

FEATURE STORIES ~

Food Trivia ~ Food Quotes ~ Famous Mississippians

Historic post-war home and Presidential library of Confederate President Jefferson Davis

Owned and operated by the Mississippi Division, Sons of Confederate Veterans.

About Beauvoir:

Beauvoir was the last home of Jefferson Davis and it was the site of his retirement.

The house was built by **James Brown**, a wealthy plantation owner from Madison County, Mississippi. Construction on the house was started in late 1848 and was completed in 1852. The home was built as a summer home for Brown's wife and his (eventually 13) children and was called **Orange Grove**, due to the Satsuma Oranges being grown on the property. Mr. Brown died in 1866 and his widow continued to own the property until 1873 when she was forced to sell the property at public auction to pay and satisfy the taxes due on her husband's estate. **Frank Johnson**, a land speculator purchased the house for taxes and then sold the house and property three months later.

The James Brown Years

1848 - 1873

A planter, from Madison County, Mississippi, **James Brown,** bought a tract of land facing the Gulf of Mexico on September 2, 1848 from **John Henderson** of Pass Christian, Mississippi. The contract and agreement required $900 in cash and a note for

$1,100 to be paid upon delivery of a deed with clear title to the land. Under the contract, Brown could, prior to receiving the title, construct a residence on the land.

James Brown acted as his own architect and construction superintendent in building the house. He brought slaves from his Madison County plantation to perform the routine work, and he built a sawmill on the property. Skilled work was done by carpenters and decorators from New Orleans. Most of his lumber was cut from trees on the property or in nearby Handsboro, although cypress lumber came from the Back Bay swamps. Slate for the roof was imported from England.

135

Brown completed the house by 1851, but he still had not received title to the land. This was finally obtained on July 16, 1855 by bidding the property for $3,000 at a Harrison County Court auction. Meanwhile, Brown had added two small tracts to the property, one bought from **G. Didier** on October 12, 1852, and the other from **W. H**. and **M. D. Teagarden** on December 27, 1852.

A four room cottage to the rear of the house was already on the property, and it was used by the Brown family during the construction. Later, it served Brown and other owners, including **Jefferson Davis**, as a kitchen and servants' quarters.

Brown also constructed two small cottages, originally identical in plan, one east and one west of the house. The cottage to the east is now known as the **Library Cottage**, but Brown also used it as an office and as a school room for his children, who were taught by a governess. The west cottage, now known as the **Hayes Cottage**, was first a Guest House, but became known as a **Circuit Rider's House** due to frequent use by the Methodist circuit rider serving the area.

Brown owned **Beauvoir** until his death. **Beauvoir** was never a plantation, due to its infertile soil, which consists of sand and a thin layer of decayed vegetation. **Beauvoir** was a coastal home for the Brown family, while they continued to operate their Madison County plantation. In May, 1873, the property was sold under order of the United States Court for the Southern District of Mississippi **to Frank Johnston** (afterward the state's attorney general) of Jackson, Mississippi.

Sarah Dorsey was the next owner of the property and when she first looked out over the Mississippi Sound from the front porch of the house, she said *"Oh my, what a beautiful view - that's what I am going to call this property: **Beauvoir!*** (Which is French for beautiful view or beautiful to look at). From that point on - the property was known as **Beauvoir.**

The Sarah Ann Ellis Dorsey Years -1873-1879

Sarah Ann Ellis was a childhood friend of Varina Howell, wife of **Jefferson Davis**. She was the daughter of a wealthy Louisiana planter who maintained his home in Natchez and who also owned plantations in Mississippi and Arkansas. She had known Davis most of her life and often visited in the home of his elder brother, Joseph, at Hurricane Plantation on the Mississippi River, south of Vicksburg. Sarah Ann married Samuel Worthington Dorsey, a native of Maryland, who managed her properties well after her parents died.

Sarah Dorsey purchased 600 acres, including **James Brown's** house, on July 7, 1873 from **Frank Johnston**, and after the death of her husband, **Sarah Dorsey** made her home at **Beauvoir**. She gave the house the name it still bears, signifying its "beautiful view." A cousin, Mrs. Cochran, made her home with **Sarah Dorsey** at **Beauvoir**.

Dorsey had completed her education in England and was a woman of exceptional educational standing. She corresponded with numerous intellectual and literary figures all over the world. She even held membership, which was rare for a woman, in the New Orleans Academy of Science. She wrote many magazine articles and six novels: **Agnes Graham** was serialized in 1863 in the Southern Literary Messenger and was published in book form in 1869. **Lucia Dare** was published in 1867, **Athalie** in 1872, and **Panola** in 1877. Two other novels, **Vivacious Castine** and **The Vivians** were written for the Church Intellegencer and were never published in book form. Her finest work was a biography of **Governor Henry W. Allen** of Louisiana, a close friend of the Dorseys. This book, published in 1866, bears the title **Reflections of Henry W. Allen.**

Sarah Dorsey spent less than six years at **Beauvoir,** selling the property to **Jefferson Davis** on February 19, 1879.

While **Jefferson Davis** was still a United States senator, his wife, Varina, selected several lots on the Mississippi Gulf coast for a future retirement home. On a business trip to Montgomery, Alabama in late 1875, Davis decided to take a look at those lots with his present needs in mind.

Arriving that night, he took a room in a small inn at Mississippi City. The next morning, he hired a horse and buggy to take a look at the property. The lots were covered with bushes, and the fences were gone. He then drove to the east to visit his old friend,

Sarah Dorsey, at **Beauvoir**. He found she had left the previous Saturday to visit her Louisiana plantations, but he did look over her property. He wrote that it was *"fine place,"* having a *"large and beautiful house, and many orange trees yet full of fruit."* He had no idea, on this day of November 18, 1875, that he was visiting the place where the last dozen years of his life would be spent.

His next trip to the Gulf Coast was a year later. The **Tilden–Hayes** presidential election controversy was raging. Davis travelled from New Orleans to visit relatives near Biloxi and to find a place on the coast where he could write undisturbed. He considered putting a small cottage on his lots, and he hired a man to clear the bushes, although he remembered that before he left her in England, Varina had told him not to get a house on the Gulf Coast.

When **Sarah Dorsey** heard that Davis was on the coast, she invited him for a visit. Arriving at **Beauvoir** in December, Davis was impressed by the peaceful atmosphere. The house was surrounded by live oaks, magnolias, and cedars, with Spanish moss festooning the live oaks. The sea lay in front of the house, and behind it was an orange grove. Beyond it was a pine forest, crossed by a running brook, on the banks of which grew wild azalea, bay, yellow jasmine, and sweet olive. There were six acres of scuppernong grapes. The Louisville & Nashville Railroad cut through the property, and north of the railroad was a virgin forest of long-leaf pine.

When Dorsey discovered that Davis was seeking a place to write his long-delayed book, she showed him her east cottage, which consisted of one room with a pillared gallery completely surrounding it. She urged that the rear gallery could be closed and could become a bedroom and dressing room, while the large room could be lined with bookshelves.

Dorsey agreed to $50.00 per month for board, including provision for Davis' servant, Robert Brown. Davis paid for the carpentry expense of readying the east pavilion for use. Dorsey arranged for **Major W. T. Walthall**, Davis' secretary, to board nearby. The arrangement was ideal. **Major Walthall** had left a large number of official letters and documents with a Mrs. Leovy in South Carolina during the flight from Richmond. There were retrieved, and, by February, 1877, Davis, Walthall, and Dorsey were all hard at work on Davis' book. Dorsey volunteered her services as Davis' amanuensis on the book, and her talents and literary experience were very valuable.

Davis also brought his 20-year-old son, **Jefferson Davis, Jr.**, to **Beauvoir**, and he occupied one of the two small rooms built on the rear gallery of the east cottage. Jeff, Jr. assisted in taking dictation for the book. Mrs. Davis remained in Europe until October, 1877, when she sailed for New York. Both Davis and Jeff, Jr. went to Memphis to greet her on her arrival there, but, she still refused to live on the Gulf Coast and made her home with her daughter Margaret in Memphis. Eventually, conditions there became too crowded, and, with extreme reluctance, she finally left for **Beauvoir.**

At first she was somewhat resentful of the help **Sarah Dorsey** had provided on Davis' book, and she soon became busy taking over the duties of amanuensis. Once established at **Beauvoir**, to her surprise, she began to like it there. After a few weeks on the job, she wrote to a friend in Paris that **Sarah Dorsey** *"makes us very comfortable...I am very fond of her but do not like the climate..."*

In October of the following year, Davis received a hard blow. His fourth and last son, Jeff, Jr., died of yellow fever in Memphis. The Davis's had six children, four boys and two girls, and now only the daughters, Margaret and Winnie, remained.

While Davis was writing **The Rise and Fall of the Confederate Government**, many Confederate leaders came to **Beauvoir** to assist him by clarifying various historical points. During the Christmas season of 1877 **General Jubal A. Early** visited Davis. **Sarah Dorsey** approached **General Early** about Davis' financial condition. She told Early that she had learned that Davis was almost destitute. She also said that she felt that she did not have long to live, and that she intended to leave her entire estate to Davis. But she warned Early that he must not let Davis know of her intentions because he would not permit it if he knew her plans.

In February, 1879, **Sarah Dorsey** offered to sell Beauvoir to **Jefferson Davis**, and on February 19, the title was passed to Davis for $5,500, to be paid in three installments, the first of which was paid immediately. Dorsey then moved to New Orleans.

Following **General Early's** visit, and well before the sale of **Beauvoir** to Davis, **Sarah Dorsey** made her will on January 4, 1878, leaving her estate to **Jefferson Davis**. It is noteworthy that after her death, Davis paid the two remaining installments due on **Beauvoir** in order to liquidate debts owed by Dorsey's estate. Consequently, Davis did buy **Beauvoir**, and he paid for it in full.

Apparently, **Sarah Dorsey** had known for some time that she had cancer, which seems to have prompted her will and the sale of **Beauvoir** to Davis. By June of 1879, her doctors knew that she would not live much longer, and she died in the early morning of July 4, 1879. **Jefferson Davis** and other prominent Southerners accompanied her body to Natchez for burial beside her husband.

In her will, **Sarah Dorsey** stated:

"I owe no obligation of any sort whatever to any relative of my own. I have done all I could for them...I therefore give and bequeath all my property, real, personal, and mixed, wherever located and situated, wholly and entirely, without hindrance or qualification, to my most honored and esteemed friend, Jefferson Davis, ex-president of the Confederate States, for his sole use and, in fee simple forever; and I hereby constitute him my sole heir, executive, and administrator. If Jefferson Davis should not survive me, I give all that I have bequeathed to him to his youngest daughter, Varina. I do not intend to share in the ingratitude of my country towards the man, who is in my eyes, the highest and noblest in existence."

Jefferson Davis continued writing **The Rise and Fall of the Confederate Government** after purchasing **Beauvoir.** After the two volumes were completed, Davis began to travel around the South and to write magazine articles.

A universal amnesty bill pending in Congress was slated to pass some 11 years after the war. **Senator James G. Blaine** from Maine rose at the last minute to offer an amendment reading:"*...with the exception of Jefferson Davis.*" offered to promote his candidacy for president. A storm of protest arose, a Kentucky newspaper expressing it well: "The idea of making **Jefferson Davis** a vicarious sufferer for acts for which he is no more answerable than thousands of his followers is one which every honorable Southern man will resent." But the amendment passed and **Jefferson Davis** alone remained a non-citizen. But Blaine did not become president ~ his reputation became stained by his involvement in a major railroad scandal, and crowds throughout America marched down streets shouting: *"Blaine! Blaine! Continental liar from the state of Maine!"* But he was an American citizen, while Davis was not.

Many people urged Davis to apply for a pardon, so that the Mississippi legislature could elect him United States senator. At the time, all senators were elected by their state legislature, not by the people. But Davis would not apply, and he avoided politics. The Mississippi legislature, on March 10, 1884, in a joint meeting of both houses, honored Davis, who spoke to that body:

"It has been said that I should apply to the United States for a pardon, but repentance must precede the right of pardon, and I have not repented. Remembering, as I must, all which has been suffered, all which has been lost, disappointed hopes and crushed aspirations, yet I deliberately say, if I were to do it all over again, I would again do just as I did in 1861."

Some were fearful that he would give offense to the North, but they were satisfied when he continued:

"...Our people have accepted the decree. It therefore behooves them...to promote the general welfare of the Union, to show the world that hereafter, as heretofore, the patriotism of our people is not measured by lines of latitude and longitude, but is as broad as the obligations they have assumed and embraces the whole of our ocean-bound domain."

During his later years, Davis made numerous trips in which large crowds honored him in ceremonials. In contrast to the criticism he received when the Confederacy fell, Davis was greeted with tremendous ovations. In 1886, in trips to Montgomery and Atlanta, his reception surpassed any which he had previously received. He always spoke of the fact that the United States was now one country and on the theme of reconciliation. Despite this, some Northern newspapers claimed to see danger for the country. However, not all Northern newspapers were so obtuse. The Springfield, Massachusetts Republican noted Southerners' *"unswerving purpose, bravery, and resolution"* and said:

"And when the end came, it was the defeat of men devoted to what was in their estimation a patriotic purpose...Now they gather to commemorate the lost cause, with no desire to recall it, only to recognize it for what it was to them, to assert it to the world and go about their affairs again."

"That is the way we read the honors to Jefferson Davis...How could we respect the Southern people if they did not believe in the thing they undertook to do...if they did not honor their leaders and their soldiers, nor exalt their services and their sacrifices? They do well to cherish the sentiment that hallows their story."

This perceptive paper understood that the South was not refighting the war, but was merely giving expression to its love and reverence for those who had sacrificed so much.

In 1887, following a speech in Macon, Georgia, Davis became seriously ill. When he recovered, he considered his days of public speaking over. But a convention of young men was held in March, 1889 at Mississippi City, only six miles from **Beauvoir**, and a delegation asked him to address them. He began his remarks with: *"Friends and fellow citizens,"* but he stopped and said:

"Ah, pardon me, the laws of the United States no longer permit me to designate you as fellow citizens, but I am thankful that I may address you as friends. I feel no regret that I stand before you a man without a country, for my ambition lies buried in the grave of the Confederacy."

He continued with these memorable words for his young audience:

"The faces I see before me are those of young men; had I not known this I would not have appeared before you. Men in whose hands the destinies of our Southland lie, for love of her I break my silence, to speak to you a few words of respectful admonition. The past is dead; let it bury its dead, its hopes and aspirations. Before you lies the future ~ a future full of golden promise; a future expanding national glory, before which all the world shall stand amazed. Let me beseech you to lay aside all rancor, all bitter sectional feeling, and to take your places in the ranks of those who will bring about a consummation devoutly to be wished ~ a reunited country."

A Time for Mourning

Jefferson Davis left **Beauvoir** for the last time in early November, 1889 for a trip to Brierfield, his plantation on the Mississippi River below Vicksburg. He went by train to New Orleans, arriving in sleety rain. Although he caught a severe chest cold, he boarded the steamer Laura Lee for the trip to Brierfield. But when the steamer arrived late at night in Brierfield, Davis was too ill to get up, so he continued on to Vicksburg, docking in the morning. That afternoon, he left Vicksburg for Brierfield, arriving after dark. He lay ill for four days, and the plantation manager secretly wired Mrs. Davis, who left at once for New Orleans. **Jefferson Davis** boarded the steamer Leathers, commanded by his friend, **Captain Leathers**, for the trip back to New Orleans. Meanwhile, Mrs. Davis boarded a northbound steamer commanded by Captain Leathers' son. During the night as the ships were about to pass one another, young Leathers learned that Davis was aboard his father's ship. He brought his ship alongside and transferred Mrs. Davis to the other steamer. When Davis awoke, he was amazed to find Mrs. Davis at his bedside.

When the ship docked at Bayou Sara, above Baton Rouge, two doctors examined Davis and diagnosed him as suffering from acute bronchitis, complicated by malaria. When the ship reached New Orleans, a number of prominent men met it, among them was **Dr. Chaille**, the dean of the medical faculty of Tulane University, and **Justice C. S. Fenner**, to whose home on First Street Davis was taken. A noted New Orleans physician, **Dr. C. J. Bickham**, joined Dr. Chaille, and the two concurred in the diagnosis of the Bayou Sara doctors. Lingering for about three weeks, Davis died on December 6, 1889.

Varina Davis decided that her husband should be buried in New Orleans, choosing the tomb of the Army of Northern Virginia at Metairie Cemetery as his burial site. The funeral ceremonies have been called "**The South's Greatest Funeral**."

Special trains brought thousands to New Orleans from all over the South. The city was crowded with prominent Confederates, both civilian and military, while private soldiers and private citizens poured into the city. A number of **Jefferson Davis'** former slaves also made the journey. One of them, **William Simpson**, wept openly at the funeral. When asked by a Northern reporter how he felt about Davis, Simpson replied: *That I loved him, this shows, and I can say that every colored man he ever owned loved him.*

Less than four years later, in May, 1893, **Jefferson Davis** was removed from the tomb in Metairie Cemetery, and a special train furnished by the L & N Railroad carried his body to Richmond Virginia. Huge crowds and flowers marked the course of the train as it wound its way across the South. He rests today in Hollywood Cemetery, surrounded by his family. It is appropriate that his final resting place be in the city of his greatest labor as the only President of the Confederate States of America.

Jefferson Davis catafalque, a ceremonial platform used to carry the remains of **Jefferson Davis** in the 1889 funeral procession is on display in the Confederate Museum at Beauvoir.

A Wife and Daughter's Responsibility

Because **Sarah Dorsey's** will had provided that Winnie should inherit **Beauvoir** in the event that **Jefferson Davis** died prior to Dorsey, Davis decided to leave **Beauvoir** to his youngest daughter, Winnie.

Winnie Davis was born **Varina Anne Jefferson Davis** in Richmond, Virginia on June 27, 1864, during her father's presidency. She became known as **"The Daughter of the Confederacy"** and was a favorite of Confederate veterans at their reunions after the war.

Like so many associated with **Beauvoir**, **Winnie Davis** followed literary pursuits. Besides writing a number of articles and poems published in national magazines, she wrote three novels: **An Irish Knight of the 19th Century**, based on the life of **Robert Emmett**, published in 1888; **The Veiled Doctor**, published in 1895; and **A Romance of Summer Seas**, published in 1898 and considered her best work.

On September 18, 1898, **Winnie Davis** died at Narragansett Pier, Rhode Island. Her death was attributed to malarial gastritis. Her grave is near her father's in Hollywood Cemetery, Richmond, Virginia.

Upon Winnie Davis' death, the ownership of **Beauvoir** reverted to **Mrs. Jefferson Davis.** Mrs. Davis had returned to **Beauvoir** very tired and worn after her husband's funeral. She found several first draft chapters of an autobiography which **Jefferson Davis** had begun, and she quickly realized that she had an important task to perform ~ letting the world know what sort of man Davis had been. Inspired by this idea, she plunged into the work of massive proportions, totaling 1,632 pages. It was published by the Belford Company as **Jefferson Davis, Ex-President of the Confederate States of America, a Memoir by His Wife.**

During the period when Winnie owned **Beauvoir**, an offer by a hotel corporation of $90,000 for the property had been firmly refused. Both Winnie and Mrs. Davis wanted **Beauvoir** to become a shrine to the memory of **Jefferson Davis**. After Mrs. Davis acquired ownership, she also refused offers for the property. However, in 1903, she sold **Beauvoir** for the token sum of $10,000 to the **Mississippi Division, Sons of Confederate Veterans** with the stipulation that it would be operated as a Confederate soldiers' home, with the house itself becoming a shrine to the memory of the former Confederate President.

A Shrine to the Memory of Jefferson Davis

When Mrs. Davis decided to sell **Beauvoir, Mrs. A. McC Kimbrough,** a long-time close friend to Jefferson and **Varina Davis,** began what many have been called her life's work ~ the preservation of **Beauvoir** as the **"Mount Vernon of the Confederacy."** She began an incredible volume of correspondence, newspaper appeals, talks, personal appeals, and every conceivable means to accomplish this end. Her activities even included the writing of a song to help raise funds.

Finally, after it was arranged for the **Mississippi Division, Sons of Confederate Veterans** to buy **Beauvoir,** Mrs. Kimbrough helped that organization raise the purchase price. No other person compares with her in the accomplishment of this dream, and it is hardly possible to give Mrs. Kimbrough as much credit as she deserves for her efforts.

In making the sale, Mrs. Davis made several provisions to assure the carrying out of her intentions. They were:

A home for ex-Confederate soldiers was to be provided.

The Mississippi Division, Sons of Confederate Veterans were to own, manage, and preserve the property as "a perpetual memorial sacred to the memory of **Jefferson Davis**, the only president of the Confederate States of America, and sacred to the memory of his family and **'The Lost Cause**;'" and, no part of the property may be sold or transferred in any manner except to the state of Mississippi, and, in that event, all other conditions shall remain in full force.

Beauvoir continues to be operated as a shrine to **Jefferson Davis**, and, as the deed permits, *"to the memory of the ex-Confederate soldiers and sailors, their wives and servants, or to the memory of the Confederate Cause."* Two separate museums are maintained, the Davis Family Museum and the Confederate Museum. Emphasis in all operations is placed on **President Jefferson Davis.**

It was almost a full century before Davis became a fellow citizen of these young men. **Senator Mark Hartfield** of Oregon introduced a Senate Joint Resolution returning citizenship posthumously to **Jefferson Davis**. It would, he said, right a "glaring injustice in the history of the United States." Passed unanimously by a voice vote, the resolution was successfully sponsored in the House of Representatives by **Representative Trent Lott** of Mississippi, whose district included **Beauvoir.** On October 17, 1978, **President Jimmy Carter** signed the resolution into law. **Jefferson Davis** was no longer a non-citizen in the land of his birth ~ a nation he had served as an army officer, a Congressman, a wounded Mexican War hero, a United States senator, and a secretary of war.

Although **Beauvoir** suffered extensive damage from Hurricane Katrina, it is now open for tours. For more information Visit their website - www.beauvoir.org

BLESSING OF THE FLEET

The Blessing of the Fleet is a tradition that began centuries ago in Mediterranean fishing communities. The practice is predominantly Catholic and a blessing from the local priest was meant to ensure a safe and bountiful season. However, there are numerous instances where the "Blessing" was initiated by an Episcopalian minister.

In most United States ports, the event was brought by immigrants who held strongly to their Catholic religious beliefs. Three of the most well known Gulf ports are **Biloxi, Mississippi & Bayou La Batre, Alabama** and **Tarpon Springs, Florida**. The events that are part of the ritual vary by community and range from a simple ceremony to a multi-day festival including a Catholic mass, Parades, Pageantry, Dancing, Feasting and Contests. The Blessing of the Fleet is held at coastal fishing communities throughout much of the world. The actual blessing used at Biloxi's first Blessing ceremony took place in 1929. George Higginbotham, a longtime Biloxi resident described the first ceremony to a local newspaper reporter in 1998. Sunday Mass was conducted by the parish priest from an altar constructed on the shore of Biloxi's Bay. The fishermen tied their decorated boats together in the bay and the priest stepped from deck to deck, blessing the boats.

The current ceremony is larger and more mobile. The shrimp boats form a procession out in the Mississippi Sound and file past the anchored *"Blessing Boat"* where the officiating priest and bishop stand, sprinkling holy water on the boats and giving the blessing for each one.

For more information on the **Blessing of the Fleet in Biloxi, Mississippi –**

BROADCAST MEDIA PERSONALITIES FROM MISSISSIPPI

Robin Roberts, TV/ Media personality for Good Morning America -ABC
Chris McDaniel (born 1971), talk radio host, (Laurel)
Norman Robinson (born 1951), news anchor, (Toomsuba)
Doug Russell (born 1972), sportscaster, (Jackson)
Tavis Smiley (born 1964), talk show host, (Gulfport)
Shepard Smith (born 1964), newscaster, (Holly Springs)
Oprah Winfrey (born 1954), talk show host, (Kosciusko)
Bill Evans (born 1960) Senior Meteorologist – WABC – TV New York (Meridian)

Marlin Miller

MARLIN MILLER ~ WOOD SCULPTOR

About the Artist

Marlin Miller lives in Fort Walton Beach, Florida with his wife, Rene and their five children. He is originally from Manson, Iowa where he grew up working on the family farm. He joined the Air Force and traveled around the world. While stationed in Hawaii, he graduated from Hawaii Pacific University with a minor in art.

Marlin is a fourth generation artist who has developed a unique style of flowing marine life into driftwood. He is an award winning sculptor who has his work on display in galleries, restaurants and homes of private collectors around the world.

Katrina Sculpture Project

Marlin started the "Katrina Sculpture Project" in 2007. He has spent over a year donating his time and resources to carve large oaks that were killed by the storm. So far, he has completed over 30 sculptures along hwy 90 on the Mississippi Gulf Coast. Some of his creations tower more than 3 stories into the sky. The project has been featured on many television stations, radio programs, magazines and newspapers around the country.

Marlin's fascination with the ocean and arts has come together with this collection of original wood sculptures.

Marlin is available for interviews and demonstrations nationwide.

Contact Marlin by Email: **marlin@marlinmillergallery.com**

Katrina Sculpture Project

For more information and to view Marlin's **Sculpture Gallery** go to **Marlinmillergallery.com**

Eagle carving dedicated to Col. Lawrence Roberts

Memorial Park in Pass Christian

Marlin Miller placed a stainless-steel plaque at the base of the tree he'd carved in honor of Col. Lawrence Roberts and the Tuskegee Airmen

The plaque reads:

"An American Hero, Tuskegee Airmen, Class of 1944K, Devoted Husband and Father.

The eagle, carved with chainsaws, stands at the end of a tunnel of Live oaks leading into the Pass Christian Park, and Miller said, "If you had seen this tree before I carved it, it was already an eagle."

Miller said when he started the carving project it represented the residents' determination and spirit to rebuild after the storm. The country had forgotten about the Coast, but he said the carvings are bringing attention again.

MO-JOE FOUNDATION

Mo-Joe foundation was started in August 2008. Our purpose is to promote tourism along the Mississippi Gulf Coast and give back to Coastal communities, such as and other non-profits that promote tourism. The Foundation works with marketing groups and media to develop premiere events on the Mississippi Gulf Coast, marketing the beautiful Golden Highway 90. The **Mo-Joe foundation** has established a reputation for excellence all over the Gulf Coast and tri-state area of Mississippi, Alabama and Louisiana as a major tourism for special events.

In the year 2008, the Legend of MO-JOE was born and the first MO-JOE Festival was established on Back Bay in D'Iberville, Mississippi. The Festival and the Mardi Gras Bed Race were named a Southern Travel Treasures by AAA's Magazine, AAA Southern Traveler, in its first year because of its appeal to the typical AAA members in 2,100,000 homes in Arkansas, Louisiana, and Mississippi.

Teamed with Demp Group, a premiere, full-service, marketing, consulting, and event planning firm located on the Mississippi Gulf Coast, **Mo-Joe foundation** will feature eight new events in 2009-2010, promoting tourism for the Coast.

Demp Group has established a reputation for excellence as a dependable firm that performs exceptional work for an impressive list of clients along the Gulf Coast region and tri-state area of Mississippi, Alabama, and Louisiana. Demp Group has joined teams with **Mo-Joe foundation** in developing and marketing MO-JOE events.

We want to thank all of our corporate sponsors, vendors, and volunteers for their love of the Mississippi Gulf Coast and the Golden Highway 90.

For more information on how you can support **Mo-Joe foundation**, call us at 228.238.7606 or e-mail us at Millie@MoJoeFoundation.com.

Mardi Gras Mo-Joe Madness

Mardi Gras is a big deal in the Mid-West. Every year thousands of people flood the streets of St. Louis, ready to celebrate this long standing annual tradition. As much of a spectacle as the festival is, it pales in comparison to the parades that crowd the streets in the city where it all began. Exactly which city holds the title of the "Birthplace of Mardi Gras" is a subject of great debate. Both Mobile, Alabama and New Orleans, Louisiana lay claim to ownership of the first Mardi Gras parades. Regardless of where the rich tradition began, it can be seen in all of its glory, nowhere more, than in these two cities, as well as the expanse of highway, known as the Golden Highway 90, that stretches between them and along the coast of Mississippi. It is here on this stretch of beautiful highway that a new Mardi Gras tradition is taking hold.

In February of 2008, the Biloxi, Mississippi area hosted the first annual Mardi Gras Bed Race, a fundraiser that benefits the Salvation Army and their efforts around the nation. It is only fitting that it is in this part of the country that a new parade has emerged in exactly this fashion, with race contestants donning costumes and riding homemade beds through the streets. What is the area's connection to such a spectacle? It begins like this:

The Legend Of Mo-Joe

In the late 1600s French explorers, Pierre Le Moyne Sier d'iberville and his brother Jean Baptiste de Bienville, arrived in present-day Mississippi attempting to establish a permanent settlement in Louisiana. After meeting friendly Native Americans of the Biloxi, Bayougoulas and Houma tribes, Le Moyne's intentions began to change. The Indians spoke of a mighty river in the west near their village. Le Moyne was able to successfully navigate the North Pass into the Mississippi River. Because of this voyage, Le Moyne eventually was credited with the formation of many areas, including D'Iberville, Mississippi and Baton Rouge, Louisiana. Soon afterward, Le Moyne and his men established a large settlement, Fort Maurepas, near present-day Ocean Springs, Mississippi. Once the stronghold was complete, Le Moyne departed for France to gather supplies and further help, leaving Savole de le Villantry and his brother Bienville in charge in his absence.

It is from these famous French explorers that we have many of today's Mississippi coast lines. It is from that same expedition that we also have the legend of another French explorer who is said to have accompanied the men on that very trip. His name was Maurice Joubert de LaBelle, and legend tells that he was member of Le Moyne's crew on the journey to Louisiana. The Indians that inhabited the Mississippi Coast at that time know more about the LeBelle legends than any other source. Known simply to them as Mo-Joe, because of their inability to pronounce his name, the Indians spoke of LeBelle as a rambunctious man that was colorful, both literally and figuratively. They described him as having a jovial personality that was always talking and that lived a vivacious lifestyle. Legend tells that Mo-Joe LeBelle was well liked among the native tribes and would frequently interact and socialize.

The most famous of the Indian tales of Mo-Joe is of the night Mo-Joe, accompanied by his Indian friends; was carried atop his bed mattress through the paths of the villages. Dressed in multi-colored clothes, Mo-Joe is said to have been drinking happily, shouting, singing, and tossing beads, necklaces and other priceless French trinkets, of which is said to have had many, into the crowds of people who had gathered to watch his one-man parade. It is said that, from that famous parade, they have never recovered all of the priceless pieces of treasure that Mo-Joe flung from his carried mattress top. Legends tell that the treasure is still there, scattered among the area that has, today, become the golden Highway 90 from Pascagoula to Waveland along the Mississippi Gulf Coast.

Little else is known of the man the Indians called Mo-Joe, except that his name has carried on in the area of the Mississippi Gulf Coast. Mo-Joe showed up again in the south in the early 20th century. This time, however, it was not a man, but instead a feeling or idea that inhabited the name. In 1957, as the musical phenomenon known as the Blues began to pick up speed in the southern United States, a Mississippi native, McKinley Morganfield, a.k.a. Muddy Waters, reintroduced the name mojo to the region. This time in a song called "Got my mojo working." Mojo was considered a charm or a trick. He described it as working mojo, or charm, on someone. In 1926, Newbell Niles Puckett published this definition in his Folk Beliefs of the Southern Negro:

"The term mojo is often used by the Mississippi Negroes to mean 'charms, amulets, or tricks', as 'to work mojo' on a person or 'to carry a mojo'."

Whether or not this term had any connection to the Mo-Joe legend of the Indians is unclear. Regardless, Puckett's mojo is certainly in the same vain as the man the Indians called by the same name.

In present day Mississippi, as the 2010 Mardi Gras season approaches, it is appropriate that we celebrate the third annual Mardi Gras Bed Race, atop our own beds the way Mo-Joe is said to have once on his. It is also fitting that, in the same area the Mo-Joe bed legend is said to have occurred, that in 2010 we celebrate the second annual Mo-Joe Day, a day of and for the people. Just like Mo-Joe's is said to have been hundreds of years ago.

Credits

Pierre Le Moyne, Sier d'iberville – www.olemiss.edu

Jean Baptiste de Bienville — www.wikipedia.org

Base of operations at Biloxi — www.datasync.com

"Ghost dance" — www.everyculture.com

Treasure hunt — www.canadian-republic.ca

McKinley Morganfield — www.phrases.org

Blake.dempgroup@yahoo.com

The Real Mo-Joe

Sounds to me like Mo-Joe rode the very first float on the entire gulf Coast, so is it possible that he is *Mr. Mardi Gras* himself? I would be willing to bet that Mo-Joe was also the first man to hand out sugar beads (Beads for kisses) and I wouldn't doubt it if he was the first to throw a moon pie to the revelers; after all, he only had so many beads, coins and trinkets so when those were gone, what else did he have? That's right, moon pies, because we all know that moon pies have been around forever.

They say that Mardi Gras started in Mobile and that New Orleans Mardi Gras is the most famous and that may be true, but there is a good possibility that both cities got the idea from Mo-Joe himself; after all, he was the first *good ole boy* on the Gulf Coast and certainly the most well known party boy; so he certainly set the standards for what Mardi Gras is all about, and let's not forget his attire, a combination of ruffles, buckles and local native garb; sounds like he designed the very first Mardi Gras costume as well.

By now you probably think Mo-Joe was nothing more than a party animal but there was much, much, more to him than most people knew. Mo-Joe loved making people laugh, even at his own expense and he loved everyone, not just during the carnival season, but every other day of the year; of course he partied every day of the year so I suppose that would account for why he loved everybody, sounds like my kind of guy.

Now I could go on and on about Mo-Joe because there are many more tales to tell but the best way to get to know him is to join the Krewe of Mo-Joe and follow in his footsteps. For more information, go to www.mojoefest.com

THE KATRINA DOLPHINS

In August 2005, **Hurricane Katrina** slammed ashore along the **Mississippi Gulf Coast,** sweeping out to sea, the resident dolphins of the **Marine Life Oceanarium** in **Gulfport, Mississipp**i.

Though this landmark institution was completely destroyed, two dolphin families found their way through the devastation into the Gulf of Mexico. Following their rescue, these 16 dolphins were given a new home at **Dolphin Cay**, a state-of-the-art habitat with expert marine mammal care.

Under the watchful, around-the-clock eye of **Dolphin Cay's** expert Marine Mammal Specialists, the *"Katrina Dolphins"* have made a remarkable recovery.

In the early fall of 2007, Lee and I had the opportunity to visit **Atlantis**, on **Paradise Island** in the Bahamas. Not only were we able to attend a *"Live with Regis and Kelly"* show, we were also in a position to find out what our *Katrina Dolphins* were up to.

Now, we are not only proud to report that our famous *Katrina Dolphins* are doing extremely well, but would love a visit from their friends on the **Mississippi Gulf Coast**.

Lee and I watched a show that featured *The Katrina Dolphins* and needless to say, we were quite impressed, and why not, after all, these Dolphins came from **Mississippi**. In fact, I was so impressed that I decided to include *The Katrina Dolphins* in my *Strawberry Fairy* series.

For any of you out there that have never been to Atlantis, please go. Lee and I have been twice and are planning another trip next year. **Paradise Island** is the perfect setting for **Atlantis** and our **Katrina Dolphins** could not be in a more ideal environment.

Everyone is so gracious and helpful that you really don't want to leave.

Dolphin Cay Atlantis

Dolphin Cay was constructed on more than 14 acres—about the size of ten American football fields. And that means plenty of room to relax and play, whether you are a guest or one of our year-round resident dolphins.

More than seven million gallons of crystal clear Bahamian sea water flow continuously into the lagoon through an open system, providing the dolphins, under our care, with a constant supply of fresh, natural saltwater.

The pristine, white sand beaches of **Dolphin Cay** are reserved exclusively for dolphin interaction participants and their companions.

If spending a day with dolphins is your idea of paradise, there's no place on earth like **Dolphin Cay at Atlantis**.

Our multi-million dollar state-of-the art habitat is one of the newest and largest in the world, with exciting interactions that let you swim and play alongside dolphins in a lagoon fed by the warm waters of the Caribbean.

Home to a playful pod of Atlantic Bottlenose Dolphins rescued from **Hurricane Katrina, Dolphin Cay** welcomes anyone visiting the islands to join in on their fun.

The Katrina Dolphins are all doing great! Four calves born here at Atlantis, listed below are their names and their respective mothers along with their birthdates, all four are females.

CALF – MOTHER – BIRTHDATE

Runner – Kelly – April 4th 2007 (named after the late Butch Kerzner who was an avid runner)

Missi – Michelle – April 17th 2007 (named by a student from Mississippi)

Bimini – Jackie – June 6th 2007 (named by a student from the Bahamas)

Palmer – Tamra – June 11th 2008 (named after our Chief Operating Officer who retired in 2008)

All are doing extremely well and are continuing to learn new behaviors and are interacting with our guests on a daily basis.

Along with the dolphins, we still have **10 California sea lions from Gulfport Mississippi** that are participating in a variety of interactions and appearances throughout the resort including our new Sea Lion Interaction Program that offers our guests an opportunity to get into the water with one of our sea lions for a very unique perspective of these amazing animals.

Our Marine Mammal Specialists blend extensive training with their own unique island flair to make a day at **Dolphin Cay** entertaining and fun.

The dolphin interactions last 90-120 minutes with about 30 minutes in the water, and begin with an orientation hosted by a member of this lively, knowledgeable team. Then it's out to the beach, where they'll introduce you to some of the dolphins under our care, who aren't shy about showing off their incredible athletic abilities and playful natures.

With these specialists as your hosts, the energy is always welcoming and happy, and the experience expertly guided.

Dolphin Cay is home to one of the most advanced marine mammal care and rescue facilities of its kind. Comparable to medical labs found in hospitals, the Atlantis Marine Mammal facility is a state-of-the-art microbiology lab able to provide sophisticated care on site.

A team of experienced veterinarians works closely with the Marine Mammal Specialists to help monitor the health and well-being of each dolphin. The daily records, observations and data regarding the behavior and physiology of the dolphins are shared with other researchers, marine biologists and universities.

Whether you're interested in learning more about the dolphins you can swim with at **Dolphin Cay** or just want the fun to last a little longer, our interactive Education Center is worth the visit.

Here you'll find electronic stations where you can read about our dolphins rescued from **Hurricane Katrina**, or learn more about dolphins in the wild and what you can do to help protect them.

For more information on Dolphin Cay Atlantis – www.atlantis.com

LAKE VISTA

Hurricane Katrina Devastates Lake Vista Community

As Told By Ken Combs, Jr.

Our preparations for Katrina were the same as for previous storms. We boarded windows and doors, tidied up around the house and yard, stocked up on food, drink and other necessary emergency items; we even bought the last generator at a local Kmart at closing time that fateful day. I was proud of that generator...it was mobile with wheels and handles; however, it later proved to be useless.

Our oldest daughter Christina (23) had just married in July and all of her wedding gifts were still at our house. What a mistake that proved to be, little did we know that Katrina would help herself to all of our possessions.

My wife, Edie, Christina; our 19 year old daughter, Jourdyn, our 12 year old son, Ken III, my mom, my sister and I all decided to ride the storm out at our place. Christina and my sister each brought their small dogs, as well. My late father, Ken Combs, Sr. was ill at the time and was safe at Gulfport Memorial Hospital.

We didn't sleep much that night...we kept up with all the hurricane updates and began to worry as Katrina became a monster, moving closer and closer to our coast. Early the next morning, on August 29th, 2005, the beast came roaring in. We lost power shortly before sunrise and it was pretty eerie hearing the sounds of howling winds and tree limbs snapping; yet not being able to see what was coming our way.

Daylight soon broke and brought about a false sense of security. We ventured out onto our backyard screen porch facing the golf course and watched in shock as trees were felled by Katrina's fury.

Suddenly, our porch began to collapse and we scurried back inside where we felt safe once again. Looking back, I have to laugh when I remember that I was rushing so fast to get back inside, I spilled my breakfast cereal all over the den floor...I was so concerned about that spill at the time, not even imagining that soon the entire den would look like a bowl of cereal and chocolate milk. It wasn't long before the screen porch completely caved in. So to take our minds off the devastation taking place outside, we began making plans to rebuild a new porch, keeping positive thoughts that the rest of our house would be spared. It was about mid-morning by this time and we were oblivious to the water rising because the windows and doors were boarded, blocking our view to the outside and even if we could see out, the wind driven rain was so powerful, we would not have been able to see anything anyway. At first we thought all the water that began seeping in under the doors was from rain; little did we know that the flood had just begun. Water began seeping in under the doors first; then under the foundation and corners of the home. We initially put towels down to try and stop it but soon surrendered. I remember Edie joking that she would finally be able to get the floors she wanted! That proved to be prophetic.

It's a pretty helpless feeling as you see your home being inundated with dirty flood water and there's absolutely nothing you can do about it. The water was steadily rising at this point. Looking out our sliding glass doors it felt like we were in an aquarium. The water was a few feet deep at this point and the doors appeared to be bending from the water pressure against them. A few years ago we had a fence in our backyard that borders the golf course. I removed that fence and cleared all the shrubs/brush along the fence line. Now there was nothing to protect us from the hurricane force winds and the water being driven in by these winds.

Soon, the waves began crashing into our home from Katrina's southerly winds. We had six vehicles at our home at the time and car alarms began sounding from flood waters reaching the electrical systems. It was weird to see trunks, windows, and doors opening automatically...must be a safety element. The water was about waist deep by now and we were considering our next move. We tried to enter the garage from the home but the water pressure made it difficult to open the door. We finally forced the door open but the big garage door was beginning to buckle from the water and was ready to collapse. By now, panic was beginning to set in. When the water reached my chest I could see the fear in my mom's eyes.

In the height of the storm we noticed that some of our neighbors were retreating to a two story home across the street. I believe my son was one of the first to say, "let's go". I made one last check of the home before I left...the wind and water were doing a number on the rear of the house by this time and you could hear the damage being dealt. Ken grabbed Edie's hand and said, "let's go, Mom". Everyone else helped my mom across the street. Keep in mind that we were practically swimming in chest/neck deep water by this time and the winds were howling. The waters were extremely rough and the swells knocked us off our feet several times. Debris was flying at us like missiles from all angles. I especially remember the big green pine cones hitting like bombs in the waters all around us. I also remember encountering the "balls" of fire ants in the water. That was rather unpleasant but luckily just a nuisance.

We finally made it over to the two story house, but the front door was damaged and wouldn't open. We had to get out of the elements and to the second floor of that home. The windows on the first floor were low profile and ground level...meaning that we would have to swim under water, through the window, to enter the home. My mom, a very petite lady cannot swim and is afraid of the water; however, she was a real trooper, as we helped her through this very frightening experience.

We finally made it inside and headed upstairs. Several families from other homes in the neighborhood were already there and believe me, we were all relieved to be out of the water. But relief soon gave way to fear as we watched the water rushing through the first floor, realizing that the home might collapse at any given moment from the pressure of the water; the large pine trees surrounding the home were a definite danger, as well.

Since I had managed to somehow keep my cell phone dry, I called 911 to let first responders know where we were. When I finally got through and the operator said that they were receiving hundreds of calls just like mine, I thanked her and hung up.

Some of the guys at the house had a small skiff so, despite the raging storm, we pulled it over to my house to retrieve all the food, drink and supplies that were still available. When I entered my house I got an idea of what kind of damage had already been inflicted and it was disturbing to say the least. I could hear destruction occurring as the swells were hitting the back eave of the house. Furniture and personal belongings were floating all around the house.

A strong gasoline odor was evident…we had numerous cans for the generator in anticipation of electrical failure…the cans were partially submerged and bobbing throughout the house. We managed to salvage some ice chests, gathered up whatever we could and headed back across the street as the fury of the storm continued.

The time spent on the second floor of our neighbor's home seemed like an eternity, but we are forever indebted to our neighbors because their house provided shelter for my family, as well as several other families, during what proved to be the most devastating storm to ever hit the United States. Those of us that weathered the storm together will always share a special bond with one another.

At last, mid to late afternoon the waters had subsided to a manageable depth and though the winds were still very gusty, we returned to our home to find total devastation. It was shocking to see everything in ruins. Walls and doors had been washed out. Windows were broken, everything below the water line was destroyed and the ceilings were in terrible shape. This was a very emotional scene for all of us.

We soon composed ourselves and decided to assess my parent's home across the golf course. The water was still deep in areas, and at times we encountered neck deep water while crossing certain areas of the course. I remember Mom, at one point, wrapping her arms around a tree because the winds were so strong.

We finally made it to Washington Avenue and spoke with a National Guard colonel. He said the situation was extremely grave and offered us a ride. He got us as close to my parent's house as possible and for that we were grateful. We walked the final few blocks; encountering an injured gentleman on the way…he cut his leg severely trying to navigate the flood waters.

We finally made it to our parent's house; my oldest sister had remained there during the storm and was thankfully safe.

Once again, the heartbreak set in; Hurricane Katrina had completely destroyed my childhood home and my Mom was devastated. This was the beginning of many emotional moments we shared together.

Next we decided to check on my sister's home near the middle school. A great neighbor offered to take us there in a vehicle his father had brought to him after the storm, but again, the roads were blocked so we had to walk several blocks to get there. Upon arriving we discovered that part of my sister's roof was gone and the home's interior had sustained major damage. Again; another emotional scene.

The day had finally come to a close and we ended up staying across the street at my sister's friend's house for the night; and what a great friend she was. She provided us with great food and a dry place to sleep. She even lent us a vehicle to use the next day to check on our dad in the hospital and thankfully he was okay.

We then drove to our youngest sister's house across town in a vehicle provided by another great friend. She had sustained minimal damage so we stayed at her house that night and the next day, we evacuated to Oxford, Mississippi. Her son was attending school there and we all rented a home together.

The local Red Cross in Oxford was already prepared for everyone and provided much needed relief.

A local church even took us under its wing, and provided a refreshing spiritual touch.

While in Oxford, we began the insurance nightmare by filing out our initial claims. We, like so many others, started with FEMA.

We remained in Oxford for about ten days before heading back home to literally rebuild our lives.

We stayed at my sister's house for another month before a FEMA travel trailer arrived in our front yard and we lived in it for about a year before being able to finally move back into our home; mid August 2006.

What a year it was!

Lake Vista Community – After the storm

Ken and Edie's daughter, Christina and her husband are both nurses. He was employed at Ocean Springs Hospital at that time and had volunteered to work the shift leading up to Katrina's arrival. With communications down after the storm's landfall, we had no idea of what may have happened to him...and he feared the worst for us, also. He left the hospital the afternoon of the 29th and drove the best he could and got as close as possible to our neighborhood. While we were assessing the situation at our house, he surprised us by wading through the subsiding flood waters. He was obviously relieved that we were OK but the concern he exhibited told another story. He and Christina (newlyweds) shared an emotional moment together as he stated that the Biloxi/Gulfport coastline was completely wiped out. He is from the Point in Biloxi and was devastated to know that his childhood home and city had been obliterated.

Most of us in Lake Vista lived in travel trailers in our front yards for a year or more after the storm, this provided a great opportunity for each of us to get to know our neighbors even better than we did before Hurricane Katrina.

Prior to the storm I was guilty of mostly just waving to my neighbors as I would come and go from home; however, *"Neighbors helping neighbors"* became the norm immediately following the storm and is even stronger today. We have supported each other and cried together during the tough times; and we have partied and laughed together during the happy times. We all still stop and chat with each other on a regular basis. It has been amazing to watch our neighborhood transition into what is has become today. *"Love thy neighbor"* is truly what our community is all about.

The neighbors banded together and formed a Neighborhood Watch program with the Gulfport Police department and to this day, we still have frequent "meetings" (parties). We have created a contact list and inform the neighbors of pertinent information via e-mail and phone calls.

Before Hurricane Katrina, the golf course adjacent to our neighborhood was called TraMark. After Katrina, we were instrumental in renaming the golf course Bayou Vista Golf Course...recognizing our sister community Bayou View and Lake Vista.

The neighbors frequently gather to do our environmental part by walking the access road and ridding it of trash.

Lake Vista recently adopted South Vista Drive and signs have been approved and will be erected (similar to the "Watch" signs) along that road stating the adoption. Katrina may have destroyed our houses and material things but she only strengthened our spirit and resolve. Our homes and relationships are stronger than ever. The future is bright in Lake Vista. New young families with young children are moving in and being welcomed with open arms. I love this neighborhood and am proud to call it home.

Chicken & Rice

1 pound chicken thighs
2 cans cream of mushroom soup
4 cups chicken broth

Salt/pepper
4 cups rice/instant

Boil chicken until cooked. De-bone. Combine chicken, broth, soup & salt/pepper.

Bring to a boil. Add rice. Cover and remove from heat. Let sit for 5 minutes.

Edie Combs

Hot Crab Dip

2 pkgs. cream cheese (softened)

2 cans crabmeat

4 tablespoons grated onion

2 tablespoons milk

1 teaspoon salt

½ teaspoon pepper

2 tablespoons horseradish sauce

Mix and bake 375° for 30 minutes

Edie Combs

Stuffed Portabella Mushrooms

2 whole portabella
mushrooms/stems removed

2 shallots

1 small container small shrimp
(salad size)

1/2 cup parmesan reggiano

1/4 cup Italian bread crumbs

Salt & pepper to taste

1 egg to bind

2 tsp butter

Chopped parsley

Sauté shrimp, shallots, chopped stems, parsley and salt and pepper in butter until tender. Let cool slightly. Add bread crumbs, eggs and most of cheese; mix until incorporated. Stuff caps with mixture. Top with remaining cheese. Grill in preheated grill with lid closed for 25 minutes on medium to low heat. Great as an appetizer or main course.

Sandra Chapman

Paneed Wild Turkey

Salt & pepper

Plain flour/seasoned with salt & pepper

Wild turkey breast

Butter/oil

Slice turkey breasts into one inch strips; season to taste with salt and pepper. Use the flat smooth side of a meat tenderizer to pound each strip flat (about the thickness of a veal cutlet) Lightly coat each strip with seasoned flour just before frying. Heat oil or butter in skillet. Use enough to come halfway up cutlet. Fry on each side until golden brown. Serve with favorite marinara sauce over angel hair pasta topped with mozzarella or with grilled veggies.

Sandra Chapman

Squash casserole

6 cups large diced yellow squash
and zucchini
Vegetable oil
1 large onion, chopped
4 tablespoons butter

1/2 cup sour cream
salt and pepper
1 cup grated cheddar cheese
1 cup crushed butter crackers
(recommended: Ritz)

Preheat oven to 350°. Sauté' the squash in a little vegetable oil over medium-low heat until it has completely broken down, about 15 to 20 minutes. Line a colander with a clean tea towel. Place the cooked squash in the lined colander. Squeeze excess moisture from the squash. Set aside.

In a medium size skillet, sauté the onion in butter for 5 minutes. Remove from pan and mix all ingredients together except cracker crumbs. Pour mixture into a buttered casserole dish and top with cracker crumbs. Bake for 25 to 30 minutes.

BB's Take N' Bake
Brandy Dyess
www.bbstakenbake.com

Chicken Poppy Seed Casserole

1 whole chicken, cooked and cut
into bite-size pieces (I usually
use about 6 to 8 breasts)

2 cans of cream of chicken soup
1 (16 oz) carton of sour cream

Topping

3 tablespoons of poppy seeds
1 tube of Ritz crackers, crumbled

1 to 2 sticks of butter or
margarine, melted

Combine sour cream, soup and chicken. Layer topping on bottom, then 1/2 chicken mixture, topping, rest of chicken mixture, ending with topping.

BB's Take N' Bake

www.takenbake.com

Pork and Sea Shells with Summer Vegetables

1 - 16 ounce package pasta (farfalle, fusilli, penne, or conchigilie rigate)

3 tablespoons olive oil, divided

6 boneless pork loin chops (thick cut), cut into bite sized pieces

1 yellow squash, cut into bite sized pieces

1 zucchini, cut into bite sized pieces

8 ounces fresh mushrooms, sliced

1 - 15 ounce can tomato sauce

1 - 14.5 ounce can diced tomatoes with juice

2 tablespoons tomato paste

Worcestershire® sauce to taste

salt and pepper to taste

1 green bell pepper, chopped

1 medium onion, chopped

4 cloves garlic, finely chopped

1/3 cup red wine

2 1/3 tablespoons dried basil

1 teaspoon dried thyme

1-1/2 teaspoon dried oregano

2 bay leaves

1 dash red pepper flakes

Grated Parmesan cheese

Bring a large pot of lightly salted water to a boil. Add seashell pasta, cook for 8 to 10 minutes, until al dente, and drain. Heat 1 tablespoon olive oil in a large deep skillet over medium-high heat. Place the cut up pork in the skillet, and season with Worcestershire® sauce, salt, and pepper. Cook and stir 10 minutes, or until almost done. Remove from heat, and set aside. Heat the remaining olive oil in the skillet over medium heat. Cook and stir the green pepper, squash, zucchini, mushrooms, onion, and garlic 3 to 4 minutes or until just beginning to soften. Return the pork to the skillet. Mix in the tomato sauce, diced tomatoes, tomato paste, and wine into the skillet. Season with basil, thyme, oregano, bay leaves, and red pepper flakes. Reduce heat to low, and simmer 35 minutes. Remove the bay leaves, and serve over the cooked pasta with a sprinkling of Parmesan cheese.

Serves 8

Jeff Wernikowski

Gulfport Lake Vista

Hot Tomato Grits

2 slices of bacon, chopped

2 - 14.5 oz cans chicken broth

2 large tomatoes, peeled and chopped

½ teaspoon salt

1 cup quick cooking grits

1 tablespoon butter

2 tablespoons, canned, chopped green chilies

1 cup shredded sharp cheddar cheese

Garnishes: chopped tomato, chopped green onions, cooked and crumbled bacon, shredded cheddar cheese.

Cook bacon in heavy saucepan until crisp, reserving drippings in pan. Gradually add broth, butter and salt; bring to a boil. Stir in grits, tomato and chilies; return to boil, stirring often, reduce heat and simmer 15 to 20 minutes.

Stir in cheese; cover and let stand 5 minutes or until cheese melts. Garnish as desired.

Nancy Orr

Banana Bread

½ cup softened butter

1 cup sugar

2 large eggs

¼ teaspoon baking soda

¼ cup buttermilk

2-3 large bananas

2 teaspoon baking powder

½ teaspoon salt

2 cups all purpose flour

1 teaspoon vanilla extract

chopped walnuts

Cream butter and sugar until light and fluffy. Add eggs to butter mixture and mix well. Combine baking soda and buttermilk, peel bananas and pour buttermilk mixture over them. Mash bananas in buttermilk mixture. Stir banana mixture into creamed mixture. Combine baking powder, salt and flour. Stir flour mixture, chopped walnuts and vanilla into creamed mixture. Pour into a greased 9x5x3 loaf pan and bake at 350° for about 45 minutes or until done.

Nancy Orr

Gumbo

16 cups water/seafood stock

1 tablespoon red pepper

1 ½ tablespoons Tabasco (optional)

2 tablespoons garlic powder

2 teaspoons black pepper

2 tablespoons Tony's

2 tablespoons oregano

2 tablespoons basil

2 tablespoons thyme

1 tablespoon salt

1 tablespoon parsley

2 bay leaves

Chop bell pepper, celery, onion, frozen okra.

Roux

¾ cup oil   1 ¼ cup flour

Microwave 1 ½ - 2 minutes, stir, continue until penny colored

Frying/sauce pan – tenderize vegetables, roux, chop ingredients.

1 can Rotel   ½ cup Andouille sausage (optional)

1 small can tomato paste

Add all together for 30 minutes, then add:

2 pounds crab

3 pounds shrimp

Cook 1 hour

Scott Blount

Mike's Cajun Jambalaya

Cook 3 cups of rice and let cool

Add 3 cups of well rinsed rice to your rice pot and add 1 index finger joint of water above the top of rice. Add 1 teaspoon salt and 2 tablespoons of cooking oil. Bring this to a boil and turn burner to low. Cover with lid and cook for 30 minutes.

Meat and Veggie Mix

Chop the following veggies and set aside in a bowl:

1 large yellow onion   1/2 bunch of fresh parsley

2 large bell peppers

Chop the following meats and set aside in separate bowls:

3 chicken breast cut in 1 inch cubes

1 1/2 pounds of smoked pork sausage (slice down the middle end to end then cut in 1/2 inch pieces)

2 pounds of peeled shrimp (30 to 40 count will work fine or even a little smaller)

Spice Mix (mix all the spices together in a bowl and set aside)

2 tablespoon chili powder   1/2 teaspoon ground thyme

1 tablespoon black pepper   1 tablespoon garlic powder

1 tablespoon salt   4 whole bay leaves

1/2 teaspoon crushed red pepper flakes   2 tablespoons dry parsley flakes

In a large stock pot add 1 stick real butter and 1/4 cup oil. Add chicken and stir until almost done. Add sausage and spices and stir for 3 minutes. Add shrimp and veggie mix. Stir until veggies are cooked but don't overcook!!!

Break up the precooked rice with a spoon until rice is "loose". Add the cooked veggie & meat mix to the rice mix and not vice versa. Spoon the veggie & meat and not the juice to the rice. When all the veggie & meat is added to the rice now you can add the juice to the consistency you want it to be. Not too wet but not too dry!!! Chop up 1 whole bunch of green onions and add to the rice mixture. This makes quite a bit so it works better if you spoon it out and microwave what you want heated. That will keep it fresher longer.

Make with love for the one's you love.

Mike Dougay

Submitted By Scott Blount

OHR-O`KEEFE MUSEUM

Museum History

1994 - A Mississippi citizens group with the founding support of the Knight Foundation opened the George Ohr Arts and Cultural Center.

1998 - Jeremiah O'Keefe family contributes $1M to the capital campaign, kicking off the new building fund.

1998 - Frank Gehry meets with Jerry O'Keefe and agrees to design the new Museum.

2000 - City of Biloxi purchases four acres on Highway 90 as the new site of the Museum.

2003 - Groundbreaking ceremony

2005 - August 29 Hurricane Katrina destroys new construction 11 months from opening.

2008 - July reconstruction begins.

George E. Ohr

The self-proclaimed "Mad Potter of Biloxi" George Edgar Ohr (1857-1918) created a body of work from Mississippi clay which defied the aesthetic conventions of 19th century America. His extraordinary cultural legacy is now recognized for its power and integrity and for its important influence on 20th and 21st century art. Ohr's work was rediscovered in the 1960s and is admired by artists and collectors alike. In May 2009, the *Metropolitan Museum of Art* in New York celebrated the opening of the *Robert Ellison Art Pottery Collection* on the Mezzanine Balcony of the New American Wing, prominently featuring selected works by *George Ohr* and as Ohr had often predicted, his genius has at long last been recognized by the world.

Ohr was born in Biloxi, Mississippi, on July 12, 1857, married Josephine Gehring of New Orleans on September 15, 1886, in Biloxi, and died on April 7, 1918. He studied the potter's trade with Joseph Meyer in New Orleans, a potter whose family hailed from Alsace-Lorraine.

Ohr's father established the first blacksmith shop in Biloxi and his mother ran an early, popular grocery store there. In his lifetime, Ohr created over 10,000 known pots. He called himself "The Mad Potter of Biloxi" and was a showman of the style of P.T. Barnum, a contemporary. Ohr was an iconic American figure at the turn of the last century. He called his work "unequaled, undisputed, unrivaled." In 1884, Ohr exhibited and sold his wares at the World's Industrial and Cotton Centennial Exposition in New Orleans. Of the hundreds of pieces he showed, Ohr boasted "no two alike."

The 1894 fire that burned most of Biloxi also destroyed Ohr's workshop, and it has been noted that Ohr's post-fireworks show tremendous "energy" and "fluidity."

Ohr had a healthy self-image during his lifetime while many others in the art world did not accept him or his pots, and considered him a boasting eccentric. In the early 1900s, the Arts and Crafts Movement and its leaders (such as William Morris) advocated that an artist should display control and perfection in all art forms. Ohr displayed little obvious perfectionism in his art or control in his person, antagonizing art leaders nationally and political leaders at home. Ohr's work is now seen as ground-breaking and a harbinger of the abstract sculpture and pottery that developed in the mid-20th century. Ohr's pieces are now relatively rare and highly coveted.

A notable feature of Ohr's pottery is that many items have thin walls, metallic glazes, and twisted, pinched shapes. To this day potters marvel at Ohr's porcelain-thin walls and unusual glazes. No one has been able to replicate them using a pottery wheel, which is how Ohr made his works. Ohr dug much of his clay locally in southern Mississippi from the Tchoutacabouffa River. Tchoutacabouffa is the Biloxi tribe's word for "broken pot."

The *Ohr-O'Keefe Museum of Art* is committed to promoting and preserving the unique legacy of Biloxi potter *George E. Ohr* and the diverse cultural heritage of the Mississippi Gulf Coast, reflecting his independent, innovative, and creative spirit. This mission is served by presenting compelling exhibitions and educational experiences viewed from a fresh perspective relevant to our community, the region, and the nation with a strong focus on ceramic arts.

The Ohr-O'Keefe Museum of Art Campus is home to a remarkable blend of architectural styles which span over a century of history. *The Pleasant Reed Interpretive Center* and the *Creel House* are each examples of 19th century regional vernacular architecture. The five new structures are designed by *Frank Gehry*, one of the 21st century's most innovative and admired architects. The new campus was fifteen months from opening when Hurricane Katrina struck on August 29, 2005.

Set within a grove of ancient Live Oak trees, *Frank Gehry* designed the *Ohr-O'Keefe* project as a series of six small pavilions woven among the trees and connected by an open brick plaza, creating an inviting and lively arts campus that maintains the existing park setting and encourages pedestrian circulation throughout the site. The entire project will employ a micro-pile foundation system intended to minimize impact on the root systems of the Live Oak trees. The use of local materials, the use of references to the local vernacular, and the scale and placement of each of the pavilions on the site, represent sensitive responses to the conditions of the site and to the context of the surrounding area. The 25,000 square foot *Ohr-O'Keefe Museum* campus will provide facilities for art exhibition and education, and cultural and community events.

The pavilions that comprise the *Ohr-O'Keefe Museum* of Art are the *Welcome Center*, the *Exhibition Gallery*, the *Gallery of African American Art*, the *George E. Ohr Gallery*, and the *Center for Ceramics*. In addition, two historic buildings are also located on the campus: the *Pleasant Reed House* was destroyed in Katrina and has been replaced by the *Pleasant Reed Interpretive Center*; the *Creel House* was severely damaged by Katrina and moved to the site for renovation.

The Pleasant Reed Interpretive Center

The *Pleasant Reed Interpretive Center* opened in September, 2008, as a reconstruction of the original house built by *Pleasant Reed* in the 1880s and 1890s. On August 29, 2005, the original structure and all furnishings were destroyed by Hurricane Katrina.

The Pleasant Reed Family

Pleasant married Georgia Anna Harris in 1884, and they were known to their family and friends by the nicknames of "Plez" and "Georgie". Emanuel, the first of their five children, was born in 1886. Receipts show that the couple rented housing during the first years of their marriage. In May of 1887 the Reeds contracted with Jacob Elmer, a local merchant and developer, in the purchase of a small lot of land on Elmer Street. Benjamin Reed also bought property on Elmer Street in 1887, the same year that his son Pleasant began to build. Over the next four years, Pleasant Reed paid for the purchase of his land. By 1891, Reed retired his debt to Elmer in part by exchanging labor for cash. Families of other ethnic and religious backgrounds joined the Reeds on Elmer Street during this period, making it a diverse, multi-racial neighborhood.

Pleasant Reed provided for his family by working primarily as a carpenter, but he also took on other work that put him in the category of "Jack of all trades." Few of Reed's clients are specifically known, but receipts in the family collection identify construction jobs both large and small performed for local merchants and others. Additional income for the family came from a variety of sources. A hand-made wooden net shuttle was found among the tools contained in Pleasant's tool chest. Pleasant's brother, Benjamin, was a fisherman, and it was likely Benjamin who taught Pleasant to make fish nets which they used and also sold to other local fishermen. Apart from her role as wife and mother, Georgia Reed contributed to the family income by occasionally performing domestic work for other families in the community.

By all appearances, Pleasant Reed could not read and write, relying instead on his wife Georgia to interpret documents and letters that required his attention; Georgia's skilled penmanship suggests that she had been well-schooled as a girl, something that was not common under slavery. The value of an education denied their father was impressed on the Reed's children, who, according to family members, all received at least an elementary education. The Reed children probably attended the city's first "Colored" public school, which opened on Main Street in 1886, a few blocks from the Reed home on Elmer Street. It is not known if any of the children were able to continue their education to the high school level, but the opportunity to do so was available. The children of Pleasant and Georgia Reed made contributions to the Biloxi community on their own account.

Sons Paul and Percy entered the military service during World War I, and then returned to Biloxi to marry and raise families. Percy's only known occupation was that of a laborer, but

Paul followed his Uncle Benjamin's example and worked as a boatman. Theresé remained in her parent's home, working as a domestic servant and later as a cook while helping to take care of her mother and father. A story maintained by the Reed family is that in the early 1920s, Theresé was engaged to be married to a fisherman, only to lose her fiancé to an accident or a storm at sea. Her continuing grief over this tragedy has been cited by family members as the cause of her reclusive and brusque character as an adult, wearing only black clothes on the rare occasions when she was seen in public.

Pleasant instilled in his children the value of hard work and citizenship, in spite of the boundaries imposed on their lives by the system of segregation. Though Biloxi was considered more progressive than many areas in the South, the system of segregation still ruled. Pleasant consistently paid his $2.00 annual poll tax to maintain his privilege to vote, in spite of the fact that the expensive tax was intended to discourage his participation as a voter (the $2.00 per year that Reed invested in his voting privilege translates to an equivalent tax of over $60.00 today). He also showed his determination by paying his property taxes to keep his hard-won home, sometimes having to swap his labor to maintain the city streets as payment. His determination and hard work gained him respect in his community among both its white and black citizens, and in return, his services as a carpenter were consistently in demand.

Rising From Slavery

Before the Civil War, slave ownership on the Mississippi Gulf Coast was not a common occurrence. Slavery was more prevalent north of the coast, in farming areas such as Hattiesburg, MS, near the Enon plantation of John B. Reed, owner of Pleasant Reed's father Benjamin Reed (1813-1908) and his family. Unfortunately, due to the slave trade, it is difficult to trace the Reed family ancestry back beyond the plantation, but we do know that Pleasant was the fourth son born to Benjamin and Charlotte Reed. George Reed Sr. was Pleasant's older brother and the first Reed family member to leave Enon for the Mississippi Gulf Coast. George moved to Biloxi in 1869, four years after the Civil War ended. Other members of the family followed George and by 1871 the entire Reed family was in Biloxi.

An elderly George was interviewed in the 1930s for a project called "The Slave Narratives". These narratives were oral histories conducted with aging African Americans who had once been slaves. Noted American writers conducted and transcribed the interviews for the Work Project Administration under *President Franklin Roosevelt*. Unfortunately for the accuracy of history, the interviewees were often encouraged to talk in a cliché-like dialect popular in tales of that time. Yet, the recollections still hold historical value, providing insights into the lives and beliefs of freedmen. In Slave Narrative 241, "Uncle George" Reed tells of the booming timber industry on the Gulf Coast: "I was married right here in (18)'78 and the church was built some time before, about (18)'69 or '70. I hauled the first timbers here for it." George Reed also discusses other topics including the hanging of one Jim Copeland and his admiration for General Custer, whom Reed once saw in New Orleans and credited for his freedom: "Yessir, he fought to make us free."

The Pleasant Reed Interpretive Center is a reconstruction of the original house built by Pleasant Reed in the 1880s and 1890s. In 2002, the relocation of the Pleasant Reed House to the new campus of the Ohr-O'Keefe Museum of Art was intended to insure that this cultural and educational resource would be used to tell the story of this modest but remarkable family that was a significant part of Biloxi's history.

On August 29, 2005, the *Pleasant Reed House* and the original furnishings were destroyed by Hurricane Katrina. The Board of Trustees of the *Ohr-O'Keefe Museum of Art* was determined to continue honoring the legacy of Pleasant Reed and his family. In 2006 the board voted to replicate the *Pleasant Reed House*, as the *Pleasant Reed Interpretive Center* so that the generations to follow could continue to learn about this remarkable man. Working from Reed's original plans the house was reconstructed on the site of the *Ohr-O'Keefe Museum of Art*. The interior of the house was changed to accommodate tours and exhibitions while the exterior is an exact model of the house Pleasant Reed built. The *Pleasant Reed Interpretive Center* is now open by appointment.

O'Keefe Legacy

Jeremiah "Jerry" O'Keefe has been and continues to be a central and dynamic force in bringing the Ohr-O'Keefe Museum of Art from vision to reality. Jerry and his children gave the first major gift to the Ohr-O'Keefe capital campaign in 1998 in memory of Jerry's wife, Rose Annette Saxon O'Keefe. In recognition of and gratitude for the family's ongoing contributions, which today have exceeded 1.8 million dollars, the George Ohr Museum was renamed the Ohr-O'Keefe Museum of Art in honor of Annette O'Keefe.

Gulfport-Biloxi International Airport

GULFPORT-BILOXI INTERNATIONAL AIRPORT

The Gulfport-Biloxi area is the second largest metropolitan area in the State of Mississippi. Our deep water port, airport, interstate highway system, stable military, space and oceanographic agencies, ship building and tourism industries have contributed greatly to the growth and balance of our economy.

History

Originally constructed in 1942 to train B-25 and B-29 flight crews for WWII, Gulfport Field was conveyed from the War Department to the City of Gulfport in 1949 for use as a civil airport. The City negotiated airline service contracts with Southern Airways and later National Airlines to provide passenger and cargo service to the Coast beginning in the early 1950's. Through the late 1970's, Southern Airways continued as the primary airline, followed by successors Republic and Northwest into the 1990's.

Beginning in 1953, the Mississippi National Guard developed a training activity which has grown into a high-tech Combat Readiness Training Center, one of four in the Nation. Military traffic has expanded each year, and now more than 20,000 Air Guard and Reserve flight personnel are trained at the base annually. Within 10 minutes, supersonic fighters and in-flight refuelers can simulate a combat environment over the Gulf of Mexico or at Camp Shelby in Hattiesburg, MS. Additionally, the Army National Guard established the Aviation Classification Repair Depot operation which repairs several types of combat and transport helicopters for military activities throughout the Southeast and Puerto Rico.

In 1977, the Cities of Gulfport and Biloxi and the County of Harrison joined together to establish Gulfport-Biloxi Regional Airport Authority, and directed the Airport Authority Commissioners to manage airport facility development. The mission of the Airport Authority is to provide a high quality, safe public airport in order that the Coast citizens and supporting communities receive a sustained and superior return on their investment. During the two following decades, passenger growth increased fourfold and the Airport Authority completed $46 million in capital improvements, 80% of which funds came from Federal Airport Improvement Program funds. Due to casino destination resort growth and a 130% increase in Coast hotel rooms, passenger boardings grew 400% during the 1990's and the economic impact of the Airport exceeded $600 million annually.

On August 29, 2005, Hurricane Katrina left a destructive path across the Mississippi Gulf Coast and at the Airport with many facilities damaged or destroyed. At that time, the Airport had initiated a major terminal expansion and scheduled completion was delayed by two years due to the storm. The grand opening of the terminal expansion was held in 2008 with the Airport increasing its capacity from one million to 2.4 million annual passengers. Other facilities repaired or replaced included the rental car service center, air cargo facility, and a new general aviation area. New items consisted of a parking garage with covered walkway, two hotels, new Air Traffic Control Tower (scheduled to open 2012), and numerous infrastructure improvements. Total investment at the Airport in the four years after Hurricane Katrina totaled $287 million including $147 million of private investment.

Entering the new millennium, Gulfport-Biloxi International Airport is served by seven commercial airlines, offering frequent, non-stop jet service to eight major cities connecting to over 2,000 flights throughout the United States and the World. As a result of competition, airfares are competitive and passenger boardings are growing. New general and corporate aviation facilities are under construction as general aviation continues to be a major contributor to the Airport's aviation service resource. The Airport also offers a 46,000 sq. ft. air cargo facility which accommodates domestic and international air cargo in Foreign Trade Zone No. 92. Major runway, taxiway and lighting system improvements are also underway to assure continued growth of commercial and military users.

In sum, the Airport is rich with aeronautical history and the Airport Authority is actively developing the Airport to meet the current and future needs of the Mississippi Gulf Coast. With nearly 1,700 acres of property and two runways, Airport environs height and hazard zoning in place, and 170 acres available for expansion of the passenger terminal complex, Gulfport-Biloxi has the land area, airspace zoning, facilities and instrument approaches in place to sustain double-digit growth for twenty years and beyond for domestic and international airlines, the military and general aviation.

Long Beach's early economy was largely agriculture-based. Logging initially drove the local economy, but when the area's virgin yellow pine forests became depleted, row crops were planted on the newly cleared land.

A productive truck farming town in the early 20th century, citizens of Long Beach proclaimed the city to be the "Radish Capital of the World." The city was especially known for its cultivation of the Long Red radish variety, a favorite beer hall staple in the northern US at the time. In 1921, a bumper crop resulted in the shipment of over 300 train loads of Long Beach's Long Red radishes to northern states.

Eventually, the Long Red radishes for which Long Beach was known fell into disfavor, and the rise of the common button radish caused a dramatic decline in the cultivation of this crop in the area.

ROBIN ROBERTS & GMA

Robin Roberts is a household name along the Mississippi Gulf Coast, whether you watch *Good Morning America* or not. My husband Lee and I just happen to be dedicated viewers of *GMA* and rarely miss a show and yes it is true that if you watch *GMA* long enough, you will feel as if the personalities are your family.

Diane Sawyer, who makes you smile when she eats because she truly enjoys food, is like the sister you wish you had. Her compassion and sincerity are obvious in her interviews.

Chris Cuomo, who looks so much like my brother and reminds me of Jerry Seinfeld, because of his quick wit and dry humor, is like the member of your family that you can't wait to see on Thanksgiving, or any other family get-together for that matter.

Sam Champion, though he is always smiling and always laughing, he still seems a little shy. Very kind and caring and someone you would definitely want as your friend.

Robin Roberts, well what can you say about *Robin Roberts*? Mississippi Gulf Coast home town girl, dedicated, full of Southern charm, very well mannered, great friend, loving daughter, sister and aunt? I guess you could say all of these things about Robin and all of us on the Mississippi Gulf Coast do.

When Robin says *The Pass* or *Mississippi* or *Family* or *Friends*, her face lights up like the *Biloxi Lighthouse*. Robin is a true *Magnolia*.

Robin and GMA – After Katrina

Good Morning America partnered with the Salvation Army and AmeriCorps to rebuild the city of *Pass Christian, Mississippi*, Robin Robert's hometown, after *Hurricane Katrina* devastated the *Mississippi Gulf Coast*.

All of us on the *Mississippi Gulf Coast* thank *Robin Roberts* and *Good Morning America* for bringing so much focus to our coast. We appreciate each and every one of you.

WLOX – TV

ABC affiliate on the Mississippi Gulf Coast

WLOX remained on the air during Hurricane Katrina, even though the studios were heavily damaged in the storm, and continued to broadcast non-stop for more than 12 days afterward. WLOX created an award-winning two-disc DVD set about the storm entitled *"Katrina: South Mississippi's Story"*.

In 2006 **WLOX** received the *Edward R. Murrow National Award* in the category of continuing coverage, for its around-the-clock coverage of *Hurricane Katrina* and its aftermath. **WLOX** also received a Southern Regional Emmy Humanitarian award in June 2006.

News Director Dave Vincent tells their story...

For more than 12 days, **WLOX** employees banded together & provided exceptional coverage of Hurricane Katrina, despite personal danger & ultimately great personal loss. **WLOX** News broadcast 24/7 for 12 straight days, delivering life saving information to the people of South Mississippi. Our news coverage went wall to wall when it became apparent that Hurricane Katrina would gravely impact South Mississippi. Katrina's winds & deadly 30 foot plus tidal surge did not stop our coverage. Neither did her massive path of destruction nor her impact on our TV station. We continued to broadcast even when Katrina ripped off our newsroom roof, destroyed another wing of our station, toppled one of our TV towers, wiped out our Jackson & Hancock County news bureaus & forced us in the main station to evacuate to a safer section of our building.

There is no doubt that without the courageous action of WLOX employees many more lives would have been lost in this, the worst natural disaster to hit our county. In addition, we have been told by many viewers that we were their only life line during the height of the storm & in those first days after Katrina, when our community was devastated & very much like a third world country.

During our coverage, we were the source of information for our community. We told people where to find shelter, where to find food & medicine & other needed supplies. To insure that life saving information reached our community we reached out to all the radio groups on the coast & they carried our signal. Also the local newspaper contacted us & we put many of their reporters on the air. The local FOX affiliate even carried our signal for a few days. After Katrina knocked out our ability to stream, our continual coverage, on our web site, our sister stations in the Liberty chain took over the postings & helped us keep thousands of evacuees informed through wlox.com.

Hurricane Katrina left thousands of people homeless & forever changed the face of our community. Our station is a reflection of the community in which we live & work. At least 12 of our employees lost everything. Another 60 had significant damage to their homes. Everyone suffered some loss. Yet our employees continued to work putting the safety & welfare of their community above their personal situation.

Rob Stinson

BUON APPETITO

By Rob Stinson

I had the incredible experience of traveling all over Italy because of Carmelo Chirico. Carmelo owned five restaurants in the heart of New Orleans French Quarter that I had the good fortune of overseeing. Two Dante's Pizzerias, Rue Bourbon Restaurant, Buon Giorno Café and Five Star Ristorante Carmelo were the different operations. The focus was always on quality first and the belief that- "Great ingredients make great food." Carmelo was out to prove that the food served at Ristorante Carmelo was as authentic as any food in Italy. At the same time we decided that we wanted to create the best Italian wine list in America. So off we went to Italy...

We stopped at the toll gate on the Autostrada, after leaving Milano Airport, when the purring sound of twelve cylinders in perfect harmony was heard behind us. We were on our way to the Tyrrhenian Coast to travel North to Piedmont for some great wine. WHHHZZZZZ!!! A red blur of color whirled past as a Ferrari Testa Rosa flashed by us on their way to Monaco Monte Carlo, and I thought- I'm going to like Italy!

In Piedmont, the wines are incredible. Northern Italy is vastly different than South Italy. The Northern regions feature cream sauces, beef, and some of the most incredible wines in all of Italy. It is a lesson in history to trace wines in Northern Italy. Barbaresco, as an example, is a wine that was brought to Italy during the invasion of the Barbarians. Barbaresco is an area in Piedmont where I had arranged for us to stay. We were staying at the estate of Ceretto, known for their great food and wine. Barolo, Barbera, Dolcetto are a few other great red wines of this area and we indulged in them all. I found that five course meals, coupled with different wines was the norm so overindulgence became a daily routine. I fell in love with the food from Piedmont because it was so similar to superb French cuisine (don't tell the Italians that!) The start of my culinary career was training under a Cordon Bleu chef, Gerald Thabuis, and yet I truly prefer Italian food now. Working in the kitchen was a joy. I learned firsthand how to make Gnocchi, potato pasta with four cheese sauce and many others. I don't know which I enjoyed more- cooking or drinking wine. While in Piedmont, we decided to find the estate of Angelo Gaja, the premier Northern Italian wine maker. To be invited inside a winery in Italy you need an appointment. We didn't have any way to contact Gaja winery, but we decided to drive and see if we could get lucky. We drove for hours and were totally lost when a miracle happened. We were headed up a mountain where the road was so narrow that we couldn't turn around and we were forced up this treacherous trail to the top. It resembled something from a horror film when we reached the top. Huge black gates loomed ahead of us. Lost and confused we looked up and saw these old tarnished letters- G A J A. We had found the winery of Angelo Gaja by mistake, and after explaining that we had been lost for hours, we were greeted and allowed to enter the finest winery in Italy. We were treated like kings and we were served some of the finest food and wine I have ever had. Gnocchi gorgonzola, salad with porcini mushrooms and wild roasted boar were just a few of the great dishes from Barbaresco. It turned out we were able to buy several bottles of Gaja wine and those bottles retail for several thousand dollars. This was enough to pay for our entire trip and was a great beginning to the trip.

After leaving Piedmont we headed South along the coast to Tuscany. What an incredible drive. Perhaps the most beautiful scenery I have ever seen! Mountains to the left and the Tyrrhenian Sea to the right, tunnels and towns everywhere and made the drive awesome. It was amazing to me how crazy the drivers were. They passed going into tunnels where you couldn't see ahead of you and it all seemed normal to the drivers. Carmelo was used to it so we made great time as we headed South along the coast to Livorno. Pisa was on the way so we had to stop and look at this weird crooked tower. Oh yeah- the Tower of Pisa!

Before we went any further we needed to eat. We had been driving for hours and decided that we deserved a special meal. We were on the coast so obviously seafood was the food of choice. We sought out the Bistrot Seafood Ristorante in Forte dei Marmi. Incredible seafood came to our table. They brought the fish you were going to eat to be viewed at the table, so you could verify that it was fresh from the ocean that morning. What a concept! The only problem I had was a delicacy of whole small fish with tiny black eyes that looked at you while you ate them. They were cooked but it was a little unsettling. Carmelo knew the owner here and he allowed me to go into the kitchen to study the art of seafood preparation of the Coast. Full and ready to drive; we moved on…

We were headed to the winery of "The King of Wines and the Wine of Kings." The area of Bolgheri is where Tenuta San Guido was established by Mario Incisa della Rochetta, of the Antinori family. Sassicaia is the only wine in Italy that is its own region and winery in one. It is South of Livorno and near the coast. Sassicaia is a wine that has won the best wine in the world, and the winery was a must visit. The art of blending Italian grapes with French grapes have become known as "Super Tuscan" wines. Typically blending the grapes of the Chianti region, Sangiovese, with Bordeaux (French) grapes like Cabernet or Merlot makes great wine. We were served by Mr. Antinori himself, a noble man, which amazed me. The humble nature of the royal families was truly refreshing. I found that befriending the chef at these fabled old wineries was the way to learn about their regional cuisine. Incredible seafood- names which I could never remember, coupled with incredible fruit and cheese became my new favorite meal. Simple ingredients with little additives is the secret to great Italian food. Bread, cheese and wine was enough to survive on in between wineries, so loaded down with wine and food we were on our way.

Next we turned to head towards the oldest medieval castle in Italy. San Gimignano is a town that hasn't changed much in 2000 years. Eighteen of the original 52 towers still exist and this was an area known for great white wine called Vernaccia di San Gimignano. I was especially interested in this area because of the escargot. Yes, snails! I had to see these creatures that literally crawled their way to your table to be eaten. It sounds hysterical, but we stayed in the castle and in the morning I woke up early and found snails crawling everywhere. If I had my trusty sauté pan with me I would have gathered them and cooked them for breakfast- just kidding… This old town of towers had leather shops and iron works where everything was done the same way it had been done 2000 years before. This was my favorite stop in Italy, not for the food or wine, but for the history of the location. It was truly magnificent and I will go back to this city in the future.

From San Gimignano we headed into the heart of Tuscany and true wine country- Chianti. Chianti is a region of Italy where great food and wine abound. We visited so many different wineries in this area and what amazed me was the gracious nature of the people. I had spent time in France when I was young and found the people very intimidating. Everywhere we went in Italy the humble, gracious nature of the people stood out as the best feature of the areas. I cannot say enough about experiences of Tuscany but one stands out. Castello Banfi Winery. It is located at the very Southern tip of Montalcino, which is known for great Brunello wine. Banfi has a renovated castle where you can stay and drink their wine and sample great Tuscan food. There have been so many books written about Tuscany and I know why now. Rolling hills, green pastures, incredible wineries are everywhere. I don't think there is another place I would rather retire than Tuscany. We had such a great experience at Banfi but one story still sticks in my mind. We were allowed to sample some of the finest balsamic vinegar at Banfi. In a tiny crystal bottle was a 50 year old sample of balsamic vinegar- sweet, tangy, rich and dark in color- it was unsurpassed in quality. I watched while the owners of the winery ate ice cream topped with this vinegar. It seemed unnatural but it was incredible! What a flavor. I was elated when they allowed me to take a bottle of this home. The sad ending to the story of 50 year old balsamic vinegar was that I dropped it on my brick flooring in my kitchen and the stain is still there- What a waste!!!

Moving South, we headed to Orvieto. Perhaps the prettiest city I have ever seen, Orvieto is situated on top of a mountain. Many of the cities in Italy are placed where they could defend themselves in the advent of attack. We mentioned earlier that Italy had been overrun by the Barbarians, and there were many others over the years of history. Orvieto was a protected city with a magnificent Duomo (Cathedral) in the center. As is typical in Italy, many cities are formed around a beautiful church which was the gathering spot of the citizens. Orvieto is also the name of a famous white wine which was a necessary addition to our wine list. Light and crisp, this wine is readily available in most American wine stores but it is simple and a perfect wine to start a meal. Wonderful veal dishes and light pastas were the favorite here, but the use of truffles was extraordinary. Learning to cook and garnish with truffles was the highlight of my culinary trip. I had never seen the freshness of such a wonderful addition to pasta as these truffles of Orvieto. Driving down the mountain of Orvieto was a sad event because I knew we were heading to Rome and it would be from there we would fly home. While waiting for our flight we could wine and dine on classic traditional food. There are some great dishes from Rome and my favorite is penne pasta Amatriciani. It is a dish flavored with pancetta (Italian bacon), onion, garlic, Romano cheese and tomato. I served it every day and I was contented to see that our recipe at Ristorante Carmelo was as good if not better than the version I tasted in Rome. With this accomplishment under my belt we headed home and planned the next visit to Italy. Ciao!

MARITIME & SEAFOOD INDUSTRY MUSEUM

The Maritime & Seafood Industry Museum was established in 1986 to preserve and interpret the maritime history and heritage of Biloxi and the Mississippi Gulf Coast. It accomplishes this mission through an array of exhibits on shrimping, oystering, recreational fishing, wetlands, managing marine resources, charter boats, marine blacksmithing, wooden boat building, net making, catboats/Biloxi skiff, shrimp peeling machine and numerous historic photographs and objects.

The Museum has brought life to local maritime history and heritage by replicating two 65' two masted Biloxi Schooners. Examples of living maritime history, they sail the Mississippi Sound and waters of the north central Gulf of Mexico almost daily. The Museum also conducts year round educational programs and a summer Sea-n-Sail Adventure Camp which teaches youth about local maritime heritage.

Recently completed is the Wade Guice Hurricane Museum within a museum, featuring 1400 square feet of exhibit space and a state of the art theatre. The Art gallery will feature regional and national maritime artists with exhibitions rotating throughout the year.

The Museum has an extraordinary collection of priceless photographs and artifacts which tell a story from the time of the first Indian residents to the growth as a world renowned seafood processing center.

Restoration Project – Post Hurricane Katrina

The Maritime & Seafood Industry Museum facility was totally devastated during hurricane Katrina. Several of the displays, exhibits, artifacts and memorabilia were also virtually destroyed.

An approximate $8.0 million is a conservative estimate to reconstruct some of the exhibits and displays. The lost authentic artifacts and memorabilia were priceless.

The organization is currently planning to reconstruct the historical museum with new exciting amenities that will make this project the marque attraction of the Mississippi Gulf Coast.

Commitment

Without its volunteers, the Museum would not be able to effect its wide variety of programs. They are the primary reason for the success of many activities - assisting the staff of the annual

Sea-n-Sail Adventure Camp, serving as crew members on the museum's schooners, securing and preserving artifacts, and helping with the annual museum drawdown and other fundraising efforts. The museum cannot truly fulfill its preservations and education mission without its docents. To become a museum docent, please call 435-6320.

Surrounded by numerous hands on exhibits, Sea Campers enjoy learning about local heritage and culture. A happy Sea Camper proudly displays a catch made with a Biloxi cast net. The cast net has been used locally to catch seafood for almost 300 years.

Preservation

The museum contains hundreds of one-of-a-kind artifacts of the historic Biloxi seafood industry. The preservation of these objects is one of the primary functions of the museum. The Maritime & Seafood Industry Museum is the only institution carrying out this mission on the Gulf of Mexico.

We celebrate 300 years of history with a $2 million expansion and renovation completed in February of 2003

Our Vision

The Maritime & Seafood Industry Museum's Restoration Project, under a Public/Private Cooperative Initiative possesses significant economic, tourism, education and historical preservation benefits. Additionally, its planned location, the Tullis Toledano Manor site adjacent to the Ohr-O'Keefe Museum, complements the estimated one billion dollar Harrah's development - Margaritaville.

Cultural & Education Center

The Maritime & Seafood Industry Museum plans to reconstruct a world-class facility that encompass approx. 40,000 square feet of exhibit/gallery space for high-tech interactive displays, mini conference & meeting rooms, a community performing arts theatre, a unique national attraction entitled - *"Into the Storm"*, two Hurricane memorials, United States Coast Guard Memorial Pavilion, and state-of-the-art summer camp facility.

Into The Storm

"Into the Storm" is a unique hi-tech experience incorporating state-of-the-art visual, audio and sensory special effects that creates an exceptionally entertaining and everlasting impression.

This one-of-a-kind experience includes the sounds, wind conditions, and storm surge that simulate the experience of a Gulf Coast hurricane but in a safe and non-threatening manner.

US Coast Guard Memorial Pavilion

An open-air memorial pavilion, dedicated to the heroic achievements of the US Coast Guard will be one of the highlight attractions on the Museum's campus. This 3,000 square feet facility is envisioned to represent imagery of the former Museum's facade, which was originally the US Coast Guard station on Biloxi's Point Cadet. This memorial pavilion will also be a popular site for public ceremonies, social events, receptions and photo opportunities.

Showcase Theatre

The Showcase Theatre will be developed for multiple usages; A featured attraction for the Museum that will show documentary films, a standalone theatre for special features, a performing arts facility for community productions and a corporate meeting facility

- 10,300 square feet of exhibit area
- state of the art amphitheater
- Wade Guice Hurricane Museum within a museum
- Art Gallery
- research library
- classrooms

New Exhibits

- Recreational Fishing
- Wetlands
- Managing Marine Resources
- Charter Boats
- Catboats/Biloxi Skiff
- Laitram Peeling Machine
- The Biloxi Schooner

For more information www.maritimemuseum.org

LEARN AND LAUGH

At The Lynn Meadows Discovery Center

At the Lynn Meadows Discovery Center, Mississippi's only children's museum, visitors can crank a crane, touch a tornado, sort seafood, cross a creek, understand a pulley fully, tromp in tree houses, take tea for two, star on a show and much more.

The Discovery Center, located in the former Mississippi City Elementary School, constructed in 1915 and an architectural exhibition itself, offers 15,000 square feet of indoor exhibit space and six acres of outdoor play space with picnic tables. The child/adult friendly interactive exhibits include an amazing two-story indoor Super, Colossal, Climbing Sculpture simulating the sea- an international travel exhibit, Celebrate the World We Share — Mexico, offering children an introduction to the culture of another country - a History Hotel full of the treasures and secrets of Mississippi City in 1898 - a true Mississippi grocery, Winn-Dixie Morning Market, where visitors can find a little bit of everything - young Investi-Gators can report environmental news in Wonder-full Wetlands, a television studio —What It's Like To Be Me where visitors take the challenge and walk in another child's shoes — board a turn-of-the century steam engine train, the Outback Express, at the Dolan Avenue Depot — the Porthole where bananas come in and chickens go out - a Bear Camp Bayou for children under four - and A Matter of Science where science is not only hands-on, but FUN! And to complete the picture, The Pelican Porch Café and Bayou Bait Shop, is an outdoor restaurant exhibit where you never gain an ounce - Bear Creek, features an outdoor, "woodsy" cabin with a running stream to explore and a wooden child-size train, Bubblemania, a summer exhibit about the science and art of bubble making, and our pride and joy, The Tree House Village, just for play!

WINGS Performing Arts Program involves young people in programs and productions throughout the year. The program was selected as one of twelve recipients for the nationally prestigious Coming Up Taller Award that was presented by Former First Lady Laura Bush. On the state level, the WINGS program was also chosen to receive the Governor's Award for Excellence in the Arts. The new WINGS Performing Arts and Education Center at the Lynn Meadows Discovery Center that opened in 2009 was a $3 million project, complete with a state of the art Viking demonstration and teaching kitchen. This new addition offers a unique venue for special event rentals- weddings, receptions, corporate retreats or family reunions.

The Lynn Meadows Discovery Center is located at 246 Dolan Avenue in Gulfport, 1 ½ blocks off US Hwy. 90. The Discovery Center is open Tuesday through Saturday, 10:00-5:00. For more information call 228-897-6039, or visit the website www.lmdc.org.

Mission

The Lynn Meadows Discovery Center expands a child's world by encouraging shared learning experiences to enrich the minds and hearts of children and adults through interactive and entertaining exhibitions and programs.

Through activities designed to simulate the real world of South Mississippi, children have the opportunity to learn about the past and the present; it is with a better understanding of themselves and their community that children can grow to be responsible, global citizens.

History

Today, more than 400 children's museums throughout the United States break the rules of traditional museums encouraging visitors to touch, talk, have fun and learn. In a children's museum, the audience rather than the objects are key. The exhibits are catalysts for questions, exploration and discovery and the entire experience is a playground for the mind. The Lynn Meadows Discovery Center is the first children's museum in Mississippi.

From its inception, The Lynn Meadows Discovery Center has been a community project. With initial funding in 1991 from Gulfport Junior Auxiliary, co-founders Rose Alman and Carole Lynn Meadows have led the team to make the dream a reality. The Mississippi City Elementary School, constructed in 1915 and an architectural exhibition itself, offers 15,000 square feet of indoor exhibit space, six acres of outdoor play space including a tree house village, a woodsy cabin on a stream and meeting rooms for workshops as well as camps and birthday parties.

Hurricane Katrina

On August 29, 2005, Hurricane Katrina devastated the MS Gulf Coast resulting in the "worst natural disaster in US history". The Lynn Meadows Discovery Center stood defiantly among the old live oaks, but the storm surge reduced the entire first floor of exhibitions, Artist Studio and staff office to rubble. The Education Building was destroyed, the pavilion was left a shell and the gymnasium multipurpose spaces were flooded.

The first floor exhibits have been replaced, the office refurbished and repaired and the main museum building reopened on June 6, 2006. The Education Building was demolished and the Pavilion has been renovated and provides three multipurpose rooms. Phases II and III of the building project, with a $3 million budget, was completed with the opening of the WINGS Performing Arts and Education Center on April 23, 2009. Phase IV of the construction will include renovation of the gym into a performing arts center for youth.

GULF COAST WRITER'S ASSOCIATION

By: Philip L. Levin

President, GCWA

www.gcwriters.org

Founded in 1975, the Gulf Coast Writers Association (GCWA) sponsors a diverse range of activities aimed at fulfilling our mission of "promoting writers." At our monthly meetings we offer opportunities to network with successful writers and editors, with the occasional guest speaker. Authors may share what they've written for public enjoyment. All meetings are free and open to the public.

GCWA produces a quarterly magazine, the *Magnolia Quarterly*, showcasing the fiction, poetry, and prose of our members. It offers contests as well. With a distribution of 150, it's a small-time publication, but there's nothing like the joy of seeing your work in print, as well as the opportunity to share your publication with friends and relatives.

In today's world, Internet opportunities have become a primary source of communication. GCWA offers two email lists, one free and open to the public, where announcements about local writing events are shared, and a second one for members, where we provide links to writing contests, markets, websites, agent information, etc. We keep an active website www.gcwriters.org with our calendar, a monthly "featured writer of the month," and individual sites for each published author in our group to display and sell their work. We also announce our members' events, such as book signings, publications, and speeches.

GCWA provides many additional opportunities for writers, such as our annual literary contest called 'Let's Write' each spring. We put out an anthology as well. The first "Teacakes and Afternoon Tales," in 2008 was followed by "Sweet Tea and Afternoon Tales." 2009.

If you're a writer on the Gulf Coast, the Gulf Coast Writers Association should be part of your adventure.

Dr. Philip L. Levin

E-mail: writerpllevin@gmail.com

Chekhov wrote, "Medicine is my wife, writing my mistress." Twelve hour shifts, over thirty years in the emergency room, I create my livelihood saving lives, fighting disease. It's fulfilling in so many ways, providing perspective and reassurance of the meaning of life. Yet I've always needed this something else, a drive to communicate my experiences and my dreams. A completed story is a thrill, like the joy of a special lover, in whose bosom I find tantalizing pleasures otherwise incomplete.

I come by my writing skills from both sides of my ancestry. My mother, Beatrice S. Levin, has published almost 20 books and thousands of articles. As well as being the author of scores of scientific works, my father, Franklyn K. Levin, edited the magazine Geophysics for several years, and still is frequently consulted for his editorial skills.

I've always been a writer. During college I edited the college newspaper. I paid much of my medical school tuition from articles I sold. During my residency in Corpus Christi, Texas, I was the associate editor and a main contributor to "Coastal Bend Medicine." Those years also saw me complete the first draft of my mystery novel.

Raising my family and tackling my career were my focus, with few publications during my thirties and forties. Once the children were off in college, I settled down to learning the craft and submitting to contests and markets. I published "Inheritance" in 2007, followed the next year by my children's photo-book, "Consuto and the Rain God."

Much of my production now is in short stories and short articles. I published four stories in anthologies in 2009, and had several contest successes. I'm writing articles for the state medical journal and editing the writing group's magazine "Magnolia Quarterly." I lecture about writing, being the guest speaker in writing groups from North Carolina to Florida and throughout Mississippi.

As one can see from my website, I also love to document my travels with photography. I take medical missionary trips to Africa, South America, and Latin America, providing unique venues and perspectives. I've had a few prize winning photographs, but, like my writing, it is more for the fun than the successes.

I hope you have the opportunity to read a few of my stories, perhaps purchase a novel, or find a photo you love. Please contact me; talk about writing or photography, or maybe arrange for me to give a talk to your group. Consider joining our organization, Gulf Coast Authors at www.gcwriters.org.

My wife and I can host you in times of need, but it's my mistress whose delights I'd like to share.

In the Fine Print

by Philip Levin

Joel rippled through the manuscript; trying to suppress his hands' trembling.
"What kind of contract is this? It's sixty pages and full of fine print."

The demon ginned. "It's a standard contract. You said you'd sell your soul for a million bucks. For a soul like yours, I'd have offered a hundred grand, tops." He shrugged his black shoulders, his hairy palms held upward. "But the boss says offer you the million."

"I needed the million bucks yesterday." Joel looked at his watch. "Big Al's thugs will be here any minute."

The demon spat on the floor, singeing the carpet. "I got delayed by a nymph. Take it or leave it, don't make no difference to me."

The glass window reading "Attorney" shattered as Joel wrote rapidly. "Here, sign this." He pushed a paper across the desk to the demon, who pulled out a pair of reading glasses from a skin fold in his belly.

"Million dollars for one soul. What's this scribble on the bottom?"

"Just a little fine print about how to distribute the payment. Could you hurry please?"

Two big men in ski masks and overcoats burst into the room. The demon made his mark on the contract, and grabbed Joel's hand. Using a sharp claw, he pricked Joel's thumb, pressing a bloody print on the paper.

"Done," the demon said with a grin, as an assault of bullets riddled Joel.

Joel's naked muscles sagged. He found himself in a cold black cavern, fires burning in little smudge pots on various rock outcroppings. "This place is going to be hell on my sinuses," he thought.

He walked up to a smoldering demon hunched over a large book. "Hello there."

The demon's glowing eyes stared at him. "I was just registering your arrival, Joel."

"That's exactly what I wanted to talk to you about. Do you have a copy of my contract there?"

The demon flipped a few pages in his book. "Not a standard contract," he growled.

Joel nodded. "That's right. Can you read the fine print on the bottom?"

The demon studied it. "It's written in Hebrew. It says…… yeah, I can read it. Okay, you're out of here."

The world around Joel was dark and warm, quiet and safe. Then the walls began to close upon him. There was a terrible squeezing and his head burst into a cold bright light. Someone stuck something in his mouth. Another squeeze and he was out, crying loudly.

"It's a boy!" the doctor shouted. "What name did you choose?"

"Joel, after his grandfather," Joel's new mother cried happily.

"And look at the time!" the doctor said. "It's exactly midnight. That means Joel wins the million dollar prize for the first baby of the century! Congratulations! You've been twice blessed."

Tamales with Cheese

What does a bachelor know about cooking? Simplicity, that's what. Here is one of my favorite recipes, a tasty meal in two minutes. Costs about a buck.

Ingredients: One Can of Hormel Tamales. A bit of leftover shredded cheese, preferably not too moldy).

Directions: Open can. Unpeel tamales onto a microwave-safe plate. Sprinkle on the cheese. Cover with plastic wrap, (do not skip this step). Microwave for one minute. Throw away wrap.

Philip L. Levin

Inheritance, a murder-suspense thriller

Consuto and the Rain God, a children's Chinese Fable

www.doctorsdreams.net

Jam Sandwich Cookies

½ cup shortening	½ teaspoon salt
½ cup of sugar	½ baking powder
1 egg	¾ cup strawberry or peach
½ teaspoon almond extract	preserves
1 ½ cups sifted flour	

In a bowl, cream the butter or shortening and sugar until light and fluffy. Beat in the egg. Add almond extract. Add sifted combined flour, salt and baking powder. Batter will be soft. Spread half the batter into a well-greased and floured baking pan (8 inch). Spread with the preserves, top carefully with the remaining batter. Bake in a 400° oven until nicely browned, about 30 minutes. Let cool in pan, cut into squares to serve. Frost squares if desired.

Mary Mariotti

Books by Celine Rose Mariotti

"Olivia Macallister, Who Are You?" – children – (ghost story)

Through Celine's Eye" – Poetry

Upcoming book – "Katrina – A Tempest Storm – Collection of Poems, Short Stories and Essays"

Available at http://crmenterprises-homebusiness.com

Midnight Cake

½ cup butter or shortening	1 ½ cups, sifted, flour
1 ¼ cups of sugar	1 teaspoon baking powder
2 eggs (beaten)	1 teaspoon baking soda
½ cup cocoa	½ teaspoon salt
1 cup hot water	1 teaspoon vanilla

In a bowl cream the butter or shortening. Blend in the sugar and beat until fluffy. Beat in the eggs one at a time. Place the cocoa in a small bowl and gradually stir in the hot water, mixing until smooth. Sift together the flour, baking powder, baking soda, and salt. Add the dry ingredients to the creamed mixture alternately with the cocoa. Add vanilla. Pour into a greased and floured square pan (9x9x2 inches). Bake 350° oven until cake tester inserted in the center comes away clean, 55 minutes. Cake may be cooled in the pan or turned out upon a rack.

Mary Mariotti

Books by Celine Rose Mariotti:

"Olivia Macallister, Who Are You?" -children - (ghost story)

"Through Celine's Eyes" - Poetry

Upcoming book - "Katrina-A Tempest Storm-A Collection of Poems, Short Stories and Essays"

Available at - http://crmenterprises-homebusiness.com

James Willis' Banana Pudding

2 sliced bananas	2 cups of milk
1 package of vanilla wafers	1/3 cup of flour
1 tsp of vanilla flavoring	2/3 cup of sugar
6 large eggs	

Crack and separate six eggs. Put egg yolks, milk, flour and sugar into a mixing bowl, stir until everything is thoroughly combined. Transfer mixture to a medium size pot. Place on low heat and slowly stir, continuously. The mixture will slowly thicken from the bottom up, so be sure to stir the bottom of the pot to lift pudding or it will burn. When mixture is thick, remove pot from heat. Let the pudding sit while you prepare the serving dish.

At the bottom of your serving dish, put in one layer of vanilla wafers and on top of the vanilla wafers put one layer of sliced bananas. Scoop some of the pudding on top of the banana slices. Put another layer of vanilla wafer and banana, then more pudding. Continue this process until the serving dish is full. Chill the banana pudding for 2-3 hours. Pudding serves 6-8 people.

Elzater Moffett

James Willis Hill was my dad. He made a mean Banana Pudding. He is also the inspiration for my books. I thought using his recipe was appropriate.

My book titles are:

Too Hot for Picking Peas

Available now at Barnes & Noble.com & Amazon.com

I don't want to go to sleep

Available May 17 at Authorhouse.com, Barnes & Noble.com & Amazon.com

FAMOUS MISSISSIPPIANS

Robin Roberts, TV/ Media personality for ABC, Pass Christian

Lance Bass, singer, Laurel

Theodore Bilbo, public official, Poplarville

Craig Claiborne, columnist, restaurant critic, Sunflower

Bo Diddley, guitarist, McComb

Charles Evers, civil rights leader, Decatur

Medgar Evers, civil rights leader, Decatur

Brett Farve, football player, Kiln

William Cuthbert Faulkner, author, New Albany

Shelby Foote, historian, Greenville

Richard Ford author, Jackson

Barry Hannah, author, Clinton

Elizabeth Lee Hazen, inventor,

Beth Henley, playwright, actress, Jackson

Jim Henson, puppeteer, Greenville

Faith Hill, singer, Jackson

James Earl Jones, entertainer, Arkabutla

Simbi Khali, actress, Jackson

B. B. King, guitarist, Itta Bena

Willie Morris, writer, Jackson

Brandy Norwood, singer, actress, McComb

Walter Payton, football player, Columbia

Elvis Presley, singer, actor, Tupelo

Charley Pride, country singer, Sledge

Leontyne Price, soprano, Laurel

William Raspberry, columnist, Oklaona

Jerry Rice, football player, Starkville

LeAnn Rimes, country music, Jackson

William Grant Still, composer, Woodville

Conway Twitty, country music, Friars Point

Sela Ward, actress, Meridian

Muddy Waters, singer, guitarist, Rolling Fork

Eudora Welty, author, Jackson

Tennessee Williams, playwright, Columbus

Oprah Winfrey, talk-show host, Kosciusko

Richard Wright, author, Natchez

Tammy Wynette, country music star, Tupelo

Red Barber (1908–1992), sportscaster, Columbus

Ron Franklin (born 1942), ESPN sportscaster, Jackson

Matt Barlow, heavy metal singer, Biloxi

Edward Charles Edmond Barq, entrepreneur and co-creator of Barq's Root Beer, Biloxi

Jimmy Buffett, singer and writer, Pascagoula

Jefferson Davis, US Army General and West Point graduate; U.S. Secretary of War (Defense); first and only President of the Confederate States of America, Biloxi

George E. Ohr, artist who broke new ground in the late 1890s with his experimental -modern clay forms – Ohr – O'Keefe Museum – Biloxi, Mississippi

FAMOUS FOOD QUOTES

He may live without books - what is knowledge but grieving?
He may live without hope - what is hope but grieving?
He may live without love - what is passion but pining?
But where is the man that can live without dining?

Edward R. Bulwer-Lytton "Lucille"

Avoid fruits and nuts. You are what you eat.

Jim Davis (Garfield)

America knows nothing of food, love, or art.

Isadora Duncan

Some people wanted champagne and caviar when they should have had beer and hot dogs.

Dwight D. Eisenhower

One can say everything best over a meal.

George Eliot

Let the stoics say what they please, we do not eat for the good of living, but because the meat is savory and the appetite is keen.

Ralph Waldo Emerson

One must ask children and birds how cherries and strawberries taste.

Johann Wolfgang von Goethe

When the stomach is full, it is easy to talk of fasting.

Saint Jerome

A smiling face is half the meal.

Latvian Proverb

Food is an important part of a balanced diet.

Fran Lebowitz

If the people have no bread, let them eat cake.

(attributed to) Marie Antoinette

At a dinner party one should eat wisely but not too well. And talk well but not too wisely.

W. Somerset Maugham

Kissing don't last: cookery do!

George Meredith

We may live without friends; we may live without books
But civilized men cannot live without cooks.

Owen Meredith

Americans can eat garbage, provided you sprinkle it liberally with ketchup, mustard, chili sauce, Tabasco sauce, cayenne pepper, or any other condiment which destroys the original flavor of the dish.

Henry Miller

One must eat to live, not live to eat.

Moliere

It's difficult to believe that people are still starving in this country because food isn't available.

Ronald Reagan

You can tell a lot about a fellow's character by his way of eating jellybeans.

Ronald Reagan

Nothing stimulates the practiced cook's imagination like an egg.

Irma Rombauer

Life is like an onion: You peel it off one layer at a time, and sometimes you weep.

Carl Sandburg

Dost thou think, because thou art virtuous, there shall be no more cakes and ale?

William Shakespeare

If music be the food of love, play on.
Give me excess of it, that, surfeiting,
The appetite may sicken, and so die.

William Shakespeare "Twelfth Night"

When men reach their sixties and retire they go to pieces. Women just go right on cooking.

Gail Sheehy

Serenely full, the epicure would say, Fate cannot harm me; I have dined to-day.

Sydney Smith "Recipe for Salad"

I prefer Hostess fruit pies to pop-up toaster tarts because they don't require as much cooking.

Carrie Snow

Bachelor's fare: bread and cheese, and kisses.

Jonathan Swift

The most remarkable thing about my mother is that for thirty years she served the family nothing but leftovers. The original meal has never been found.

Calvin Trillin

Nothing would be more tiresome than eating and drinking if God had not made them a pleasure as well as a necessity.

Voltaire

All happiness depends on a leisurely breakfast.

John Gunther

Cabbage: A vegetable about as large and wise as a man's head.

Ambrose Bierce

An idealist is one who, on noticing that roses smell better than a cabbage, concludes that it will also make better soup.

H. L. Mencken

Cheese-milk's leap toward immortality.

Clifton Fadiman

Research tells us that fourteen out of any ten individuals like chocolate.

Sandra Boynton "Chocolate: The Consuming Passion"

Venice is like eating an entire box of chocolate liqueurs in one go.

Truman Capote

Strength is the capacity to break a chocolate bar into four pieces with your bare hands -- and then eat just one of the pieces.

Judith Viorst

Never drink black coffee at lunch; it will keep you awake all afternoon.

Jilly Cooper

Only Irish coffee provides in a single glass all four essential food groups: alcohol, caffeine, sugar, and fat.

Alex Levine

If this is coffee, please bring some tea; but it this is tea, please bring me some coffee.

Abraham Lincoln

I think if I were a woman I'd wear coffee as a perfume.

John Van Druten

If there hadn't been women we'd still be squatting in a cave eating raw meat, because we made civilization in order to impress our girl friends. And they tolerated it and let us go ahead and play with our toys.

Orson Welles

A cucumber should be well sliced, and dressed with pepper and vinegar, and then thrown out, as good for nothing.

Samuel Johnson

Give me a fish, I eat for a day. Teach me to fish, I eat for a lifetime.

Robert Louis Stevenson

There are five elements: earth, air, fire, water and garlic.

Louis Diat

I am not a glutton - I am an explorer of food.

Erma Bombeck

Glutton: one who digs his grave with his teeth.

French Proverb

When we lose, I eat. When we win, I eat. I also eat when we're rained out.

Tommy Lasorda

The appetite grows with eating.

Francois Rabelais

My doctor told me to stop having intimate dinners for four, unless there are three other people.

Orson Welles

The pedigree of Honey

Does not concern the Bee

A Clover, any time, to him,

Is Aristocracy.

Emily Dickinson

A spoonful of honey will catch more flies than a gallon of vinegar.

Benjamin Franklin

I doubt the world holds for anyone a more soul-stirring surprise than the first adventure with ice cream.

Heywood Broun

When one has tasted watermelon he knows what the angels eat.

Mark Twain

Vegetables are interesting but lack a sense of purpose when unaccompanied by a good cut of meat.

Fran Lebowitz "Metropolitan Life"

"This recipe is certainly silly. It says to separate two eggs, but it doesn't say how far to separate them."

Gracie Allen

"I've been on a constant diet for the last two decades. I've lost a total of 789 pounds. By all accounts, I should be hanging from a charm bracelet."

Erma Bombeck

"I told my doctor I get very tired when I go on a diet, so he gave me pep pills. Know what happened? I ate faster."

Joe E. Lewis

About 85% of women are responsible for cooking the family dinner, and 84% wish they didn't have to.

"The age of your children is a key factor in how quickly you are served in a restaurant. We once had a waiter in Canada who said, 'Could I get you your check?' and we answered, 'How about the menus first?'"

Erma Bombeck

"I went into a French restaurant and asked the waiter, 'Have you got frog's legs?' He said, 'Yes,' so I said, 'Well hop into the kitchen and get me a cheese sandwich.'"

Tommy Cooper

FOOD TRIVIA

A honey bee must tap two million flowers to make one pound of honey.

Astronaut John Glenn ate the first meal in space when he ate pureed applesauce squeezed from a tube aboard Friendship 7 in 1962.

Aunt Jemima pancake flour, invented in 1889, was the first ready-mix food to be sold commercially.

California's Frank Epperson invented the Popsicle in 1905 when he was 11-years-old.

Capsaicin, which makes hot peppers "hot" to the human mouth, is best neutralized by casein, the main protein found in milk.

Chocolate contains phenylethylamine (PEA), a natural substance that is reputed to stimulate the same reaction in the body as falling in love.

During the Alaskan Klondike gold rush, (1897-1898) potatoes were practically worth their weight in gold. Potatoes were so valued for their vitamin C content that miners traded gold for potatoes.

During World War II, bakers in the United States were ordered to stop selling sliced bread for the duration of the war on January 18, 1943. Only whole loaves were made available to the public. It was never explained how this action helped the war effort.

Fortune cookies were invented in 1916 by George Jung, a Los Angeles noodle maker.

Goulash, a beef soup, originated in Hungary in the 9th century AD.

Hostess Twinkies were invented in 1931 by James Dewar, manager of Continental Bakeries' Chicago factory. He envisioned the product as a way of using the company's thousands of short-cake pans which were otherwise employed only during the strawberry season. Originally called Little Shortcake Fingers, they were renamed Twinkie Fingers, and finally "Twinkies."

In 1860, 'Godey's Lady's Book' advised US women to cook tomatoes for at least 3 hours.

In 1926, when a Los Angeles restaurant owner with the all-American name of Bob Cobb was looking for a way to use up leftovers, he threw together some avocado, celery, tomato, chives, watercress, hard-boiled eggs, chicken, bacon, and Roquefort cheese, and named it after himself: Cobb salad.

In 1976, the first eight Jelly Belly® flavors were launched: Orange, Green Apple, Root Beer, Very Cherry, Lemon, Cream Soda, Grape, and Licorice.

In 1995, KFC sold 11 pieces of chicken for every man, woman and child in the US.

Laws forbidding the sale of sodas on Sunday prompted William Garwood to invent the ice cream sundae in Evanston, IL, in 1875.

Louis XIV (1638-1715), was recorded to eat "four soups, a pheasant, a partridge, a plate of salad, sliced mutton with garlic, two lumps of ham, a plate of pastries, fruits and preserves" at one sitting.

Mayonnaise is said to be the invention of the French chef of the Duke de Richelieu in 1756. While the Duke was defeating the British at Port Mahon, his chef was creating a victory feast that included a sauce made of cream and eggs. When the chef realized that there was no cream in the kitchen, he improvised, substituting olive oil for the cream. A new culinary masterpiece was born, and the chef named it "Mahonnaise" in honor of the Duke's victory.

Mushrooms have no chlorophyll so they don't need sunshine to grow and thrive. Some of the earliest commercial mushroom farms were set up in caves in France during the reign of King Louis XIV (1638-1715).

Persians first began using colored eggs to celebrate spring in 3,000 B.C. 13th century Macedonians were the first Christians on record to use colored eggs in Easter celebrations. Crusaders returning from the Middle East spread the custom of coloring eggs, and Europeans began to use them to celebrate Easter and other warm weather holidays.

Potato chips were invented in Saratoga Springs in 1853 by Chef George Crum. They were a mocking response to a patron who complained that his French fries were too thick.

Sliced bread was introduced under the Wonder Bread label in 1930.

Sweetbread is neither sweet, nor bread. It is a dish made up of the pancreas or the thymus gland of a calf or lamb.

Swiss steak, Chop Suey, Russian dressing, and a Hamburger all originated in the US.

Tequila is made from the root of the blue agave cactus.

The Agen plum which would become the basis of the US prune industry was first planted in California in 1856.

The bubbles in Guiness beer sink to the bottom rather than float to the top as in other beers.

The California grape and wine industries were started by Count Agoston Haraszthy de Moksa, who planted Tokay, Zinfandel, and Shiras varieties from his native Hungary in Buena Vista in 1857.

The difference between apple juice and apple cider is that apple juice is the juice of the fruit only, and apple cider is the whole apple-skins, seeds, and all- which gives it the fuller body and deeper color. The juice is pasteurized and the cider is not.

The English word "soup" comes from the Middle Ages word "sop," which means a slice of bread over which roast drippings were poured. The first archaeological evidence of soup being consumed dates back to 6000 B.C., with the main ingredient being Hippopotamus bones!

The first ring donuts were produced in 1847 by a 15 year old baker's apprentice, Hanson Gregory, who knocked the soggy center out of a fried doughnut.

The hamburger was invented in 1900 by Louis Lassen. He ground beef, broiled it, and served it between two pieces of toast.

The ice cream soda was invented in 1874 by Robert Green. He was serving a mixture of syrup, sweet cream and carbonated water at a celebration in Philadelphia. He ran out of cream and substituted ice cream.

The Pillsbury Bake-off has been held every year since 1948.

The pound cake got its name from the pound of butter it contained.

The sandwich is named for the Fourth Earl of Sandwich (1718-92), for whom sandwiches were made so that he could stay at the gambling table without interruptions for meals.

The vintage date on a bottle of wine indicates the year the grapes were picked, not the year of bottling.

The white part of an egg is the albumen.

The white potato originated in the Andes Mountains and was probably brought to Britain by Sir Francis Drake about 1586.

The world's first chocolate candy was produced in 1828 by Dutch chocolate-maker Conrad J. Van Houten. He pressed the fat from roasted cacao beans to produce cocoa butter, to which he added cocoa powder and sugar.

Van Camp's Pork and Beans were a staple food for Union soldiers in the Civil War.

Vanilla is the extract of fermented and dried pods of several species of orchids.

Watermelon, considered one of America's favorite fruits, is really a vegetable (Citrullus lanatus). Cousin to the cucumber and kin to the gourd, watermelons can range in size from 7 to 100 pounds.

When Catherine de Medici married Henry II of France (1533) she brought forks with her, as well as several master Florentine cooks. Foods never before seen in France were soon being served using utensils instead of fingers or daggers. She is said to have introduced spinach (which "à la Florentine" usually means) as well as aspics, sweetbreads, artichoke hearts, truffles, liver crépinettes, quenelles of poultry, macaroons, ice cream, and zabagliones.

When honey is swallowed, it enters the blood stream within a period of 20 minutes.

When potatoes first appeared in Europe in the seventeenth century, it was thought that they were disgusting, and they were blamed for starting outbreaks of leprosy and syphilis. As late as 1720 in America, eating potatoes was believed to shorten a person's life.

When Swiss cheese ferments, a bacterial action generates gas. As the gas is liberated, it bubbles through the cheese leaving holes. Cheese-makers call them "eyes."

Chocolate

A recent study indicates when men crave food, they tend to crave fat and salt. When women crave food, they tend to desire chocolate.

The daughter of confectioner Leo Hirschfield is commemorated in the name of the sweet he invented: Although his daughter's real name was Clara, she went by the nickname Tootsie, and in her honor, her doting father named his chewy chocolate logs Tootsie Rolls.

Aztec emperor Montezuma drank 50 golden goblets of hot chocolate every day. It was thick, dyed red and flavored with chili peppers.

Chocolate contains phenylethylamine (PEA), a natural substance that is reputed to stimulate the same reaction in the body as falling in love.

Chocolate syrup was used for blood in the famous 45 second shower scene in Alfred Hitchcock's movie, Psycho, which actually took 7 days to shoot.

1824: John Cadbury, an English Quaker, begins roasting and grinding chocolate beans to sell in his tea and coffee shop. In 1842 Cadbury's Chocolate Company in England creates the first chocolate bar.

1875: A Swiss chocolate maker, Daniel Peter, mixes Henri Nestle's con- densed milk with chocolate and the two men found a company to manufacture the first milk chocolate.

1894: Milton Hershey adds a line of chocolate to his caramel manufacturing business.

Soon he invents the Hershey Bar by experimenting with milk chocolate. Hershey's Cocoa appears next.

1897: Brownies are first mentioned in print, listed for sale in the Sears, Roebuck and Co. catalogue.

About 1900: A machine called the enrober is invented to replace the task of hand-dipping chocolate.

1930: Franklin Mars invents the Snickers Bar.

1939: Nestle introduces semisweet chocolate morsels.

1940: The Mars Company invents M&M's for soldiers going to World War II.

Chocolate was introduced into the United States in 1765 when cocoa beans were brought from the West Indies to Dorchester, Massachusetts.

Cocoa butter is the natural fat of the cocoa bean. It has a delicate chocolate aroma, but is very bitter tasting. It is used to give body, smoothness, and flavor to eating chocolate.

Columbus brought cacao (chocolate) beans back to Spain on his fourth voyage in 1502.

German chocolate cake did not originate in Germany. In 1852, Sam German developed a sweet baking bar for Baker's Chocolate Co. The product was named in honor of him -- Baker's German's Sweet Chocolate.

In 1900, Queen Victoria sent her New Year's greetings to the British troops stationed in South Africa during the Boer War in the form of a specially molded chocolate bar.

In Hershey, Pennsylvania, the streetlights along "Chocolate Avenue" are in the shape of Hershey Kisses.

It's a common myth that chocolate aggravates acne. Experiments conducted at the University of Pennsylvania and the U.S. Naval Academy found that consumption of chocolate -- even frequent daily dietary intake -- had no effect on the incidence of acne. Professional dermatologists today do not link acne with diet.

One plain milk chocolate candy bar has more protein than a banana.

Per capita, the Irish eat more chocolate than Americans, Swedes, Danes, French, and Italians.

Pet parrots can eat virtually any common "people-food" except for chocolate and avocados. Both of these are highly toxic to the parrot and can be fatal.

The botanical name of the chocolate plant is Theobramba cacao, which means "Food of the Gods."

The daughter of confectioner Leo Hirschfield is commemorated in the name of the sweet he invented: Although his daughter's real name was Clara, she went by the nickname Tootsie, and in her honor, her doting father named his chewy chocolate logs Tootsie Rolls.

The earliest cocoa plantations were established in 600 AD, in the Yucatan, by the Mayans.

The fruit of the Cacao tree grow directly from the trunk. They look like small melons, and the pulp inside contains 20 to 50 seeds or beans. It takes about 400 beans to make a pound of chocolate.

The Imperial torte, a square chocolate cake with five thin layers of almond paste, was created by a master pastry chef at the court of Emperor Franz Joseph (1830 - 1916).

The melting point of cocoa butter is just below the human body temperature -- which is why it literally melts in your mouth.

The term "white chocolate" is a misnomer. Under Federal Standards of Identity, real chocolate must contain chocolate liquor. "White" chocolate contains no chocolate liquor.

The theobromine in chocolate that stimulates the cardiac and nervous systems is too much for dogs, especially smaller pups. A chocolate bar is poisonous to dogs and can even be lethal.

The world's first chocolate candy was produced in 1828 by Dutch chocolate-maker Conrad J. Van Houten. He pressed the fat from roasted cacao beans to produce cocoa butter, to which he added cocoa powder and sugar.

Coffee

Adding sugar to coffee is believed to have started in 1715, in the court of King Louis XIV, the French monarch.

Advertisements for coffee in London in 1657 claimed that the beverage was a cure for scurvy, gout and other ills.

Beethoven, who was a coffee lover, was so particular about his coffee that he always counted 60 beans each cup when he prepared his brew.

Before the first French cafe in the late 1700's, coffee was sold by street vendors in Europe, in the Arab fashion. The Arabs were the forerunners of the sidewalk espresso carts of today.

By 1850, the manual coffee grinder found its way to most upper middle class kitchens of the U.S.

Citrus has been added to coffee for several hundred years.

Coffee as a medicine reached its highest and lowest point in the 1600's in England. Wild medical contraptions to administer a mixture of coffee and an assortment of heated butter, honey, and oil, became treatments for the sick. Soon tea replaced coffee as the national beverage.

Coffee Recipe from: 'Kitchen Directory and American Housewife' (1844)

"Use a tablespoonful ground to a pint of boiling water [less than a quarter of what we would use today].

Boil in tin pot twenty to twenty-five minutes. If boiled longer it will not taste fresh and lively.

Let stand four or five minutes to settle, pour off grounds into a coffee pot or urn.

Put fish skin or isinglass size of a nine-pence in pot when put on to boil or else the white and shell of half an egg to a couple of quarts of coffee."

Coffee was first known in Europe as Arabian Wine.

During the American Civil War the Union soldiers were issued eight pounds of ground roasted coffee as part of their personal ration of one hundred pounds of food. And they had another choice: ten pounds of green coffee beans.

During World War II the U.S. government used 260 million pounds of instant coffee.

Frederick the great had his coffee made with champagne and a bit of mustard.

Hills Brothers Ground Vacuum Packed Coffee was first introduced in 1900.

Iced coffee in a can has been popular in Japan since 1945.

In 1670, Dorothy Jones of Boston was granted a license to sell coffee, and so became the first American coffee trader.

In 1727, as a result of seedlings smuggled from Paris, coffee plants first were cultivated in Brazil. Brazil is presently by far the world's largest producer of coffee.

In 1900, coffee was often delivered door-to-door in the United States, by horse-pulled wagons.

In 1990, over 4 billion dollars of coffee was imported into the United States.

In early America, coffee was usually taken between meals and after dinner.

In Japan, coffee shops are called Kissaten.

In the 14th century, the Arabs started to cultivate coffee plants. The first commercially grown and harvested coffee originated in the Arabian Peninsula near the port of Mocha.

In the 16th century, Turkish women could divorce their husbands if the man failed to keep his family's pot filled with coffee.

In the year 1763, there were over 200 coffee shops in Venice.

In the year 1790, there were two firsts in the United States; the first wholesale coffee roasting company, and the first newspaper advertisement featuring coffee. .

It was during the 1600's that the first coffee mill made its debut in London.

Italians do not drink espresso during meals. It is considered to be a separate event and is given its own time.

Latte is the Italian word for milk. So if you request a latte' in Italy, you'll be served a glass of milk.

Lloyd's of London began as Edward Lloyd's coffeehouse.

Milk as an additive to coffee became popular in the 1680's, when a French physician recommended that cafe au lait be used for medicinal purposes.

Raw coffee beans, soaked in water and spices, are chewed like candy in many parts of Africa.

The Arabica is the original coffee plant. It still grows wild in Ethiopia. The Arabica coffee tree is an evergreen and in the wild will grow to a height between 14 and 20 feet.

The Arabs are generally believed to be the first to brew coffee.

The Civil War in the United States elevated the popularity of coffee to new heights. Soldiers went to war with coffee beans as a primary ration.

The coffee filter was invented in 1908 by a German homemaker, Melitta Benz, when she lined a tin cup with blotter paper to filter the coffee grinds.

The drip pot was invented by a Frenchman around 1800.

The Europeans first added chocolate to their coffee in the 1600's.

The first coffee drinkers, the Arabs, flavored their coffee with spices during the brewing process.

The first commercial espresso machine was manufactured in Italy in 1906.

The first Parisian cafe opened in 1689 to serve coffee.

The French philosopher, Voltaire, reportedly drank fifty cups of coffee a day.

The heavy tea tax imposed on the colonies in 1773, which caused the "Boston Tea Party," resulted in America switching from tea to coffee. Drinking coffee was an expression of freedom.

Turkey began to roast and grind the coffee bean in the 13th Century, and some 300 years later, in the 1500's, the country had become the chief distributor of coffee, with markets established in Egypt, Syria, Persia, and Venice, Italy.

Until the 18th century coffee was almost always boiled.

Until the late 1800's, people roasted their coffee at home. Popcorn poppers and stove-top frying pans were favored.

William Penn purchased a pound of coffee in New York in 1683 for $4.68.

THE HISTORY OF GAMBLING

Gambling has existed since ancient times, and there is evidence that most cultures supported it in some form or another.

Gambling has played a role in the history of nations. Around the year 1,000 A.D., King Olaf of Norway and King Olaf of Sweden are said to have come together to decide on the ownership of the district of Hising, a relatively isolated area claimed by both countries. Because the dispute could not be resolved diplomatically, the two kings agreed to roll a pair of dice. On their first rolls, both kings got double six; on their second rolls, the Swedish king came up with two sixes and the Norwegian king rolled six on the first die. The second, however, is said to have cracked, showed seven. Norway received the territory, and the two kings reportedly departed on good terms.

It is said that gambling was so popular during the Middle Ages that some countries prohibited their soldiers from participating in games, since the gambling activities prevented them from carrying out their proper duties. **King Henry VIII** of England, for example, is said to have banned gambling when he determined that his soldiers were devoting more time to gambling and less time to working on drills and marksmanship.

Playing cards may have developed in China, since the Chinese developed both paper and money made from paper. In fact, the Chinese are said to have come up with the practice of shuffling paper money about 900 A.D. This may have evolved into the practice of shuffling cards. Playing cards then apparently spread to the Mameluke Empire. Since the Mamelukes were Muslim, they did not decorate their playing cards with human forms; instead, their cards were decorated with intricate designs. When the cards made their way to the Mediterranean countries, card makers began distinguishing cards with the royal ranks of noblemen who frequented the royal court. The French took out one of the men and added a queen card sometime in the 1500s. **This "French Pack"** of cards became the prototype of the 52-card deck we use today.

CASINO GAMING

Casino gaming is the largest part of the commercial gambling market. Casino gaming continues to grow in popularity, fueled by the creation of new casino destinations and the expansion of existing casino locales.

A casino is usually characterized by the offering of banked games. Banked games are where the house is banking the game and basically acting as a participant. That is, it has a stake in who wins.

In 1638, the government of Venice decided that if they ran a gambling house themselves they could better control it and, while they were at it, make a lot of money. Thus, they authorized the opening of not just any *ridotto*, but **The Ridotto**, a four-story gambling house with various rooms for primitive card games and a selection of food and beverages to keep the gamblers happy **The Ridotto** was important for two reasons -- *it was the world's first government-sanctioned gambling house, and the first that was open to the general public.* High stakes games meant that the clientele were still generally rich people, but in principle, the **Ridotto** makes Venice the birthplace of the casino. The idea spread throughout Europe as people either thought of it themselves or copied it from the Italians. Indeed, most popular modern casino games were invented in France. As for the word itself, a casino was originally a small clubhouse for Italians to meet in for social occasions. The closure of large public gambling houses like the **Ridotto** pushed gambling into these smaller venues, which flourished

HISTORY OF GAMBLING
IN THE USA

Historians have classified the early American settlers into two groups, the English who brought along the English traditions and beliefs, and the Puritans. Although the Puritans came from England, they came to the new world intending to create a "better" society and discard the values of their mother country. To them, the new world represented an opportunity for establishing a society grounded on religious Puritan values and strict Christian beliefs.

Entire colonies were established along the guidelines and beliefs of one group or another. In particular, different attitudes towards gambling were enforced. In New England and Pennsylvania, Puritan attitudes toward gaming and recreation were adopted. The Puritan-led Massachusetts Bay Colony outlawed not only the possession of cards, dice, and gaming tables (even in private homes), but also dancing and singing. This stance was relaxed slightly over the following years so as to allow casual gaming as long as it was for "innocent and moderate recreation" and not as a trade or calling. This hostility towards the professional gambler is a common theme in the history of U.S. gambling.

In other colonies, English attitudes towards gambling and recreation prevailed. These settlers brought with them the view that gambling was a harmless diversion. In these colonies, gambling was a prevalent, popular and widely accepted activity. Legal gambling tended to be those types that were considered proper gentlemen's diversions, such as cards, dice and animal racing games. It is widely held that the appeal of gambling was heightened by the frontier spirit. The desire to explore new worlds is similar to gambling. Both rely heavily on high expectations, risk taking and opportunism.

Casino gaming started slowly. Taverns and roadhouses would allow dice and card games. The relatively sparse population was a barrier to establishing exotic gaming houses. But as the population increased, by the early 1800s lavish casinos were established in more densely populated areas of the young republic. As previously mentioned, gambling and the frontier lifestyle shared similar foundations -- a spirit of adventure, opportunity, and risk taking. During the early 1800s gambling in the lower Mississippi Valley became a legitimate and organized enterprise. The Mississippi River and connected waterways were major avenues of trade for farmers and merchants and the river boats carried passengers who held significant quantities of cash and goods. The south tended to have a more open attitude towards gaming, reflecting the Spanish, French, and early Virginian traditions. New Orleans quickly became the capital for gambling in

America and the birthplace of many popular old-west gambling games, including faro, brag, hazard, bluff (poker) and blackjack, each evolving from popular French, English and other European games of skill and chance that originated in the Renaissance and beyond.

"Gambling is inevitable. No matter what is said or done by advocates or opponents of gambling in all its various forms, it is an activity that is practiced, or tacitly endorsed, by a substantial majority of Americans."

-- Commission on the Review of National Policy toward Gambling, 1976, p.1.

In 1973, the Commission on the Review of National Policy toward Gambling was created to study gambling in the United States. The Commission began its report with the above statement.

The act of gambling may actually predate documented history

Cards and Kings

The four kings on a standard pack of playing cards actually represent famous kings from history. The king of spades represents the biblical king, David and the king of clubs represents Alexander the Great. And for the red team, Julius Caesar is supposedly depicted by the king of diamonds, while the king or hearts is purported to represent Charles the Great, king of the Franks, otherwise known as King Charlemagne.

These historical links go back almost 500 years to the time when the modern pack of cards was designed in France. The suits themselves apparently equate to four historical cultures with clubs, spades, diamonds, and hearts representing Greece, the Middle East, Rome, and the Holy Roman Empire respectively.

Dice

The six-sided dice also have a fascinating history. Traditionally carved from animal bones, they have been used by man as a means of predicting the future as well as the outcome of games of chance. These lucky cubes have been fashioned from all kinds of materials ranging from fruit pits, ivory, jewels, and even human teeth. The oldest known dice were uncovered by archaeologists in Iraq where they were possibly used with a game similar to the modern game of backgammon. These dice were made from baked clay and are approximately 5,000 years old.

Slot Machines

Slot machines have been with us for over 100 years with the earliest version attributed to American Charles Fey. Fey devised the first slot machine in San Francisco in 1899 and it comprised a three-slot device containing an image of the famous Liberty Bell, a well-known symbol from the American Civil war. In fact, Fey's machines were so popular that for many years slot machines were called Bell machines.

The bar symbol, which is the other classic slot machine design, is derived from the logo of the Bell Fruit chewing gum company. The gum was delivered through slots in a machine designed by Herbert Mills of Chicago in 1910. The use of fruit symbols is also linked to the Mills machine as these represented the different gum flavors produced by the Herbert Mills Company. The fruit flavors gave rise to the other common name for these devices - fruit machines.

Roulette Wheel

The roulette wheel was invented by the French inventor Blaise Pascal. Pascal was actually trying to create a perpetual movement machine, but ended up with the roulette wheel - not a bad rap.

The double 00 position found on American Roulette Wheels were added only when roulette found its way to the United States of America. Previous to this the wheel only had the single 0 position, but the American casino owners didn't feel that the house had enough of an edge with this and so added the extra position.

The chap that added the original one 0 position was named Francois Blanc; he was also responsible for setting up the first casino in Monte Carlo. It was rumored that in order to learn the secrets of roulette Mr. Blanc actually made a pact with the devil. The evidence lies in the wheel itself: If you add all the numbers of the board together you come to the sum of the devil, 666.

Row 5 is the worst row to bet on; statistically speaking row 5 is the least likely row to win.

Einstein apparently commented that, "you can't beat a roulette table unless you steal from it".

Roulette has played a part in many a flick, the most famous of which being James Bond's 'Diamonds are forever', and of course Casablanca where we found our hero, Rick, fixing the wheel for a destitute client to win big and be able to escape to America.

HISTORY OF GAMBLING ON THE MISSISSIPPI GULF COAST

Biloxi's casino history dates back to a period in the 1940s, when open technically illegal gambling took place in a casino within the Broadwater Beach Resort. Open gambling ended during the 1950s. The Mississippi Gulf Coast became known as the "Poor Man's Riviera", and was frequented by Southern families interested in fishing expeditions during the summer. Commercially, Biloxi was dominated by shrimp boats and oyster luggers.

In the early 1960s, the Gulf Coast again emerged as a prime alternative to Florida, as a southern vacation destination among Northerners, with Biloxi a center of the focus. Biloxi hotels upgraded their amenities and hired chefs from France and Switzerland in an effort to provide some of the best seafood cuisine in the country.

With the introduction of legal gambling in Mississippi in the 1990s, Biloxi was again transformed. It became an important center for casinos, and the hotels and complexes brought millions of dollars in tourism revenue to the city.

For more information on the history of gambling on the Mississippi Coast:

http://mshistory.k12.ms.us/

CASINOS

The Mississippi Gulf Coast has become home to many casino resort hotels, with 24-hour gambling, championship golf courses, luxury spas, world class entertainment, and a wide variety of casual, as well as, fine dining restaurants.

Casinos are a major employer and revenue source in the state of Mississippi, offering gaming comparable to Las Vegas and Atlantic City.

Some of the casinos offer supervised activities for children and some are complete resort complexes with golf courses and hotels as part of their package.

With 11 casinos to choose from-and more on the way, the Mississippi Gulf Coast's 24-hour non-stop gaming offers it all!

- **IP Casino Resort** re-opened on December 22, 2005, formerly **<u>Imperial Palace</u>.**
- **Isle of Capri Casino Resort** re-opened in late December 2005.
- **Palace Casino Resort** re-opened in late December 2005.
- **Beau Rivage Resort & Casino**-opened August 29, 2006 on the first anniversary of Hurricane Katrina.
- **Boomtown Casino** re-opened in 2006.
- **Hard Rock Hotel & Casino**, which had initially hoped to open for post-Katrina business in the summer of 2005, but opened later than expected in June 2007.
- **Treasure Bay Casino** Resort re-opened in summer 2006.
- **Grand Biloxi** re-opened and has built a casino in its formerly named Bayview Hotel
- **Island View Resort** is nearby Gulfport's only casino and home to one of world-famous chef **Emeril Lagasse's** restaurants, **The Fish House**
- **Hollywood Casino**s is located in Bay St. Louis and includes an on-site golf course and movie cinema decor.
- **The Silver Slipper** was the first land-based casino to open following Hurricane Katrina. This beachfront resort is located just outside Bay St. Louis, west of Biloxi.

MARDI GRAS TRIVIA AND HISTORY

What is Mardi-Gras?

Mardi Gras, also known as Fat Tuesday, is the celebration leading up to lent. Mardi Gras season officially begins on Twelfth Night, or the Feast of the Epiphany, and concludes on Shrove Tuesday, just before Ash Wednesday and the beginning of lent. Traditionally it is a time of feasting and celebrations before the onset of the upcoming sacrifices. In the old days, and too many Catholics today, this mostly meant the eschewing of meat. Hence Mardi Gras or Fat Tuesday, which in years past was known as Boeuf Gras, in homage to the last feast of meat before the Lenten season. In other areas of the world, the celebration is known as Carnival, from the Latin for "farewell to flesh."

Where did Mardi Gras begin in the United States

Mobile, Alabama is where Mardi Gras began and is still celebrated in grand style today. Visitors to Mobile can view dazzling Mardi Gras costumes as well as other Fat Tuesday historical memorabilia, year round, at the **Museum of Mobile** located at 355 Government Street (334-208-7569).

Most of the towns along the gulf coast of Mississippi and Louisiana celebrate Mardi Gras, the largest celebration of course, being New Orleans.

The King Cake

A king cake is a traditional Mardi Gras treat, brightly decorated in the colors of Rex: purple, green and gold. The cake, which is similar to a coffee cake, contains a tiny baby doll hidden within one of the slices. Custom dictates that the "lucky" recipient who gets the piece with the baby throws the next Mardi Gras party or brings the next cake.

HISTORY OF MARDI GRAS ON THE MISSISSIPPI COAST

Biloxi, Mississippi was the first City in Mississippi to host an official Mardi Gras parade in 1908 with 17 floats.

The first king and queen were *King d'Iberville* and *Queen Ixolib*, (Biloxi spelled backwards) In 1916 a group organized in Biloxi, Mississippi, named themselves the *Biloxi Literary and Carnival Association*, which became the *Gulf Coast Carnival Association,* chartered in 1946 and still participating and hosting parades today. In 1929 other coast cities joined in the tradition and started forming their own Krewes and hosting parades and balls.

Gulf Coast Carnival Association traces its roots back to 1908 and Biloxi's first Mardi Gras parade, which included 17 floats, 150 flambeau carriers, the new 12-piece Herald Newspaper Band, a grand marshal, the mayor and the councilmen. The monarchs were the first King d'Iberville and Queen Ixolib.

In 1929, the Biloxi celebration expanded to include other cities along the Mississippi Gulf Coast.

Mardi Gras Museum - Biloxi

Phone: 228-435-6245; Web Site: www.biloxi.ms.us

My Mardi Gras Memories

I suppose one of my happiest memories from childhood was walking to the Mardi Gras Parades with my mother and sister and later on with my friends.

We lived near downtown Mobile, Alabama, where the parades took place so there was not much of a chance that we would miss one unless it rained, of course. Oh, but that didn't keep my mother from making sure we still got to watch the parade and feel almost as if we were there. I can remember her pulling the television away from the wall, standing behind it and when a float would appear on the television screen, we would yell *throw me something, mister* and she would throw candy & moon pies over the top of the television. Later on in my adult life, I actually carried on the tradition with my own children.

Mardi Gras is still the height of the Southern Social season with two weeks of parades followed by spectacular formal balls and Lee and I have attended our share of both.

MISSISSIPPI TRIVIA

The Mississippi River is the largest in the United States and is the nation's chief waterway. Its nickname is *Old Man River*.

In 1963 the **University of Mississippi Medical Center** accomplished the world's first human lung transplant

Mississippi suffered the largest percentage of people who died in the Civil War of any Confederate State. 78,000 Mississippians entered the Confederate military. By the end of the war 59,000 were either dead or wounded.

The oldest game in America is stickball. **The Choctaw Indians of Mississippi** played the game. Demonstrations can be seen every July at the Choctaw Indian Fair in **Philadelphia**.

The world's largest shrimp is on display at the Old Spanish Fort Museum in **Pascagoula.**

The world's largest cactus plantation is in **Edwards.**

H.T. Merrill from **Luka** performed the world's first round trip trans-oceanic flight in 1928.

The first female rural mail carrier in the United States was Mrs. Mamie Thomas. She delivered mail by buggy to the area southeast of **Vicksburg** in 1914.

Historic Jefferson College, circa 1802, was the first preparatory school established in the Mississippi Territory. Located in **Washington** the educational institution is also the site where tradition holds Aaron Burr was arraigned for treason in 1807, beneath what became known as **Burr Oaks**.

William Grant Still of **Woodville** composed the Afro-American Symphony.

Burnita Shelton Mathews of **Hazelhurst** was the first woman federal judge in the United States and served in Washington, the District of Columbia.

Dr. Emmette F. Izard of **Hazelhurst** developed the first fibers of rayon. They became known as the first real synthetics.

In 1884 the concept of selling shoes in boxes in pairs (right foot and left foot) occurred in **Vicksburg** at Phil Gilbert's Shoe Parlor on Washington Street.

The first bottle of Dr. Tichener's Antiseptic was produced in **Liberty.**

The first nuclear submarine built in the south was produced in **Mississippi.**

1959: **Ingalls** launched its first submarine, the **USS Blueback**. Three years later it christened its first nuclear submarine.

In May of 1930 **"Ripley's Believe it or Not"** has a cartoon of the **Singing River**.

In November of 1938, **Robert Ingalls**, a wealthy Alabama industrialist, began improvements at a 187-acre WWI shipyard site on East **Pascagoula.**

June 8, 1940, **Ingalls** launched its first ship, the **Exchequer,** a cargo vessel.

In 1871 **Liberty** became the first town in the United States to erect a Confederate monument.

Mississippi was the first state in the nation to have a planned system of junior colleges.

Leontyne Price of **Laurel** performed with the New York Metropolitan Opera.

Mississippi is the birthplace of the Order of the Eastern Star.

The rarest of North American cranes lives in Mississippi in the grassy savannas of **Jackson County**. The Mississippi Sandhill Crane stands about 44 inches tall and has an eight-foot wingspan.

Guy Bush of **Tupelo** was one of the most valuable players with the Chicago Cubs. He was on the 1929 World Series team and Babe Ruth hit his last home run off a ball pitched by Bush.

S.B. Sam Vick of **Oakland** played for the New York Yankees and the Boston Red Sox. He was the only man ever to pinch hit for the baseball great Babe Ruth.

Blazon-Flexible Flyer, Inc. in **West Point** is proclaimed to make the very best snow sled in the United States, which became an American tradition. It is called The Flexible Flyer.

The largest Bible-binding plant in the nation is Norris Bookbinding Company in **Greenwood.**

After the Civil War, famed hat maker John B. Stetson learned and practiced his trade at Dunn's Falls near **Meridian.**

Greenwood is the home of Cotton Row, which is the second largest cotton exchange in the nation and is on the National Register of Historic Places.

In 1834 Captain Isaac Ross, whose plantation was in **Lorman,** freed his slaves and arranged for them to be sent to Africa, where they founded the country of Liberia. Recently, representatives of Liberia visited Lorman and placed a stone at the Captain's gravesite in honor of his kindness.

The International Checkers Hall of Fame is in **Petal.**

The world's largest cottonwood tree plantation is in **Issaquena County.**

Natchez was settled by the French in 1716 and is the oldest permanent settlement on the Mississippi River. Natchez once had 500 millionaires, more than any other city except New York City.

Natchez now has more than 500 buildings that are on the National Register of Historic Places.

The Natchez Trace Parkway, named an All American Road by the federal government, extends from Natchez to just south of Nashville, Tennessee. The Trace began as an Indian trail more than 8,000 years ago.

The Vicksburg National Cemetery is the second largest national cemetery in the country. Arlington National Cemetery is the largest.

D'Lo was featured in "Life Magazine" for sending proportionally more men to serve in World War II than any other town of its size. 38 percent of the men who lived in D'Lo served.

Pine Sol was invented in 1929 by **Jackson** native Harry A. Cole, Sr.

Greenwood is called the Cotton Capital of the World.

Greenville is called the Towboat Capital of the World.

At **Vicksburg**, the United States Army Corps of Engineers Waterways Experiment Station is the world's largest hydraulic research laboratory.

David Harrison of **Columbus** owns the patent on the Soft Toilet Seat. Over 1,000,000 are sold every year.

At **Pascagoula** the Ingalls Division of Litton Industries uses leading-edge construction techniques to build the United State Navy's most sophisticated ships. At the state's eight research centers programs are under way in acoustics, polymer science, electricity, microelectronics, hydrodynamics, and oceanography.

Friendship Cemetery in **Columbus** has been called *Where Flowers Healed a Nation*. It was April 25, 1866, and the Civil War had been over for a year when the ladies of Columbus decided to decorate both Confederate and Union soldiers' graves with beautiful bouquets and garlands of flowers. As a direct result of this kind gesture, Americans celebrate what has come to be called **Memorial Day** each year, an annual observance of recognition of war dead.

SOUTHERN FOOD

Turnip greens and corn bread, black eyed peas and rice, fried chicken, steamed cabbage, creamed potatoes and gravy, these are just a few of the dishes I think about when I think about my childhood.

Yes, my Daddy was from New Orleans so there was often a pot of gumbo cooking on the stove and it seemed like there was a never ending supply of shrimp, fish and oysters in our kitchen; however, my Mama made sure her children remembered that there was more to living in the South, than eating seafood; although I cannot imagine why, because I never knew anyone who loved oysters and fish more than she did; however, I suppose it would have been impossible to feed small children gumbo, fish and oysters at every meal.

My Mother once told me that before there was such a thing as *baby food,* people would put on a big pot of beans, turnip greens or green beans and use the *pot liqueur* (liquid in the pot) to feed their babies, in fact, she said when the babies were old enough, they would soak a little corn bread in the liquid and feed it to the babies; maybe that's why I love turnip greens and cornbread so much and maybe that is where Irritable Bowel Syndrome came from. Can you just imagine little toddlers trying to digest turnip greens and corn bread seasoned with bacon grease and onions?

Actually, I can imagine this because I must have been one of those toddlers. I can remember my mother pouring coffee in a saucer, over a piece of bread, and feeding it to me. Now, I must have been no more than a year old, but I do remember that my mother used about a half cup of sugar and at least a fourth cup of Carnation® or Pet® milk in her coffee, so it's no wonder that my generation became addicted to sugar and fat.

Southern fried chicken, need I say more? Every Sunday we had fried chicken, potato salad and green peas, at least for dinner; supper was a different meal altogether. Sometimes we had roast and spaghetti, which was a roast cooked in a tomato gravy and served over spaghetti. Other times we had pork roast, turnip greens, cornbread and sweet potatoes; well, you get the picture; however, no matter what we had any other day of the week, Friday was seafood day. There was either fried fish or fried shrimp or both. Sometimes there were stuffed crabs, oysters and shrimp salad and of course there was always gumbo, served over rice, but then we served almost every-thing over rice. Red beans, black eyed peas, butter beans and of course gravy.

Now let's talk breads. In the south you must have bread, of some type, at each meal; and to this day, I cannot eat an egg without a piece of toast, it just somehow seems wrong.

As a little girl, I don't believe I ate very much cornbread; that is until Jiffy® corn bread mix became available and that is because I loved sugar, still do, but these days I love any kind of cornbread, sweet or not.

We never really ate sandwiches when I was growing up unless it was for an afternoon snack and that was usually peanut butter and jelly or French fry sandwiches; because my Mother cooked three hot meals a day. When she wasn't cooking, my Dad was cooking. So to say that we were exposed to a wide variety of foods is an understatement and if it was high in fat, calories and sugar, we ate it.

Now don't get me wrong, my mother cooked lots of fresh vegetables; squash, corn, field peas, okra, snap beans, cabbage, turnip greens and rutabagas and she always used bacon grease and butter to ensure they tasted wonderful, and they always did.

Desserts; who could resist a homemade pecan pie, bread pudding, pineapple upside – down cake and the ultimate; devil's food cake with chocolate icing, certainly not me; although pineapple upside – down cake was not my favorite, too much fruit in it, I suppose, and that made it seem way too healthy.

By now you know, without a doubt, that I was probably a sugarholic growing up, but you have to remember that I was the youngest of six children and by the time I came along, I'm sure my mother just gave me whatever I wanted to eat; no questions asked, the lady was tired.

I can remember my mother putting sugar on my grits and my turnip greens so I would eat them, and to this day, I still put sugar on grits and turnip greens, only now I use Splenda® in and on everything that calls for sugar or that I think needs sugar; everything, that is, except pralines. I do not believe I have ever eaten a praline, nor do I ever want to try a praline made with a sugar substitute; now that would just go against my Southern up-bringing.

Southern Food Trivia and fact

The South has given us orange juice, iced tea, Vidalia onions, chicory coffee, sweet potato pie, peanut brittle, pralines and Bananas Foster.

There are two kinds of grits: plain corn grits are dried, ground corn. Hominy grits are ground corn kernels with the hull and germ removed. By themselves, grits are bland -- yet they are eaten a variety of ways and are served for breakfast, lunch and dinner

Sweet Tea

The oldest known recipe for sweet tea dates back to an 1879 issue of Housekeeping in Old Virginia. Marion Cabell Tyree's recipe called for green tea. During World War II, traditional sources for tea in the United States were cut off, forcing tea drinkers to switch to black tea [source: Buy Southern].

Fried chicken

The Scots had a tradition of deep-frying chicken in fat. Scottish immigrants came to the South where African slaves had already introduced a tradition of frying food. Over time, deep-frying became a common way of cooking chicken and other food.

African ingredients like okra and black-eyed peas became a staple of the Southern diet, in addition to the homegrown green staples of collards, mustard, turnips and kale. Other highly used crops include pecans and peanuts, sweet potatoes and peaches.

The region's lakes, rivers, tidal pools and oceans served up oysters, shrimp, crawfish, crab and Mississippi catfish.

Prior to the Civil War, most southerners were subsistence farmers who lived off the land. Pork and chicken, not cattle, were typically raised. Farmers working outside needed a lot of calories to get through the day; therefore they indulged in big breakfasts and suppers.

Barbeque

Barbecue varies across the South. It can consist of pulled pork shoulder or ribs, either pork or beef; however, barbecue sauce is no longer a Southern thing, and everyone throughout the United States has the *World's Best barbecue sauce*, just ask them and they will tell you they have a secret ingredient that no one in the universe uses in their sauce; I know this because I have the secret ingredient, as well, and I can't tell you what it is because…well, I just can't.

Being a Southerner has less to do with whether or not you were born and raised in the south; it has more to do with how connected your soul feels to nature when you are standing on southern soil.

Everything southern feels exaggerated. The Oak trees seem to reach out to you as you approach them and while inside an Antebellum home, you can almost hear the walls whisper the secrets they have held for so many decades, the people are so open and friendly that you truly understand why so many people relocate to the south.

LINDA'S STORIES

And Recipes

Lost Bread

When I was growing up, one of my favorite things to eat for breakfast was *Lost Bread*. I had no idea why it was called *Lost Bread* until I got a little older and decided that this was a very strange name for bread that was in fact, not really lost at all. My Mother explained that when she and my Father lived in New Orleans, they loved the fresh French bread from the local bakery; however, French bread did not stay fresh very long so instead of throwing it away, they would slice it and dip it in egg and milk and fry it. She said that the French called it *Pain Perdu* which meant *Lost Bread*. Now I still didn't understand why they called it *Lost Bread* when it wasn't actually lost, but I decided it wasn't really that important because I loved it no matter what they called it. My mother used plain white bread for us, probably because there was never any leftover French bread with so many children in the house.

I made *Lost Bread* for my children when they were growing up and somewhere along the way we began calling it *French toast*. I still make it occasionally though I usually use low fat milk instead of the evaporated milk my mother used. Now the low fat milk may be better for you but it doesn't taste quite as good as it did when my mother made it.

There are many different recipes for *French Toast* these days, some call for vanilla extract or cinnamon or nutmeg and there are even stuffed *French Toast* recipes, but sometimes less is more so if you want to sample the *Lost Bread* I grew up eating, then pull out your iron skillet, open a can of evaporated milk, beat some eggs up and dip plain white bread in the egg and evaporated milk mixture and fry in a lightly buttered pan. My oldest brother liked his *Lost Bread* somewhat fluffy and so did I, but if you like yours a little firmer, well then fry it longer. After you remove the *Lost Bread* from the pan and place it on your plate, sprinkle it with powdered sugar, think of me and smile.

Yellow Squash Casserole

Growing up I didn't eat squash so when I was visiting my sister, Beverly, and she asked me to try this new recipe she had found, imagine my disgust when she told me what it was. Of course to be nice, I tried it and I absolutely loved it, in fact, it was the only way I could get my children to eat squash.

Now I have to tell you that my sister was a wonderful cook and though my mother taught me the basics, Beverly taught me to try new foods and experiment with different recipes. My sister was twelve years older than me so I would baby sit for her sometimes and she would cook foods that I never really liked before, but she had a knack for making vegetables not taste like vegetables.

The following recipe came from my beloved sister, Beverly Ann Scott, whom I miss dearly, every single day.

1 pound of yellow squash	2 tablespoons of bacon grease or
I can of cream of chicken soup	butter
1 large onion	Bread crumbs
Salt & pepper to taste	

Wash and slice squash. Dice onion and sauté`, along with squash, in skillet until tender. Pour into casserole dish. Pour soup over the top, sprinkle with bread crumbs and dot with butter. Bake for half an hour at 350 °.

Seafood Florentine Soup

The following recipe came from a restaurant my son-in-law owned. This soup was so delicious that people came from all around to sample it. Some days they used spinach and other days broccoli but it never seemed to matter because this was by far, the best seafood soup I have every eaten.

1/2 cup chopped green onions	1 cup sour cream
1/2 cup chopped green pepper	1 cup fresh sliced mushrooms
1/2 cup chopped celery	3 pounds small shrimp
1/2 cup yellow onion	2 pounds crabmeat
1/2 cup butter	Garlic to taste
Chopped fresh spinach	2 tablespoons crab base
1 can evaporated milk	1/2 cup flour
1 pint heavy cream	

Sauté` vegetables in butter until half done, add flour, mix well and set aside. Boil shrimp drain and save water. Add all other ingredients to shrimp stock. Reheat sautéed vegetables and flour. Whisk to prevent lumps. Add to shrimp stock. Simmer to desired thickness. Add Spinach and share with your closest friends.

Easy Rice Casserole

This is another recipe that my sister used to make and everyone loved it. To me it's a different and very tasty way to serve rice.

1 cup white rice

1/2 stick butter or

margarine

1 can of onion soup

1 can chicken consommé`

slivered almonds

Garlic salt to taste

2 teaspoons Parmesan

cheese

Cayenne pepper to taste

Sauté` rice in butter over low heat until rice is lightly browned. Add remaining ingredients. Bake in covered dish at 350 ° for one hour.

It takes a little time to brown the rice but trust me it is well worth the time. Even if you are not a big rice eater, I believe you will love this dish.

Hamburger Egg Rolls

Hamburger egg rolls may not sound very Oriental, but trust me they are yummy. If you still can't handle using hamburger meat in egg rolls, use shrimp or chicken. I am a seafood lover so if I say these hamburger egg rolls are delicious, you can believe they are delicious and then some. Now I cannot say I have exact measurements for this recipe so bear with me and I will try and walk you through it.

Season one pound of hamburger meat with pepper and soy sauce. Brown the hamburger, drain and set aside. Sauté` a package of fresh sliced mushrooms in a little butter and garlic powder, drain and set aside. Now I used to use fresh green onions but I now use Zatarain's green onions in the jar. Isn't cooking at home easier since Zatarain's and Tony Chachere's came to be? It's still not as much fun as eating out at the wonderful restaurants in this book, but at least it helps us make it until we get the opportunity to dine in one of our favorite restaurants on the Mississippi Gulf Coast.

Now, back to the famous *Hamburger Egg Roll Recipe*.

Sprinkle about 1/4 cup of green onions into the cooked hamburger, add the mushrooms, a can of bean sprouts (fresh if you like) a can of water chestnuts, chopped and drained, mix together and get ready to wrap. You can buy the egg roll wraps in most grocery stores and the directions for wrapping are on the package. After wrapping egg rolls, deep fry at 350 °, turning once until golden brown, and drain well. While your egg rolls are cooling, mix together some orange marmalade, a little salt, a little white vinegar, a little Worcestershire® and a little soy sauce. This is an excellent dipping sauce for these wonderful egg rolls.

By the way, if you do not wish to fry them all, you can freeze them for another time; just make sure that you separate them so that they don't stick together.

Asparagus Casserole

Yes, another recipe that came from my wonderful sister, Beverly, but hey, it caused me to like asparagus, in fact, she said it caused her own children to love asparagus.

2 tablespoons butter or margarine	*1 cup liquid (asparagus juice and milk)*
2 tablespoons flour	*1 small jar pimento*
1 can of asparagus tips	*3 boiled eggs — sliced*
1 cup grated cheddar cheese	*grated almonds*

Melt butter in pan and add flour (salt & pepper to taste) Add liquid slowly and cook until thick. Add cheese and pimento. In a buttered baking dish, add a layer of asparagus, a layer of eggs, then sauce. Repeat and add grated almonds on top.

Bake at 350 ° for about 20 minutes or until heated thoroughly.

Dixie Fried Corn

Now this is a recipe that I made for my children when they were growing up and though fresh corn on the cob is best, drained canned corn works too. Get ready to go back in time when bacon grease ruled. Heat a mixture of half bacon drippings and half vegetable oil in iron skillet (if you have one) Add the corn to hot oil and fry. As the corn begins to stick and brown, turn and mash around in pan. When half the corn is brown, lower heat and add a cup of boiling water. Salt & pepper to taste. Cover and simmer until thickened. Yum!

Potato Casserole

Now I'm sure this recipe is nothing new to anyone but it was one that my niece absolutely loved and I always made it for her. I still make it for my, oh so potato loving, husband.

1 can cream of chicken soup	*4 medium potatoes, peeled & sliced*
1 can milk or half & half1	*Salt & pepper to taste*
whole onion, sliced	*1 cup grated cheddar cheese*

Place one layer of sliced potatoes in a buttered casserole dish. Place a layer of sliced onions on top of potatoes. Pour some of the soup and milk mixture over potatoes and onions. Repeat and top with grated cheese. Bake at 350 ° for 45 minutes. Can also be baked in microwave and it saves time and energy.

Creamy Vegetable Casserole

I'm convinced that children, dogs and husbands will eat anything that has cheese in it and the following recipe is no exception.

*1 lb. bag California blend frozen
vegetables*
1/2 cup mayonnaise
2 eggs
2 tablespoons all purpose flour
1/4 cup Ranch dressing
2 cups shredded cheddar cheese

*1 8 oz. package cream cheese,
softened*
1/4 cup chopped onion
1/2 cup sour cream
2 cup stuffing mix
2 tablespoons melted butter

Preheat oven to 350 °. Spray a 2 quart casserole dish with butter spray
Thaw the frozen vegetables in boiling water then drain and set aside.
Beat the softened cream cheese and eggs until smooth. Add the next six ingredients and mix well. Stir in the vegetables and pour into baking dish. Toss the stuffing mix with melted butter and spread on top of casserole. Bake 35 to 40 minutes.

When I was 12 or so, my mom was teaching me how to make Lasagna. The recipe calls for cottage or ricotta cheese, and a slightly beat egg. Well, in saving dishes, I decided to put the egg into the empty cheese container and shake it. Unfortunately, I did not hold the lid on the container and egg flew all over the kitchen, on the ceiling and all over the cookbook! To this day, that page in the cookbook is stiff and tends to stick to the other pages.

Goulash

1 lb. ground beef
1 cup chopped onion
1 can diced tomatoes (with or
Green pepper, if desired without green chilies)

1 cup dry elbow macaroni
1 cup shredded cheddar cheese

Brown meat, onions and green pepper (if desired). Season with salt and pepper. Add undrained tomatoes and 1 cup water, bring to a boil. Stir in macaroni. Cover and simmer 10 minutes or until pasta is done. Stir in cheese. Garnish with sliced green onions and/or sour cream if desired.

Jolee Eschler Hart

Novi Michigan

The Original Blackened Turkey

The only funny story I have on cooking is my blackened turkey recipe, or I guess it's my blackened turkey incident. I was smoking my first turkey for Thanksgiving; Kathy's parents were coming down from N.C. for the first time. I put the bird on the smoker with a drip pan full of water and a good fire under it; I sat down to watch some football. The game was pretty boring and I fell asleep, when I woke, I rushed to check the smoker. The paint on the outside of the smoker was burnt off and the wooden handles were ashes on the ground. The turkey was so black I thought it was hopeless, we cut it open and it was great. Kathy's parents said it was the best turkey ever and still talk about it 20 years later.

Paul Stewart
Stewart Surveying
Mobile, Alabama

Swirl Cake

1 3/4 cups flour	1/2 cup shortening (room
1 1/2 cups sugar	temperature)
2 teaspoons double acting baking	1 cup evaporated milk
powder	(undiluted)
1 teaspoon salt	2 eggs
1 teaspoon vanilla	2 squares unsweetened chocolate

Frosting

1 1/2 cups vegetable shortening (Crisco)	1/4 cup water
1 cup sugar	1 teaspoon brandy flavoring
1/2 teaspoon salt	2 eggs

Measure flour, sugar, baking powder, soda and salt into sifter. Place shorting in mixing bowl-stir to soften. Sift in dry ingredients. Add 3/4 cups milk, mix until all flour is moist. Beat two minutes. Add eggs, remaining milk and vanilla. Beat one minute longer. Put in 9x13 greased and floured pan-pour melted unsweetened chocolate over batter in four rows and swirl thru with knife. DO NOT TOUCH THE KNIFE TO THE BOTTOM OF THE PAN OR IT WILL STICK!!! Bake at 350° for 35 to 40 minutes or until toothpick comes out clean. (don't test with toothpick through the chocolate).

Frosting:

Combine all frosting ingredients in small mixing bowl and beat at high speed for 10 minutes or until smooth and fluffy.

Todd Eschler

Sugarland Texas

Éclair Cake

Cake

2 (3 ¾ oz.) pkgs. French vanilla
pudding

2 2/3 cups milk

1 envelope unflavored gelatin

8 oz. cool whip

1 box graham crackers

Mix pudding, milk, gelatin with wire whisk for 2 minutes. Gently stir in cool whip. Place single layer of graham crackers on bottom of pan (13x9), add half the pudding mix on top of that, repeat layers, top with remaining crackers.

Frosting

2 squares Baker's unsweetened baking
chocolate

2 teaspoons white corn syrup

1 teaspoon vanilla extract

3 tablespoons margarine

¾ cup powdered sugar

3 tablespoons milk

Microwave chocolate, butter on high, 1 ½ minutes, stirring after 1 minute. Stir until chocolate is melted. Add remaining ingredients, stir until well blended. Immediately spread over graham crackers. Refrigerate at least 4 hours or overnight.

Kim Stewart

Daphne, Alabama

Peanut Brittle

2 cups sugar

¾ cup corn syrup

¼ cup water

3 cups raw peanuts

3 teaspoons baking soda

Pinch of salt

Butter a large cookie sheet. Mix sugar, water, salt and corn syrup, bring to a boil in a large, heavy saucepan. Add peanuts and cook on high, stirring constantly until peanuts begin to pop and mixture appears to start scorching, cook a little longer. Add baking soda, mixture will puff up. Stir vigorously. Pour onto buttered cookie sheet. When cool, break into small pieces and store in airtight container.

Kim Stewart

Daphne, Alabama

Aviation - A Childhood Dream

Patrick Raymond Repka

Patrick Raymond Repka was born, May 15[th,] in Pecos, Texas; his boyhood dream was to become a pilot. As a child, he watched every aviation movie available and built dozens of model airplanes.

His early years in the Air Force were spent going to night school to complete his degree and get his private pilot license. Patrick was accepted into Air Force flight school in 1973 and graduated in 1974 in the top 5% of his class. Early on, he was recognized as an exceptional pilot.

In 1977, while stationed in the Philippines Patrick Repka was selected as a flight examiner aircraft commander in low altitude parachute extraction system (LAPES). There were approximately six people in the world with this qualification. He was also part of an elite force flying special missions for the CIA.

Upon his return to The United States; in 1982, Repka became a flight examiner for the Hurricane Hunters at Keesler Air Force Base in Biloxi, Mississippi; then in 1986, he became an instructor- pilot with Lockheed Aircraft in Yemen and Saudi Arabia. In 1987 Repka flew for Southern Air Transport in Central and South America as well as in Africa; while there, he was selected to inaugurate many new procedures due to his expertise.

In 1990, Mr. Repka went to Angola and flew cargo missions in that brutal civil war for ten years. **He also flew for the United Nations, International Red Cross, and Catholic Relief Services. He participated in humanitarian missions in Ethiopia, Sudan, Uganda, Somalia, Rwanda, Liberia, Sierra Leone and Namibia**. During that period of time, he was severely injured and the airline had four out of seven airplanes shot down.

Mr. Repka's final mission was in Colombia, South America; his position was *Lead Pilot* in the US State Department International Law enforcement and Narcotics.

Repka has more flying hours as a pilot in C 130 "Hercules" than anyone else in the world. Patrick Raymond Repka Retired in 2006 in Ocean Springs, Mississippi, where he resides with his wife, Claudia.

Pat Repka's Famous Salsa

6 large ripe, peeled, seeded and
chopped tomatoes

6 peeled, seeded and chopped
tomatillos

1 large chopped onion

3 chopped scallions

12 fresh seeded and chopped
jalapeno peppers

1 bunch chopped cilantro

1 3-oz package pine nuts

1 fresh lime

1 teaspoon salt

1 teaspoon chili powder

½ teaspoon oregano

1teaspoon black pepper

Combine all ingredients, squeeze the fresh lime into the mixture and stir thoroughly. Refrigerate one hour and serve. Makes approximate 2 quarts. It can be kept in the refrigerator for up to 1 week.

Patrick Repka,

Ocean Springs, MS

Pat Repka's Seafood Gumbo

1 cup of chopped parsley

1 ½ cups chopped green bell pepper

1 ½ cups, chopped celery

2 (28 oz.) cans diced tomatoes

1 (16 oz) package Andouille sausage,
sliced into ¼ inch pieces

2 bay leaves

2 tablespoons salt

1 tablespoon ground pepper

½ teaspoon oregano

1 cup chopped green onion

1 ½ tablespoons, chopped garlic

2 (16 oz.) packages frozen, cut okra

½ teaspoon rosemary

½ teaspoon thyme

3 ½ pounds peeled, clean and
deveined shrimp

1 pound picked crab meat

1 quart shrimp, fish or chicken stock

Combine tomatoes, okra, bell peppers, celery, green onion, garlic, bay leaves and all spices with the stock into a large pot. Bring to a boil and cook on medium heat for 10 minutes. Add the crab meat and bring back to a boil. Add the shrimp and bring back to a boil. Spoon in roux, stirring thoroughly as you add. Simmer for 15 minutes and serve with white rice. Sprinkle slight amount of file'.

White Rice

2 cups rice

4 cups water

2 tablespoons butter

2 chicken bouillon cubes

In a large saucepan, sauté rice, with butter, stirring often, on low to medium heat. After 5 minutes add the water and the bouillon cubes and bring to a boil. Stir, reduce heat to simmer and cover tightly. Simmer for 20-25 minutes. Turn heat off and leave covered for 15 minutes.

Roux

1 ½ cups flour

1 ½ cups vegetable oil

2 cups chopped yellow or white onions

Combine flour and oil in a heavy pan and cook on medium - high heat. Whisk thoroughly and often. When mixture turns reddish brown add the onions and stir thoroughly. Remove from heat. Stir every 5 minutes as mixture cools.

Patrick Repka, Ocean Springs, MS

Currently being served at the Ocean Springs Oyster House & Seafood Restaurant on Government Street

Shrimp / Crawfish Potato Salad

This is great to use from a shrimp / crawfish boil. If you want to do a boil for the potato salad, here it is:

5 pounds shrimp or crawfish

4 pounds small red potatoes

6 corn ears

4 onions peeled and quarter

4 heads of garlic with the button (1/2 inch) cut off

1 pint liquid shrimp boil or 1 bag dry shrimp boil

½ cup of rock salt

Boil potatoes, onions, garlic, shrimp boil and salt for 20 minutes in a quart of water. Add shrimp and crawfish, bring back to a boil. Turn off heat and let stand 5 minutes, drain and cool (do not overcook shrimp / crawfish).

Potato Salad

Contents of shrimp / crawfish boil
1/3 cup of olive oil
1 cup mayonnaise
1 bunch parsley chopped

2 cups chopped celery with the
leaves
1 tablespoon black pepper
¼ cup of white vinegar

Peel shrimp /crawfish, cut potatoes into quarters, cut corn from cob, cut onions in ½ inch pieces and squeeze out cooked garlic. Add all ingredients in a large bowl with mayonnaise and olive oil. Chop parsley, celery, black pepper and vinegar and mix together. Add it to mixture Toss well and serve chilled.

Pat Repka, Ocean Springs, MS

Tar Babies

Marinade mixture

2 cups white vinegar
2 cups soy sauce
2 cups Worcestershire® sauce
2 cups Dale's® marinade

8 boneless and skinless chicken
breast cut in four strips each
32 brown sugar bacon slices

Marinade the chicken strips in the mixture for 1 day. Drain and pat dry. Wrap each chicken strip in a slice of bacon and secure with 1-2 tooth picks. Grill the tar babies on medium heat until the bacon turns dark brown but it is not burned. The chicken is mostly cooked by the marinade so you do not have to worry about the chicken being raw.

Claudia Repka, Ocean Springs, MS

Ceviche

1/2 pound large shrimp, peeled and
deveined
1/2 pound sea scallops, muscle
removed and finely chopped in ¼
inch dice

1 1/2 teaspoons salt
1 jalapeno, seeded and sliced, bunch

1/2 pound red snapper, or any firm
fish you like, chopped in ¼ inch
dice+ 1/2 cup fresh lime juice
1/2 cup fresh lemon juice
1/2 cup fresh orange juice
1 tablespoon sugar
1 large red onion, cut in half and
finely sliced

cilantro, leaves chopped

2 ripe mangoes, but still firm, chopped in ¼ inch dice

Bring a saucepan of salted water to a boil over medium heat. Add shrimp, until they just turn pink, and the fish and the scallops look firm, but not cooked, about 1 to 1- 1/2 minutes, then transfer to an ice bath. When cool enough to handle, chop roughly and put in a large plastic bag. In a small bowl, whisk lime juice, lemon juice, and fresh orange juice with the sugar and the salt, until they are dissolved. Stir in jalapenos, cilantro, red onion and mangoes to combine. Then, add the mixture to the bag with the scallops, the fish, and the shrimp. Put the bag in the refrigerator to marinate for at least 2 hours. Serve the ceviche in martini glasses.

Claudia Repka, Ocean Springs, MS

Crock Pot Macaroni & Cheese

(Add shrimp to if you like)

1 1/2 cups milk
1 large can evaporated milk
1 egg
1 small onion, diced
1/4 teaspoon salt
1/8 teaspoon black pepper

2 cups, uncooked, elbow macaroni
1 1/2 cups, shredded, sharp cheddar cheese (you can also add some parmesan cheese if you like)
1/2 pound of small cleaned shrimp

Spray inside of crock pot with cooking spray. Measure milk into a 4 cup, or larger, mixing bowl, add evaporated milk, egg, salt, pepper and mix well. Pour mixture into crock pot. Add cheese and macaroni. Stir gently to blend mixture together. Cook on low for 3 and 1/2 hours or till macaroni is soft. Add shrimp with about 1 hour left in the cooking time. Do not overcook the macaroni or it will dry out.

Gus Pialet, Ocean Springs, MS

Jalapeno Peppers Stuffed with Hot Pepper Cheese and Sausage

Select larger sized jalapeno peppers. Cut stem end off the jalapeno and cut length wise (recommend that latex or rubber gloves be worn during cutting and cleaning process) Scrape the seeds from the jalapeno halves with a spoon. Cut hot pepper cheese pieces to a size that will fit in jalapeno and lay them in the jalapeno pepper. Use bulk ground sausage (Hot, sweet or mild Italian; Cajun; green onion or as you like). If bulk is not available use casing sausage and remove casing. With a spoon or gloved hand put sausage in and on the jalapeno pepper in a quantity that it is mounded up on top of the piece of cheese. Place on cookie sheet with sides or in a baking pan in case grease from sausage runs during baking. Bake in preheated oven at 325° for 45 minutes or sausage has and internal temperature of 160°. Serve warm or make ahead of time and reheat in microwave for a short period of time

Gus Pialet, Ocean Springs, MS

Tasty Saltine Crackers

Arrange unsalted crackers on cookie sheet and spray with olive oil (available from PAM® brand and others). Do not soak the crackers or the following ingredients will not adhere. Sprinkle the crackers with cayenne pepper, ranch dressing powder, garlic powder and a Creole seasoning of your choice. Spray the olive oil over the crackers again and sprinkle crushed red peppers over the crackers. Bake in preheated oven for 30 minutes at 200° Can be used with dips or I like them with a small thin slice of blue cheese and a small piece of thinly slice salmon topping them.

Gus Pialet, Ocean Springs, MS

Chocolate Fondue Sauce

1/2 cup evaporate milk	*dash salt*
3/4 cups sugar	*2 squares unsweetened chocolate*
1/4 cup butter	*5 large marshmallows*

Combine milk, sugar, butter and salt in pan. Add chocolate and heat until blended. Serve over fruit, ice cream, pound cake, etc. Store in refrigerator and reheat as needed.

Diane Blalock

Gulfport, Ms

Aunt Heidle's Peach Cobbler

1 stick unsalted butter	*¾ cup of milk*
1 cup self rising flower	*1 large can sliced peaches*
1 cup sugar	*1 small can pineapple chunks*

Combine all ingredients except butter. Melt butter and pour in 8 x 11 baking dish. Add all the other ingredients. Bake at 350° oven for 1 hour or until golden brown. Let stand for a few minutes before serving.

Larry Platt, Ocean Springs, MS

From Aunt Heidle Platt Smith, Green County, MS

Summer Refreshing Corn Salad

2 cans whole-kernel corn, drained

1 basket, chopped in half, cherry

tomatoes

1 chopped and peeled cucumber

1 bunch chopped cilantro

Italian dressing

salt, pepper and garlic seasoning, to

taste

Toss ingredients together with the dressing. Chill and serve.

Larry Platt, Ocean Springs, MS

From The Hire Family, Ocean Springs, MS

Roger's Louisiana Shrimp and Grits

Grits:

2 cups chicken stock

1 cup quick grits (not instant or regular)

1 cup heavy cream

1 tablespoon unsalted butter

Kosher salt and freshly ground black pepper

8 oz extra sharp grated cheddar cheese

Shrimp:

2 tablespoons extra-virgin olive oil

1 medium white onion, minced

1 garlic clove, minced (more if desired)

2 tablespoons red and/or yellow bell pepper

finely diced

½ pound andoullie sausage, sliced and

halved

½ pound Tasso finely diced

2 tablespoons all-purpose flour

1 green onion, white and green part,

2 cups chicken stock

1 or 2 bay leaves

Creole seasoning (Tony Chachere or

Blackening)

2 pounds large shrimp, peeled and deveined,

tails on

Kosher salt and freshly ground black pepper

2 tablespoons finely chopped fresh flat-leaf

parsley

chopped

To make the shrimp, place a deep skillet over medium heat and coat with the olive oil. Add the onion and garlic; sauté for 2 minutes to soften. Add the bell pepper and sausage and cook, stirring, until there is a fair amount of fat in the pan and the sausage is brown. Sprinkle in the flour and stir with a wooden spoon to create a roux. Slowly pour in the chicken stock and continue to stir to avoid lumps. Toss in the bay leaf. Put on low simmer and prepare the grits. Lightly sprinkle shrimp with Creole or blackening seasoning. With the liquid at a simmer, add the shrimp. Poach the shrimp in the stock for 2 to 3 minutes, until they are firm and pink and the gravy is smooth and thick. Season with salt and pepper; stir in the parsley and green onion. Spoon the grits into a serving bowl. Add the shrimp mixture and mix well. Serve immediately.

To make the grits, place a 3-quart pot over medium-high heat. Add the chicken stock and bring to a boil. Slowly whisk in the grits. When the grits begin to bubble, add the cheese and turn the heat down to medium low and simmer, stirring frequently with a wooden spoon. Allow to cook until the mixture is smooth and thick. Remove from heat and stir in the cream and butter, season with salt and pepper.

Roger Gardner, Biloxi, MS

Whipped Cream Pound Cake

1/2 pound butter (2 sticks)
3 cups sugar
3 cups cake flour

6 eggs
1/2 pint whipping cream (heavy cream)

Cream together butter and sugar. Add eggs, one at a time. Add flour and mix together. Fold in heavy cream that has been beaten to a creamy whip top, but not as stiff as for topping. Pour into large greased and floured cake pan and bake at 300° until toothpick inserted comes out clean

Diane Blalock
Gulfport, Ms.

Green Grape Salad

4 pounds seedless green grapes
1 - 8 ounce package cream cheese
1 - 8 ounce container sour cream
1/2 cup white sugar

1 teaspoon vanilla extract
4 ounces chopped pecans
2 tablespoons brown sugar

Wash and dry grapes. In large bowl mix together cream cheese, sour cream, sugar and vanilla. Add grapes until evenly coated. Sprinkle with brown sugar and pecans. Mix again and refrigerate until ready to serve

Diane Blalock
Gulfport, Ms.

Appetizer Cheese Biscuits

1 cup and 2 tablespoons, sifted, cake flour

3/4 teaspoons red pepper

1/2 teaspoon salt

1/2 cup butter (softened)

5 ounces extra sharp cheddar cheese, shredded

4 to 6 ounces Tabasco® sauce

1 1/4 cups rice crispies

Sift flour together with salt and red pepper. In a separate bowl, cream together butter, cheese and Tabasco® using an electric mixer. Add the flour and rice crispies. Shape into small balls and place 2 inches apart on ungreased baking sheet. Press down with fingers and bake at 350° for 15 to 20 minutes. Makes 48

Diane Blalock

Gulfport, Ms.

Lady Di's Pumpkin Cake in a Jar

2/3 cups Crisco® (solid)

2 2/3 cups sugar

2/3 cups water

3 1/3 cups flour

1/2 teaspoon baking powder

2 cups canned pumpkin

4 eggs

1 1/2 teaspoons salt

1 teaspoon ground cloves

1/2 teaspoon allspice

1 teaspoon cinnamon

2 teaspoons baking soda

1 cup chopped pecans

8 pint sized wide mouth jars with lids for sealing

wax paper circles to fit jars

Cream together, Crisco® and sugar. Beat in eggs, pumpkin and water. Set aside. Sift together, flour, baking soda, salt, cloves, allspice, cinnamon and baking powder. Add to pumpkin mix and stir. Add pecans to this mixture. Pour into greased and floured jars filling half full. Place jars upright on a cookie sheet and bake at 325° for 45 minutes. When done, remove 1 jar at a time from oven and while still warm, place waxed circle on top end of cake. Wipe sealing edge of jar and place lid on jar. Close tightly with ring. Turn jar upside down until sealed and repeat with each jar.

To Serve: Open jar and slide knife around inside jar to loosen cake. Remove from jar, enjoy.

To label for gifts: Tie with ribbon and gift tag.

Diane Blalock

Gulfport, Ms.

The Lady's Pralines

1 box light brown sugar

1/8 teaspoon salt

3/4 cups evaporated milk

2 tablespoons butter

2 cups pecan halves

Melt butter. Add sugar, salt and butter. Cook over low heat until sugar dissolves. Add pecans and cook over medium heat to soft ball stage. (234°) Remove from heat and let cool for five minutes. Stir rapidly until mixture thickens and coats pecans. Place newspaper under waxed paper and drop mixture by spoonfuls on to waxed paper. Press with spoon to form patties.

Diane Blalock

Gulfport, Ms.

Di's Crab Imperial

4 tablespoons butter

1/4 teaspoon salt

1/4 teaspoon cayenne pepper

1 pound flaked crabmeat

1 tablespoon prepared mustard

paprika

snipped parsley

1 teaspoon dried mustard

3 1/2 tablespoons mayonnaise

1/4 teaspoon lemon juice

1/4 teaspoon celery seed

chopped green pepper to taste

Blend melted butter, salt, green pepper and celery seed. Add crab meat, mustards, mayonnaise, parsley and lemon juice. Place in individual Ramekin dishes and top with melted butter and paprika. Bake at 350° for 20 to 30 minutes or until golden brown. If mixture is too dry, add small amount of cream.

Diane Blalock

Gulfport, Ms.

Broccoli & Cauliflower Salad

Chop one head of cauliflower and one bunch of broccoli into bite sized pieces and set aside.

Sauce

1/2 cup sour cream	1 teaspoon Worcestershire®
1 cup mayonnaise	dash Tabasco®
1 onion chopped	1 tablespoon vinegar
salt and pepper to taste	1 tablespoon sugar

Pour sauce over vegetables and chill overnight.

Diane Blalock

Gulfport, Ms.

Crab Cakes

1 lb crab meat	1 egg beaten
1/2 cup finely chopped celery	5 to 7 slices of toasted white
7 to 8 shallots chopped	bread
1/2 cup of fresh chopped parsley	Tabasco to taste
1/2 cup chopped bell pepper	Salt & pepper to taste

Sauté vegetables in butter and set aside. Sprinkle toasted bread with water and tear into small pieces. Combine all ingredients and shape into patties. Bake at 350° until brown

Jerry Switzer

Gulfport, Mississippi

Pecan Pie Muffins

1 box light brown sugar	4 eggs at room temperature
2 sticks margarine	2 1/2 cups chopped pecans
1 cup plain white flour	

Melt margarine, add beaten eggs mix flour sugar and pecans well — mix all ingredients together. Bake at 350° for 14 minutes for small muffins and 25 minutes for large muffins.

Jerry Switzer

Gulfport, Mississippi

French Coconut Pie

3 eggs beaten

1 1/4 cups sugar

1 stick margarine

1 teaspoon vanilla

1 tablespoon vinegar

1 1/2 cups flaked coconut

1 9 inch pie crust

Beat eggs in a separated bowl then combine all ingredients, mix and pour into pie shell. Bake at 350°for 30 minutes

Jerry Switzer

Gulfport, Mississippi

Spiced Pecans

1 egg white

1 tablespoon water

3 cups pecans

1/4 cup sugar

1/3 teaspoon ground nutmeg

1/2 teaspoon salt

1 teaspoon ground cinnamon

1/4 teaspoon ground cloves

(optional)

Beat egg white and water until very foamy. Stir in nuts, coating well, combine sugar and remaining ingredients. Sprinkle over nuts and stir until coated. Spread nuts in a lightly greased pan and bake at 300° for 25 or 30 minutes stirring every ten minutes. Yields 3 cups

Jerry Switzer

Gulfport, Mississippi